D0623576

This time it's Real

This time it's Real

ANN LIANG

Scholastic Press / New York

Library of Congress Cataloging-in-Publication Data available

ISBN 978-1-338-82711-8

10 9 8 7 6 5 4 3 2 1 23 24 25 26 27

Printed in Italy 183
First edition, February 2023

Book design by Maeve Norton

FOR ALL THE CYNICS WHO SECRETLY
STILL BELIEVE IN LOVE

CHAPTER ONE

I'm about to change into my school uniform when I notice the man floating outside my bedroom window.

No, *floating* isn't the right word, I realize as I step closer, my plaid skirt still crumpled in one hand, my pulse racing in my ears. He's *dangling.* His whole body is suspended by two metal wires that look dangerously thin, considering how we're on the twenty-eighth floor and the summer wind's been blowing extra hard since noon, kicking up dust and leaves like a mini tornado.

I shake my head, bewildered as to why anyone would put themselves in such a position. What is this—some kind of new extreme sport? A gang initiation?

A midlife crisis?

The man catches me staring and gives me a cheerful little wave, as if he isn't one faulty wire or loose knot or particularly aggressive bird away from plummeting down the side of the building. Then, still ever-so-casual, he pulls out a wet cloth from his pocket and starts scrubbing the glass between us, leaving trails of white foam everywhere.

Right. Of course.

My cheeks heat. I've been away from China for so long that I completely forgot this is how apartment windows are cleaned—the same way I forgot how the subway lines work, or how you're not supposed to flush toilet paper, or how you can only bargain at certain types of stores without coming across as broke or stingy. Then there are all the things that have changed in the twelve years that my family and I were overseas, the things I never had the chance to learn in the first place. Like how people here apparently just *don't use cash anymore.*

I'm not kidding. When I tried to hand a waitress an old one hundred yuan note the other week, she'd gaped at me as though I'd time-traveled straight from the seventeenth century.

"Uh, hello? Eliza? Are you still there?"

I almost trip over my bed corner in my haste to get to my laptop, which has been propped up on two cardboard boxes labeled ELIZA'S NOT VERY IMPORTANT STUFF—boxes I haven't gotten around to unpacking yet, unlike my VERY IMPORTANT STUFF box. Ma thinks I could afford to be a bit more specific with my labels, but you can't say I don't have my own system.

"Eli-za?" Zoe's voice—achingly familiar even through the screen—grows louder.

"I'm here, I'm here," I call back.

"Oh, good, because literally all I can see is a bare wall. Speaking of which . . . girl, are you *ever* going to decorate your room? You've been there for, like, three months and it looks like a hotel. I mean, a *nice* hotel, sure, but—"

"It's a deliberate artistic choice, okay? You know, minimalism and all that."

She snorts. I'm a good bullshitter, but Zoe happens to have a great bullshit detector. "*Is it*, though? Is it really?"

"Maybe," I lie, turning the laptop toward me. One side of the screen has been taken up by a personal essay for my English class and about a billion tabs on "how to write a kiss scene" for research purposes; on the other side is my best friend's beautiful, grinning face.

Zoe Sato-Meyer's sitting in her kitchen, her favorite tweed jacket draped around her narrow frame, her dark waves smoothed back into a high ponytail and haloed by the overhead lights like a very stylish seventeen-year-old angel. The pitch-black windows behind her—and the bowl of steaming instant noodles on the counter (her idea of a bedtime snack)—are the only clue it's some ungodly hour of the night in LA right now.

"Oh my god." Her eyes cut to my worn polka-dot sweatshirt as I adjust my laptop camera. "I can't believe you still have that shirt. Didn't you wear it in eighth grade or something?"

"What? It's comfortable," I say, which is technically true. But I guess it's also true that this ugly, fraying shirt is one of the only things that's remained consistent throughout six different countries and twelve different schools.

"Okay, okay." Zoe holds up both hands in mock surrender. "You do you. But, like, still, shouldn't you be changing? Unless you plan to wear that to your parent-teacher conferences . . ."

My attention snaps back to the skirt in my grip, to the foreign-looking WESTBRIDGE INTERNATIONAL SCHOOL OF BEIJING logo embroidered over the stiff, plasticky fabric. A knot forms in my stomach. "Yeah, no," I mutter. "I should definitely be changing."

The window cleaner's still here, so I yank the curtains closed—but not before I catch a glimpse of the sprawling apartment complex below. For a place called Bluelake, there's very little that's actually *blue* about the neat rows of buildings or curated gardens, but there is plenty of green: in the man-made lake at the heart of the compound and its adjoining lotus ponds, the spacious mini golf course and tennis courts by the parking lot, the lush grass lining the pebbled paths and maidenhair trees. When we first moved in, the whole area had reminded me of a fancy resort, which seems fitting. After all, it's not like we'll be staying here longer than a year.

While I wriggle into my uniform, Zoe snaps her fingers and says, "Wait, you're not getting out of this—tell me again why you're writing about a nonexistent boyfriend for your essay?"

"Not writing. *Written*," I correct, pulling my shirt over my head. "I've already turned it in. And it's not like I *wanted* to make up a story about my love life, but I didn't know what else to write . . ." I pause to free a strand of my long, inky hair from one of the shirt buttons. "This thing is due tonight, and it counts as part of our coursework, so . . . you know. I had to get a little creative."

Zoe snorts again, so loud this time her microphone crackles. "You realize personal essays shouldn't be made up, right?"

"No," I say, deadpan. "Personal essays should be personal? Totally news to me. Shocking. My life is a lie."

The truth is, I chose to turn my serious nonfiction assignment into what's essentially a four-thousand-word romance *because* of how personal it's meant to be. The topic itself is bad enough, inspired by this sappy book we studied in the first week of school: *In* When the Nightingales Sang Back, *Lucy and Taylor are described to have their own "secret language" that no one else knows. Who do you share a secret language with? How did it develop? What does that person mean to you?*

Even so, I might've held my nose and gone along with it, written an only lightly exaggerated piece about either one of my parents or my little sister or Zoe . . . except we have to post our finished essay on the Westbridge school blog. As in, a very public platform that anyone—any of my classmates who know me only as "the new kid" or "the one who recently moved from the States"—could see and comment on.

There's *no way* I'm sharing actual details about my closest personal relationships. Even the *fake* details are embarrassing enough: like how I'd traced the lines of this pretend boyfriend's palm, whispered secrets to him in the dark, told him he meant the world to me, that he felt like home.

". . . not even remotely concerned that people at your school might, I don't know, read it and be curious about this boyfriend of yours?" Zoe's saying.

"I've got it covered," I reassure her as I tug the curtains back open. Light floods in at once, illuminating the tiny specks of dust floating before my now-empty window. "I didn't include a name, so no one can try and stalk him. Plus, I wrote that I met this fictional dude three months ago while I was apartment hunting with my family, which is a pretty plausible meet-cute without revealing what school he might go to. *And*, since our relationship is still pretty new and everything's kind of delicate, we like to keep things private. See?" I step in front of the camera and make a grand gesture toward the air, as if the entirety of my essay is written right there in glowing letters. "Foolproof."

"Wow." An intake of breath. "Wow. I mean, all this effort," Zoe says, sounding exasperated and impressed at the same time, "just so you don't have to write something real?"

"That's the plan."

There's a brief silence, broken only by the slurp of noodles on Zoe's end and the thud of footsteps outside my room. Then Zoe sighs and asks, in a tone far too concerned for my liking, "Are you doing okay at your new school, girl? Like, are you . . . settling in?"

"What?" I feel myself stiffen immediately, my muscles tensing as though anticipating a blow. "Why—why would you say that?"

"I don't know." Zoe jerks a shoulder, her ponytail bouncing with the motion. "Just . . . vibes."

I'm saved from having to answer when Ma calls down the hall at a volume one would usually reserve for search-and-rescue missions. "Ai-Ai! The driver's here!"

Ai-Ai is my Chinese nickname, which translates directly to *love*. Fictional relationship aside, I can't quite say I've lived up to it.

"I'm coming!" I yell back, then turn to the screen. "I assume you heard that?"

Zoe grins, and I relax slightly, relieved whatever heart-to-heart conversation she was trying to have is over. "Yeah, I think the whole planet heard it. Tell your mom I said hi," she adds.

"Will do." Before I shut my laptop, I make a cheesy heart sign with my fingers; something I wouldn't be caught dead doing around anyone else. "I miss you."

Zoe blows a dramatic kiss at me in response, and I laugh. "I miss you too."

The hard knot in my stomach loosens a little at the familiar words. Ever since I left LA two years ago, we've ended every single call like this, no matter how busy and tired we are, or how short the conversation is, or how long it'll be until we can talk again.

I miss you.

It's not as good as the sleepovers we used to have at her place, where we'd sprawl on the couch in our pajamas, some Netflix show playing on her laptop, a plate of her mom's homemade rice balls balanced between us. And it's nowhere near as good as our weekend trips down by the beach, the California sun warming our skin, the breeze tugging at our salt-tangled hair. Of course it isn't.

But for now, this small, simple ritual feels enough.

Because it's ours.

Our driver has parked his car just outside the apartment complex, under the dappled shade of a willow tree.

Technically, Li Shushu isn't so much our driver as *Ma*'s driver—one of the many perks of being an executive at a super-prestigious global consulting company, and part of the sorry-for-asking-you-to-uproot-your life-almost-every-year! package—which is why he rushes out to greet her first.

"Yu Nüshi," he says, opening the door for her with a little bow. *Madame Yu.*

This kind of treatment always makes me uncomfortable in a way I can't articulate, even when it's not directed at me, but Ma just smiles at him through her sunglasses and slides gracefully into the front seat. Looking at her now, with her pale, unblemished skin and custom-made blazer and razor-sharp bob, you'd never guess she grew up fighting for scraps with six other siblings in a poor rural Chinese town.

The rest of us squeeze into the back of the car in our usual order: me and Ba beside the windows, and my nine-year-old little sister, Emily, squashed in the middle.

"To your school?" Li Shushu confirms in slow, enunciated Mandarin as he starts the engine, the smell of new leather and petrol fumes seeping into the enclosed space. He's been around me long enough to know the extent of my Chinese skills.

"To the school," I agree, doing my best to ignore the pinch in my gut. I hate going to Westbridge enough as it is, but whatever the school, parent-teacher interviews are always the worst. If it wasn't for the fact that Emily goes to the same school as me and also has her interviews this evening, I'd have made up a brilliant excuse to keep us all home.

Too late to do anything now.

I lean back in my seat and press my cheek to the cool, flat glass, watching our apartment complex grow smaller and smaller until it disappears entirely, replaced by the onrush of the inner city scene.

Since we moved back here, I've spent most of our car rides plastered to the window like this, trying to take in the sharp rise and fall of the Beijing skyline, the maze of intersections and ring roads, the bright clusters of dumpling restaurants and packed grocery stores.

Trying to memorize it all—and trying to remember.

It kind of amazes me how misleading the photos you tend to see of Beijing are. They either depict the city as this smoggy postapocalyptic world packed full of weathered, stony-faced people in pollution masks, or they make it look like something straight out of a high-budget sci-fi movie, all sleek skyscrapers and dazzling lights and dripping luxury.

They rarely capture the true energy of the city, the forward momentum that runs beneath everything here like a wild undercurrent. Everyone seems to be hustling, reaching, striving for more, moving from one place to the next; whether it's the delivery guy weaving through the traffic behind us with dozens of takeout boxes strapped to his bike, or the businesswoman texting someone frantically in the Mercedes on our left.

My attention shifts when a famous Chinese rapper's song starts playing on the radio. In the rearview mirror, I see Ma remove her sunglasses and visibly wince.

"Why does he keep making those *si-ge si-ge* sounds?" she demands after about three seconds. "Does he have something stuck in his throat?"

I choke on a laugh.

"It's just how music sounds nowadays," Ba says in Mandarin, ever the diplomat.

"I think it's kind of nice," I volunteer, bobbing my head to the beat.

Ma glances back at me with a half-hearted scowl. "Don't bounce your head like that, Ai-Ai. You look like a chicken."

"You mean like this?" I bob my head harder.

Ba hides a smile with the back of his hand while Ma clucks her tongue, and Emily, who I'm convinced is really an eighty-year-old grandma trapped inside a nine-year-old's tiny body, lets out a long, dramatic sigh. "Teenagers," she mutters.

I elbow her in the ribs, which makes her elbow me back, which sets off a whole new round of bickering that only ends when Ma threatens to feed us nothing but plain rice for dinner.

If I'm honest, though, it's in these moments—with the music filling the car and the wind whipping past the windows, the late-afternoon sun flashing gold through the trees and my family close beside me—that I feel . . . lucky. Really, truly lucky, despite all the moving and leaving and adjusting. Despite everything.

CHAPTER TWO

The mood doesn't last.

As soon as we pull up beside the Westbridge school buildings, I realize my mistake.

Everyone is dressed in casual clothes. Cute summer dresses. Crop tops and jean shorts. The teachers didn't specify what to wear this evening, and I naively assumed it'd be standard uniform, because that's what the expectations were at my previous school.

My family starts getting out of the car, and I push down a swell of panic. It's not like I'll get *in trouble* for wearing what I'm wearing—I just know I'll look dumb and stand out. I'll look like the Clueless New Kid, which is exactly what I am, but that doesn't make it any easier to bear.

"Ai-Ai." Ma taps the window. "Kuaidian." *Hurry.*

I say a quick thanks to the driver and step outside. At least the weather's nice; the wind's quieted down to more of a gentle, silky breeze, a welcome reprieve from the heat. And the sky. The sky is beautiful, a blend of pastel blues and muted pinks.

I inhale. Exhale.

This is fine, I tell myself. *Totally fine.*

"Come on, Baba," Emily is saying, already pulling Ba toward the primary school section of the campus, where all the walls are painted bright colors. Obnoxiously bright colors, if you ask me. "You *have* to talk to Ms. Chloe. I told her how you were a poet, and you do signings and stuff at big bookstores, and she was soooo impressed. She didn't believe me at first, I don't think, but then I made her search your name, and then . . ."

Emily looks *actually* fine, because she is. No matter where we go, my little sister never has any trouble fitting or settling in. We could probably ship her off to Antarctica and find her just chilling with the penguins two weeks later.

Ma and I walk in the opposite direction, where the senior classrooms are. The wide gray corridors are already pretty crowded with parents and students, some heading in, some weaving their way out. Just as I expected, a few people's eyes slide to my stiff skirt and too-big blazer, a mixture of pity and amusement flickering over their faces before they avert their gazes.

I lift my chin high. Walk faster.

This is fine.

We couldn't reach my homeroom fast enough.

It's loud inside. Classmates everywhere, teachers waiting behind rows of desks. None of them say hi to me, and I don't say hi to them either.

Even though school started almost a month ago, I haven't really gotten to know anyone. All the names and faces and classes kind of just blur together. The way I see it, we'll be graduating in less than a year anyway. There's no reason to *put myself out there*, as my past teachers all loved to recommend, and get attached to people only to grow apart months later. With Ma's job moving us around all the time, it's already happened too many times for me to keep track: that slow, painful, far-too-predictable transition from strangers to acquaintances to friends back to strangers the second I leave the school behind me.

I'd be a masochist to put myself through it again.

Besides, there are fewer than thirty kids in my whole year level, and everyone's clearly formed their own cliques already. To my right, a group of girls are squealing and embracing like it's been years since they last saw one another, not hours. And somewhere behind me, another group is deep in conversation, switching between three languages—English, Korean, and something else—within every sentence as if it's the most natural thing in the world.

Pretty on-brand for an international school, I guess.

"Ah! Look who it is!"

My English and homeroom teacher, Mr. Lee, waves me over, his eyes bright behind his thick, oversized glasses. He's been cursed with this round baby face and unruly gray-streaked hair, which has the combined, disorienting effect of making him look like he could either be in his early thirties or late fifties.

"Have a seat, have a seat," he says briskly, motioning to two chairs on the other side of his desk. Then his attention goes to Ma, and his expression grows more benevolent. The way someone would look at a cute kid in the park. "And this is . . . Eliza's mother, I'm assuming."

"Yes. I'm Eva Yu," Ma says, instantly easing into the chirpy Work Voice she uses around white people, her accent flattened to sound more American. She extends a manicured hand. "It's lovely to meet you."

Mr. Lee's brows furrow a little as he shakes it, and furrow farther when he realizes how strong her grip is. I can tell he's trying to match up his impression of Ma with whatever preconceived idea he had of her, just based on the non-Western surname.

Ma lets go first, sitting back with a small, self-satisfied smile. She's enjoying this, I know. She's always enjoyed surprising people, which happens often, because people are always underestimating her. Part of the reason she got into consulting in the first place was because a friend joked that she'd never survive in the corporate world.

"Now . . ." Mr. Lee clears his throat. Turns to me again. "Since you're new to this, let's just go over the rules real quick, yeah?" He doesn't wait for me to respond. "In the next ten minutes or so, I'll be talking to your mother about your academic performance in your English classes so far, your learning attitude, possible areas for improvement—yada yada ya. No interrupting, asking questions, or drawing attention to yourself until the very end, when I call on you. Is that clear?"

And people wonder why teenagers tend to have authority issues.

"Ah, I see you've already got the hang of it," Mr. Lee says cheerfully, waving a hand at my stony face.

I let my gaze and attention wander.

Then, across the room, I spot one of the few people here I do recognize.

Caz Song.

For all my lack of effort, it'd be hard *not* to have at least some idea of who he is: Model. Actor. God—if you were to go by the way everyone gushes over him and follows his every move, despite him never actually *doing* anything apart from standing around and looking obnoxiously pretty. Even now, in this depressing, heavily supervised setting, a substantial crowd of students has already gathered around him, their mouths agape. One girl's clutching her side in hysterical laughter at a joke he probably never made.

I resist the urge to roll my eyes.

I've never really understood the hype around him, unless it's from a purely aesthetic perspective. There *is* this certain elegance to the cut of his jaw, the slight pout of his lips, the sharp, lean angles of his frame. His dark hair and darker eyes. It's not like his features are inhumanly perfect or anything, but together, they just *work*.

Still, I get the sense that he's every bit as aware of this as all his adoring fans, which kind of ruins it. And of course the press loves him; just the other day, I stumbled across some article that deemed him one of the "Rising Stars of the Chinese Entertainment Industry."

He's leaning against the back wall now, hands shoved into pockets. This seems to be his natural state: leaning on something—doors, lockers, tables, you name it—as if he can't be bothered standing upright on his own.

But I've been staring too hard, too long. Caz looks up, sensing my gaze.

I quickly look away. Tune back into the interview, just in time to hear Mr. Lee say:

"Her English is really quite good—"

"Yeah, well, I *did* learn English when I was a kid," I point out before I can stop myself. Years of getting vaguely condescending comments about just how *good* my English is and how I *don't even have an accent*—almost always spoken with a note of surprise, if not confusion—have made this a natural reflex.

Mr. Lee blinks at me. Adjusts his glasses. "Right . . ."

"Just wanted to put that out there." I lean back in my seat, suddenly unsure if I should feel triumphant or guilty for interrupting. Maybe he really *had* meant it in your typical she-sure-knows-her-conjunctions kind of way, rather than an I-don't-expect-people-who-look-like-her-to-speak-any-English way.

Ma clearly seems to believe the former, because she shoots me a sharp look.

"Sorry. Carry on," I mutter.

Mr. Lee glances over at Ma. "So what I'm curious to know, if you don't mind, is a bit about Eliza's background before she came here . . ."

Ma nods, well prepared for this, and launches into the usual script: *born in China, moved when she was five, went to this school and that school and moved countries again . . .*

I try not to fidget, to flee. Being talked about this way makes my skin itch.

"Ah, but the best thing about having lived everywhere is that she belongs *anywhere*." Mr. Lee stretches his hands out wide in a gesture that I'm assuming represents "anywhere"—and knocks over a tissue box in the process. He pauses, flustered. Picks it up. Then, unbelievably, continues right where he left off. "You should know that Eliza is not a citizen of one country or even one continent, but rather a—"

"If you say *citizen of the world*, I'm going to throw up," I mutter under my breath, low enough for only me to hear.

Mr. Lee leans forward. "Sorry, what's that?"

"Nothing." I shake my head. Smile. "Nothing."

A beat.

"Well, since we're on the topic of Eliza's circumstances," Mr. Lee says delicately, hesitantly, and I have a terrible feeling I know what's coming. "I do worry that Eliza is having a hard time . . . adjusting."

My throat tightens.

This. This is why I hate parent-teacher interviews.

"Adjusting," Ma repeats with a frown, though she doesn't look too surprised. Just sad.

"She doesn't seem to be close with anyone in her class," Mr. Lee elaborates. The trilingual group waiting for their parents in the back choose this time to burst into loud laughter at whatever it is they're chatting about, the sound banging against all four walls. Mr. Lee raises his voice, almost yelling, "That is to say, it's somewhat concerning that she still doesn't have any friends here."

Unfortunately for me, the noise levels happen to die down again halfway through his sentence.

And of course, everyone hears every last word. There's an

awkward pause, and about thirty pairs of eyes burn holes into my skull. My face catches fire.

I rise from my seat, wincing inwardly when the chair legs squeak against the polished floor, scraping against the silence. I mumble something about using the bathroom.

Then I get the hell out of there.

In my defense, I'm generally pretty good—an expert, even—at pushing my feelings aside and disconnecting myself from everything, but sometimes it just hits me hard: this horrible, crushing sense of *wrong*ness, of *otherness*, regardless of whether I'm the only Asian kid at an elite Catholic all-girls school in London or the only new kid in a tiny cohort at a Chinese international school. Sometimes I'm convinced I'll spend the rest of my life this way. Alone.

Sometimes I think loneliness is my default setting.

To my relief, the corridor is empty. I retreat into the farthest corner, bend down into a half crouch, and take my phone out. Scroll through nothing for a minute. Feel intuitively for the rough string bracelet around my wrist, a gift from Zoe, let it comfort me.

This is fine, I'm fine.

Then I head onto the Craneswift website.

I discovered Craneswift a few years back, when I picked up one of their newsletters at a London train station, and I've been reading their stuff ever since. They don't have a massive readership, but they more than make up for it in quality and reputation.

Basically anyone who's ever been lucky enough to publish their writing through Craneswift has gone on to achieve the kind of success I could only dream of: journalism awards, prestigious nonfiction writing scholarships in New York, international recognition. All because they wrote something beautiful and profound.

Words just move me. A beautiful sentence will sneak under my skin and crack me open the way a phrase of music might, or a climactic scene from a movie. A well-crafted story can make me laugh and gasp for breath and weep.

As I settle into one of Craneswift's recently posted essays about finding soul mates in the unlikeliest of places, the familiar blue website banner glowing over the screen, I can already feel some of the weight on my shoulders easing, the tension in my body dissolving—

A door creaks open and noise spills into the hallway.

I stiffen, squint down the corridor. Caz Song steps out alone, his gaze sweeping right past me like I'm not even here. He looks distracted.

". . . all waiting for you," he's saying, a rare crease between his brows, an even rarer edge to his voice. Caz has always given me the impression of someone pulled straight out of a magazine cover: glossy and airbrushed and digestible; marketable and inoffensive. But right now he's pacing in an agitated circle, his footsteps so light they barely make any sound. "These are the *parent-teacher* interviews. I can't just do it alone."

For one confusing moment, I think he's talking to himself or trying out some weird acting technique, but then I hear the muffled female voice coming out through his phone's speakers:

"I know, I know, but my patient needs me more. Can you tell your teacher something came up at the hospital? Hao erzi, tinghua." *Good child. Behave.* "Maybe we can reschedule for next week—that worked last time, didn't it?"

I watch Caz breathe in. Out. When he speaks again, his voice is remarkably controlled. "No, that's fine, Mom. I—I'll tell them. I'm sure they'll understand."

"Hao erzi," the woman says again, and even from this distance, I can hear the odd commotion in the background. Slamming metal. The beep of a monitor. "Oh, and just before I go—what did they say about those college applications?"

Applications.

I turn the unexpected snippet of information over in my head. This is news to me. I'd figured someone like Caz would skip the college route, go down the acting path instead.

But at present, the Rising Star himself is rubbing his jaw and saying, "It's . . . fine. They reckon that if I can pull off a really great college admission essay, it should be able to make up for my grades and attendance record . . ."

A sigh hisses through the speakers. "What do I always tell you, ya? *Grades first*, grades first. Do you think the college admissions team cares if you play lead role in campus drama? Do you think they even know any Asian celebrities other than Jackie Chan?" Before Caz can reply, his mother sighs again. "Never mind. Too late now. You just focus on that essay—are you almost done?"

It might be a trick of the low corridor lights, but I swear I see Caz wince. "Sort of."

"What's *sort of*?"

"I—" His jaw clenches. "I mean, I still need to brainstorm and outline and . . . write it. But I will find a way to write it," he adds quickly. "Promise. Trust me, Mom. I—I won't let you down."

There's a long pause. "All right. Well, listen, my patient's calling for me, but talk soon, okay? And *make sure you focus on those essays.* If you put in even half as much effort into them as you do memorizing those scripts, then—"

"I got it, Mom."

Something like worry briefly pinches his features as he ends the call.

Then, as he spins to leave, he sees me squatting like a fugitive in the dark of the corridor, caught staring at him for the second time this evening.

"Oh," he says, the same time I stand up and blurt out, "Sorry!" and the rest of our sentences spill over one another:

"I didn't see—"

"I promise I wasn't trying to—"

"It's cool—"

"Just about to head in—"

"You're Eliza, right? Eliza Lin?"

"Yes," I say slowly, and even I can hear the wary edge in my voice. "Why?"

He raises a dark brow, all signs of worry now wiped clean from his face. Fast enough to make me wonder if I'd imagined them there in the first place. "Nothing. Just trying to be friendly."

An innocuous reply. Perfectly reasonable.

And yet . . .

She still doesn't have any friends here.

"Did you . . . hear what Mr. Lee said earlier?" As soon as the words leave my mouth, I want to retract them. Erase them from existence completely. There are certain things you simply shouldn't draw attention to, even if both parties are well aware of the issue. Like a bad acne flare-up. Or your homeroom teacher declaring you friendless in front of your entire class.

The fact that I don't really *need* new friends makes this no less embarrassing.

Caz considers the question for a second. Leans against the closest wall, so half his body is angled toward me. "Yeah," he admits. "Yeah, I did."

"Oh wow."

"What?"

I let out a small, awkward laugh. "I was kind of expecting you to lie about it. You know. To spare my feelings or something."

Instead of responding directly to that, he tilts his head and asks, his tone guarded, "Did *you* hear me on the phone?"

"No," I tell him without thinking, then cringe. "I mean—well—"

"Very nice of you to care about protecting *my* feelings," he says, but there's a curl of irony to his voice that makes me want to evaporate on the spot. And then an even more horrifying thought materializes: What if he thinks I'm a fan? Or a stalker? Another one of those wide-eyed, overenthusiastic classmates who follows him everywhere like a disciple, who was waiting out here just to get him all alone? I've witnessed it happen myself a dozen times before: students ducking behind literal bins or walls and springing on him the second he rounds the corner.

"I swear I didn't mean to overhear anything," I say frantically, holding up both hands. "I didn't even know you'd come out here."

He shrugs, his face impassive. "All right."

"Really," I say. "Swear on my heart."

He gives me a long look. "I said all right."

But he doesn't sound like he fully believes me either. My skin prickles, embarrassment and annoyance warming my cheeks. And then my mouth decides to make everything worse by saying the most ridiculous thing: "I'm not—I'm not even a fan."

A terse second passes, his expression shifting briefly into something impossible to read. Surprise, perhaps. I can feel my insides disintegrating.

"Good to know," he says at last.

"I mean, I'm not an *anti-fan* either," I splutter, with that dreadful, helpless, out-of-body feeling of watching a protagonist inside a horror film: when you want to scream at them to stop, but they keep moving closer and closer toward their own doom. "I'm just neutral. Nothing. A—a normal person."

"Clearly."

I clamp my mouth shut, my cheeks hot. I can't believe I'm still standing here with *Caz Song*, who apparently has a unique talent for making me feel even more self-conscious than I usually do. I can't believe we're still talking, and Mr. Lee's still inside that crowded classroom with Ma, and both of them think I'm still in the bathroom.

This is a nightmare. Time to figure out an escape strategy before I can embarrass myself further.

"You know what?" I crane my neck as though I just heard someone call for me. "I'm pretty sure that was my mom."

Caz lifts both eyebrows this time. "I didn't hear anything."

"Yeah, well, she has a soft voice," I babble, already moving past him. "Hard to pick out, unless you're really accustomed to it. So, um, I should probably go. See you around!"

I don't give him a chance to reply. I just bolt back into the classroom, ready to grab my mom and beg Li Shushu to come pick us up as soon as possible. After an ordeal this mortifying, I can never, *ever* talk to Caz Song ever again.

CHAPTER THREE

I wake up before dawn the next day, the heat heavy on my skin, my blankets twisted around me.

My phone is flashing.

237 new notifications.

I squint at it for a minute, uncomprehending, my brain still foggy from sleep. But again and again, the screen lights up, casting a soft blue glow over the bedside table, and a jolt of alarm cuts through my fatigue. No one usually messages me at this hour. And certainly no one—not even Zoe—would send me *this* many messages in a row.

239 new notifications.

240 new . . .

I kick my blankets aside, fully awake now, and check my iMessage, my confusion quickly curdling into apprehension.

Then I read Zoe's texts:

holy shit.

Holy fucking shit!!!!!!

ok i knOW IT'S THE MIDDLE OF THE NIGHT

BUT

PLS GET ON YOUR PHONE

asdfghjkklkll

girl have you SEEN THIS what the actual hELL

She's attached a screenshot below: an article. I'm almost too scared to open it, but after two seconds of staring at the screen, my heart punching holes in my ribs, I give in.

A giant, bold heading leaps out from the page:

"A Rom-Com in the Making: This Girl's Blog Post about Her Love Life Has Us Believing in Love."

My pulse quickens.

I don't understand what I'm seeing at first. I only know that there's an excerpt from my personal essay—the essay I proofread at least three times, posted only yesterday—and my own name and . . . the *BuzzFeed logo* above it all. The same BuzzFeed I used to spend hours scrolling through with Zoe, taking quizzes to find out which party snack we resembled. None of it makes sense. I have no idea how or why BuzzFeed even has my writing.

It's like coming across a photo of yourself in someone else's house, this jarring combination of "hey, this looks familiar" and "what the hell is this doing here?" It feels like I'm dreaming.

But oh god—there's more. So much more.

Apparently my essay was already spreading last night, but when someone semi-famous tweeted a screenshot and a link to my post on the school blog, it all blew up. I quickly secure my VPN and head over to Twitter, and my heart almost falls out of my chest.

Last night, I had a grand total of five followers on my lurking-only Twitter account, and I'm pretty sure two of them were bots.

Now I already have more than ten thousand followers.

"Holy fucking shit indeed," I mutter, and the sound of my own voice, low and slightly scratchy with disuse, only makes it all more surreal. None of it makes sense. It doesn't make sense that I could be sitting here on my bed, the light of my phone illuminating my plain bedroom walls, while this tweet a bunch of people have so thoughtfully tagged me in has gotten *half a million likes* and counting.

My hands are shaking as I scroll through some of the recent comments.

@alltoowell13: *maybe guys do deserve rights after all???*

@jiminswife: *I'm actually crying omg this is SO. CUTE. (pls feed us more quality content my soul needs it) ((if they ever break up i swear i'll stop believing in love))*

@angelica_b_smith: *Lmao how are teens these days writing Shakespeare-level essays abt the love of their life . . . like when i was that age i couldn't even string together a full sentence*

@drunklanwangji: *not to be dramatic or anything but i would literally die for them to just stay together and hold hands and be happy forever.*

@user387: *pLEASE someone make this into a movie i am BEGGING—*

@echoooli: *Am I the only one hella curious about who the boyfriend is? (and where can I find one??)*

I drop my phone before I can read any more, an unsettling mix of panic and euphoria shooting through my veins.

So.

This is ridiculous.

My brain feels like it's glitching. Overheating. People across the world are reading my essay and imagining me cuddling with some guy on his couch, kissing him on a balcony, whispering things like *I miss you even when you're close to me* and *You're so beautiful sometimes I can't even think straight around you.*

People have read it . . . and actually *liked* it. My words, my writing, my thoughts. Recognized some piece of themselves in it. Despite my embarrassment, I can't stop the smile from spreading across my face. *Is this what it's like to be a celebrity?* I can't help wondering briefly, through my utter disbelief. *Is this how someone like Caz Song feels all the time?*

But no—I catch myself. All this, as exciting as it is, isn't the point. Because going viral just for my writing would be one thing—a good thing, even, the stuff of modern-day fairy tales. But going viral for a "wholesome real-life love story" (@therealcarrielo's words, not mine) that's actually completely fictional is another.

I can just picture how the next BuzzFeed article would look if the truth gets out: "A Criminal in the Making: This Girl's Viral Personal Essay about Her Love Life Turns Out to Be a Total Lie."

Over the next hour or so, while the rest of the apartment stirs and the bathroom taps creak and Ma shuffles into the kitchen to turn the soy milk machine on, this is all I can think about. The BuzzFeed heading. The comments. How invested people already seem to be, how many have followed me for "updates" that I don't have . . .

Guilt soon worms its way into my chest and I want to scream.

But by some miracle, or maybe years of practice, I manage to act like everything's fine at breakfast. It just doesn't feel right to blurt out something like *Oh, by the way, I may have treated my personal essay assignment as a creative writing exercise and it somehow went viral and now over a million people think I've met the love of my life in Beijing*, when it isn't even eight o'clock in the morning yet. So I drink my homemade soy milk and eat my tea egg and try not to think about the fact that my life may have irrevocably changed over the course of one night.

". . . is killing me," Ma is saying as she cracks her egg on a bowl, the shell breaking apart with a satisfying crunch. "It's an absolute disaster."

I don't even have to pay full attention to know exactly who she's talking about: Kevin from marketing. Some recent Harvard graduate with a genius IQ and, according to Ma, zero common sense.

"Sorry—what's an absolute disaster?" I ask, hoping she'll elaborate. Some disaster-management tips would definitely come in handy right now.

"My life," Emily volunteers from the other end of the dining table. Her school uniform's on backward, and her shoulder-length jet-black hair has been tied into what I suspect *should* be a ponytail but looks more like a bean sprout instead. Clearly, Ba's been put in charge of helping Emily get ready today.

Ma rolls her eyes. "Save that attitude for your mid-forties," she chides Emily, then turns back to me. "And since when are you so interested in my work life?"

"Since always," I say innocently.

"I thought you found my job confusing," Ma points out, passing over a plate of fluffy round mantous still warm from the steamer.

"Yeah, well, that's only because your company insists on describing itself as a 'creative collaborator and leader' that seeks to 'influence culture and inspire' and deliver on 'key marketing project initiatives' or whatever." I shred half a mantou into bite-size pieces, the dough softening between my fingers. "Like, those are literally just words. But I understand what *you* do. Sort of."

Ma doesn't look too convinced by this, but she sighs and explains, "Kevin got this huge investor to sign with us."

"And that's a problem because . . . ?"

"They only signed because he told them we were on great terms with that popular tech start-up SYS." She grabs a mantou for herself and doesn't eat it. Just watches it go cold beside the egg. "Except we've never even *spoken* to anyone from SYS before. We have no connections whatsoever."

"Ah." I nod slowly, shoving down a small bubble of hysteria at the obvious parallel between Kevin's crisis and mine. "I do see how that might be challenging." Then, hoping I don't look overeager, I take a casual sip of my soybean milk and ask, "So, um, what's the plan? Are you guys going to come clean, or—"

"God, no. Of course not." Ma actually laughs, like the very idea is absurd. "No, we've been trying to get this investor on board for years. We'll just have to work in reverse: reach out to SYS and forge a connection and act like we've been close all along. Maybe if we approached one of *their* marketing teams first, or that guy from the Cartier campaign . . ." She gets this distant, almost-zealous gleam in her eye, the way she tends to whenever she's puzzling out a work issue. Then she remembers who she's talking to. "But lying is bad," she adds hastily, shooting Emily and me a stern look.

"Noted," I say, and swallow the last of my milk with some difficulty. The soybean pulp scratches my throat like sand.

When everyone's finished eating, I help Ma clean up the table, and we head down to the driver's car together, my phone burning a hole in my blazer pocket the whole way. I haven't checked it properly since this morning, but the notifications keep coming in. By the time we're dropped off at school, I have 472 unread messages and god knows how many Twitter mentions.

And then things get significantly weirder.

I'm the first person to arrive to my math class, as usual.

Not because I'm particularly punctual by nature, or because I'm in any way enthusiastic about quadratic equations, but because there's nowhere better to go. In the spare minutes before and between classes, people love gathering around lockers, blocking up halls, chatting and laughing so loud together the walls seem to tremble.

I tried hanging around once too, on my third day here, and it only made me feel ridiculous. Ridiculous and kind of sad, since I had no one to wait *for*. I ended up just standing in the middle of the corridor, my bag gripped tight in my hands, praying for the school bell to hurry up and ring.

After that, I decided I might as well wait around in the classroom, books and pens out like I'm actually studying.

I'm pretending to look over my calc notes from the other day when I hear footsteps approach. Pause, right before my desk. Then—

"Hey, Eliza."

I jerk my head up in surprise.

These two girls I've never spoken a word to in my life are smiling at me—positively *beaming*—as though we're best friends. I don't even know their names.

"Hi?" I reply. It comes out like a question.

They take this as an invitation to slide into the two empty seats beside me, still smiling so wide I can see all their pearly-white teeth. As one of them nudges the other, and a quick, meaningful look passes between them, I begin to have some idea of why they might be here.

"We read your essay," the taller, tanner girl on the left blurts out, confirming my suspicions.

"Oh," I say, unsure how else to respond. "Um, good. I'm glad."

"I just—god, I loved it so much," she continues brightly, in the manner of someone building to a big, emotional speech. "I was literally up all night reading it and—"

"It was so *cute*," the other girl chimes in, hand fluttering to her heart.

Okay. I definitely wasn't expecting *this.* Nor the small, involuntary smile tugging at my lips.

But soon they're both gesturing wildly and talking at the same time, their voices growing louder and louder with excitement:

"My favorite part was the bit at the grocery store, oh my god—"

"I had no idea you were going out with someone! You've been so low-key about it—"

"Do you have a picture of him? I mean, you don't have to show us if you don't want to, but—"

"What's his name? Does he go to our school?"

"Is he in our year level?"

"Is he in our *class*?"

They both turn, wide-eyed, to the classroom door, where more students are trickling in, as if one of the guys might suddenly step forward and declare himself my secret boyfriend. Nothing of the sort happens, of course, but people *do* slow down and stare at me like they've never really seen me before. Like they're hoping I might share something about my fake love life with them too.

The only person who goes straight to his desk at the very back is Caz Song. Hands in pockets, one AirPod in, expression of perpetual boredom on his face. Just like yesterday. He glances my way, briefly, impassively, then turns away.

And though it's really the least of my concerns, my rib cage curves inward. I'm not even sure what I was hoping for, why I imagined he'd acknowledge my existence after that one anomaly of a conversation out in the corridor. Caz Song and I are so different we might as well inhabit separate planets.

"Well?" the girl on my left prompts, drawing my attention back to her and her friend. "Is he?"

I study the two of them, searching for any signs of ill will or mockery. But they both just continue smiling, and I notice the light scatter of freckles across the taller girl's nose, the yellow butterfly clip in the other girl's wavy hair. They seem . . . nice. Genuinely friendly—

"Um, I can't tell you that," I say with a small, apologetic smile, hoping they'll leave the conversation there. "I wish I could, but, you know. We haven't been together *that* long, so we want to keep things private for now."

"Ah." They both nod slowly. Beam some more. Neither of them budges. "That's totally understandable."

Even though this is all part of the script I'd prepared when submitting my essay, it was only ever meant to be a preventative measure, not something to be shared with people across the world. It's like those life jackets they store on airplanes; nobody *actually* expects to have to use them.

As if on cue, my phone flashes again on my desk.

531 new notifications.

The taller girl sees before I can flip the screen down.

"Wow," she says as she finally starts unpacking her own stuff for class. A MacBook Air in shiny casing. Highlighters and pens with cute designs all over them. A thick planner that hardly looks used but has bright colored tabs running down the sides and a giant sticker of some K-pop group plastered on the cover. "You must've had a pretty wild morning, huh?"

"*Wild* is definitely one word for it," I say, relieved I can at least be honest about this.

"I've always wondered what it's like to go viral," the other girl muses. She has her laptop out, and nothing else. This is actually standard for students here, I've learned the hard way. At my old school, we were *only* allowed paper notes, so I didn't realize I would even need to bring a laptop until my first class at Westbridge, when everyone was working on a Google Doc and all I had was a notebook and pencil.

Yeah, not exactly the best start.

"Nadia, didn't that Douyin of yours go viral for a while the other month?" the tall girl is saying.

"The video got, like, twenty thousand views." Nadia waves a dismissive hand in the air. "That's *very* different from having like a bajillion people read your writing. Plus"—she wrinkles her nose—"I kept getting all those weird comments about my feet."

"True. We don't love that."

As the two of them break into giggles, I feel a dull pang in my chest. I'd kill to have that—to be sitting next to Zoe, laughing over some silly inside joke without worrying that I'll be leaving in a year. To feel so comfortable, at ease, at home.

Something must show on my face, because the tall girl stops and turns to me with concern. "Are you okay, Eliza?"

"Huh?" I feign confusion, then quickly pull my lips into a sheepish smile. "Yeah, of course. Just . . . thinking about the essay, I guess. And what I'm going to do about it."

The two of them make long *ah*ing sounds and nod again in total sync.

"That's a good point," the tall girl says. "You should do something about it for sure. You should— Oh! You should capitalize on the fame."

"Yes!" Nadia points one finger at me excitedly—and almost pokes my eye out. "Oops—sorry! But Stephanie's right. Whenever people go viral on Twitter, they always use it to promote themselves or boost their friend's baking account or something."

"Do you have one?" Stephanie asks, leaning over the back of her seat.

"What, a baking account?"

"Something to promote," she clarifies with a laugh. "So? What are you thinking?"

And it's silly, and beside the point, and completely unrealistic given the circumstances, but I *do* find myself thinking about it, some of my initial giddiness from this morning bubbling back up inside me. I've always dreamed of having people read my writing—read it, and actually like it—and now, for the first time ever, I have a potential readership. I have a *following.* Maybe if I published more essays while people are still paying attention, I could . . . I don't know. Jump-start a legitimate writing career. Make a name for myself. I could be a Writer, not just someone who writes.

But just as quickly as hope sprouts in my chest, I crush it back down.

People only want to hear more from me because they think my essay was real. They think I'm dating a good-looking boy who takes me out on spontaneous motorcycle rides around the city and once slow-danced with me in the middle of a grocery store aisle and texts me good night every evening before I fall asleep. They're in love with my love story.

If I want to keep writing and *capitalize on my fame*, as Stephanie says, I'll have to keep lying.

"I don't know," I say slowly. "Maybe—"

The door swings open before I can give a vague response, and everyone snaps to attention at once.

Our math teacher, Ms. Sui, strides to the front of the classroom, an intimidating sheaf of worksheets balanced on one hand, a briefcase swinging from the other. She reminds me of the teachers at my old Chinese Saturday schools. Everything about her is sharp: her gaze, her voice, the cut of her pure white blazer. Her teaching style reminds me of them too.

She doesn't greet us. She simply lets the worksheets drop to the desk with a menacing thud and calls on Stephanie to help pass them out.

We each get fifty double-sided pages of math questions printed in the tiniest of fonts, all due by tomorrow morning. This feels illegal. Someone makes a strangled noise that they quickly disguise as a cough.

Still, I'm almost grateful for the insane workload, for the focused silence that continues throughout the rest of class. I might be a good bullshitter, but I honestly don't know how many more questions I could field without letting something slip.

By the time lunch rolls around, I've spoken to more people in the past few hours than I have since I started school here. People keep coming up to me, calling for me in the busy corridors between classes, at the start of double English, even on my way to the bathroom—and now here, in the middle of the cafeteria line.

Someone taps my shoulder. "Hey, you're the girl with the essay, right?"

This is my reputation now, I guess: not "The New Girl from America" but "The Girl with the Viral Essay." I would consider it an upgrade if it weren't for my overwhelming fear of becoming known as "The Girl Who Lied" in a few days or weeks. Depending on how long I can keep pretending.

I spin around and find a whole squad of girls and three guys gaping at me.

They look a few years younger than I am, maybe year nines or tens. Some of them haven't even shed their baby fat yet, but the girls are all wearing heavy makeup and the guys have on copious amounts of hair gel in an attempt to look more Grown Up.

"Yeah," I say, smiling a little despite myself. "Yes. That's me."

"See, I *told you*," one of the girls says to the guy behind her.

The guy scowls. "She looks the exact same as her photo."

I blink. "Uh, my photo? What photo?"

The same girl's eyes widen while her friends titter. "Haven't you seen it? It's been going around everywhere—pretty flattering too," she adds hastily, in a way that makes me suspect she's lying. As we shuffle farther up the line, she fishes her phone out from her pocket and brandishes it in front of my face.

And I don't know whether to cry or laugh.

In an article for some online teen magazine (titled "Why We're All Swooning Over This Senior Student's Love Story"), someone's attached one of my old school photos from when I was still living in the States. It's actually impressive, how they managed to find the worst possible photo of me. My hair's been tied into a super-tight high ponytail that's hidden behind my head, so I pretty much look bald, and my eyes are only half-open and watery from having just sneezed.

I'd begged the school photographer—almost bribed him—to let me retake it at the time, but he'd waved me away with a cheery "Don't worry! Only your parents will see this anyway!"

Funny how that turned out.

"Wow," I say. "This is just . . . great."

"I know, right?" The girl beams, either missing my sarcasm or choosing to ignore it. "You're, like, famous now."

Famous. The word tastes funny, but not entirely in a bad way. There's something inherently *cool* about it, something flashy and shiny and desirable, all the things I never thought I could be. I just wish it were only my writing that was famous, and not me.

I make a noncommittal sound with the back of my throat and grab an empty tray. Try to focus on selecting my lunch. If there's one thing Westbridge International does well, it's the food. The school chefs serve actual three-course meals, and they change it up every day; we had pineapple fried rice and braised chicken and silk tofu earlier this week, then dim sum (complete with shrimp dumplings and fresh mango pudding and all) the day after.

Today, they're serving up roujiamo—shredded pork belly and diced scallion sandwiched in crisp, golden pieces of bing.

I heap four onto my tray and turn to go, but the kids behind me aren't done yet.

"Is it true that your boyfriend's identity is top secret?" the same girl asks.

My body stiffens, but my voice comes out smooth. "No. I mean . . . No, I wouldn't say that."

"So you can tell us who he is?" another girl pipes up.

"Also no."

Even though I can only see them out of the corner of my eye, I can practically sense their disappointment.

"Can y'all give her some space?"

This, from a girl in my year level I vaguely know. Her name starts with *S*: Samantha or Sally or Sarah . . . No, *Savannah*. She's standing at the front of the line, her tray stacked with at least six roujiamos, one hand on her hip.

After a stunned beat, the kids mumble apologies and back away. I almost feel bad for them. Savannah is one of those people who's effortlessly cool and absolutely terrifying at the same time. Her winged eyeliner alone is sharp enough to cut glass, and she's so tall I have to crane my neck a little just to look at her. It also doesn't hurt that she's dating one of Caz Song's friends; anyone with any connection to Caz Song is basically granted instant membership to the school's Super Popular, They-Could-Step-on-Me-and-I'd-Thank-Them circle.

"Um, thanks for that," I manage.

"No big deal," she says. She has a faint New York accent, and I remember hearing somewhere that she's Vietnamese American. Quite a few students around here fall into similar categories: Chinese American, Korean Australian, British Indian. All people who have grown up balancing different cultures. People like me. "Must be pretty overwhelming, huh? Getting questions like that all day."

"It's okay." I shrug, hoping to play it cool. "Could be a lot worse."

"Yeah, I mean, you could've gone viral for trying to go up a down escalator in the middle of a crowded mall only to end up falling and knocking over a mascot in a giant chicken costume."

I stare at her. "That's . . . very specific."

She laughs. "It was trending the other day. In fact, I think your post took its spot."

"That's nice? I guess?"

"Huge accomplishment," she agrees jokingly. "You should be proud."

We're standing near the cafeteria tables now, and for a moment, I debate asking if she wants to have lunch together. But that's silly. It's not like I have a great track record with keeping new friends; I can't imagine building a friendship on a deeply embarrassing lie would yield great results in any case. And like she said, her speaking up for me wasn't a big deal.

Plus, a scan of the cafeteria makes it clear that her boyfriend—*Daiki*, I remember from roll call—is waiting for her at the largest corner table, alongside Caz Song, Stephanie, and Nadia and a bunch of other loud, gorgeous, perfectly sociable people from our year level. They're laughing together at some joke Caz must've told just now, their mouths wide open, some actually doubled over in mirth. I can't help but stare for a few beats, an unwelcome, unreasonable stone of envy lodged in my gut.

"Well, thanks again," I tell Savannah with a weak half wave, eager to be alone. "Um, bye."

She looks surprised, but she nods at me. Smiles. "Anytime."

Then I leave her there. I leave the cafeteria entirely and climb the five flights of steps up to the very top of the building, my lunch tray still gripped tight in my hands. Soon, the babble of voices and clatter of plates fade away, and it's just me standing alone on the roof with warm, buttery sunlight falling around me.

For the first time since this morning, I feel myself relax slightly.

I love coming up here, not only because it's quiet and most often empty, but because it's beautiful. The rooftop is designed like a garden, with bright mandarin trees and slender bamboos and this gnarled-looking plant I can't name lining the sides and fresh jasmine flowers—Ma's favorite—blooming everywhere like little clusters of stars, sweetening the air with their scent. There are even fairy lights strung up around the railings and over the wooden swing set in one corner, though I've never stayed behind late enough to watch them glow.

The view's gorgeous too. From here, you can see the entire stretch of the school campus, and Beijing rising behind it, all that shiny glass and steel reflecting the clouds in the sky.

This is my trick to surviving new schools: Find a space like this, a place no one can disturb me, and claim it as my own.

It's especially useful now, when I need to figure things out alone.

I lower myself onto the swing and balance my tray on my lap, ripping out a large bite of the roujiamo with my teeth. Then I do the thing I've been putting off all day: I check my phone.

Generally speaking, I try to stay off social media as much as possible. Every new post from an old friend serves as a painful reminder: This is their life now, without you. This is their group of best friends, their boyfriend they didn't tell you about; this is them moving on completely. This is proof that when they said they'll remember you, stay in touch with you, they were lying. Sometimes I'll stare at an Instagram photo of someone I was close to in London, New Zealand, Singapore, at their fresh-dyed hair and wide grin and the kind of cropped jacket they wouldn't have been caught dead wearing years ago, and get the odd sense of seeing a total stranger on my feed.

But today, so many messages come flooding in that my phone freezes for a solid minute. My heart freezes as well. People I haven't spoken to in years—people from *primary school*—have reached out to me, all with screenshots or some variation of *omg you made it!* A few have followed up with questions like *How has life been?* or *It's been ages!* but the distant politeness of it all, compared with the keyboard smashes and emoji spam we used to send one another without thought, only drives another pang through my gut.

And all I can think is: *Thank god for Zoe.*

She's the only one left in my life. The only one who's stayed over the years. And the only one who's messaged me with a completely unrestrained number of exclamation marks demanding an explanation.

I shoot back a quick message promising to update her on everything the next time we call, before moving on to my inbox with quivering fingers. My mouth feels too dry. I can barely swallow.

At least twenty emails from journalists and writers for all kinds of media sites pop up, some requesting interviews, some asking for more exclusive material, including a couple selfie. I imagine myself posing with one arm around nothing but air, or one of those cardboard cutouts of a K-pop idol, and hysteria rises to my throat.

But the absurdity doesn't stop there. A few people have sent me links to think pieces inspired by my essay. "The Teen Love Story People Can't Stop Talking About: Joy in the Age of Cynicism," one reads. Another has tied the "surprising success" of my essay to the revival of rom-coms, as well as my generation's "growing disillusionment" with dating apps like Tinder. Yet another has somehow managed to drag my racial identity into their analysis, warning that the whole thing could be an elaborate ruse designed by the Chinese government to "soften the image of the rapidly emerging global superpower."

Despite the dread churning in my stomach, I can't help it; a laugh of disbelief bursts from my lips. This is by far the most ridiculous thing to have ever happened to me. That probably ever *will* happen to me, period.

But then a new email comes in with a faint ping, and my incredulity gives way to pure awe when I see who it's from.

CHAPTER FOUR

Dear Eliza,

I hope this email finds you well!

My name is Sarah Diaz. I had the tremendous pleasure of reading your viral essay "Love and Other Small, Sacred Things" last night, and I found myself extremely moved by your love story (a rare thing for a cynic like me). At times I laughed aloud; at other times I wanted to weep, in the best kind of way. All of this is to say that I think you have real potential, and I'd love to offer you an internship opportunity with us here at Craneswift. *This will be a paid position, for a total duration of six months, and I'd be most pleased to write you a letter of recommendation at the end of it, should you choose to accept . . .*

I read over the email for what must be the hundredth time on the car ride home, my breath caught in my throat.

Craneswift.

I'm scared that if I exhale, the words will dissolve. That the people at Craneswift will send me another email, telling me it was a huge mistake, that they've read over my essay again and realized their judgment was wrong.

Because this—this is everything I've ever wanted. I mean, I didn't even *know* I wanted it, since I never would've dared dream of getting to intern at Craneswift. The publication behind some of the most successful writers in the world.

And Sarah Diaz is one of the best writers they have. Maybe one of the best writers I know. I have a whole notebook filled with annotated quotes from her published essays and articles alone, carried it with me from city to city. Two years ago, she'd offered up a thirty-minute writing consultation for some kind of auction, and the highest bidder had paid over five grand for it. *That's* how badly most aspiring journalists crave her feedback.

If she really wants me to work for her—to work *with* her—then how could I say no?

But what am I going to do about my made-up relationship if I say yes?

"Jie, why are people at school saying you have a boyfriend?"

My head snaps up.

Emily is watching me curiously from the other side of the back seat. It's only the two of us in the car right now, plus Li Shushu, who's busy listening to his favorite Peking opera radio station.

Thank god. I'm not sure what I would say if Ma or Ba were here.

"I don't know," I tell her, attempting to laugh it off as a joke. "Don't listen to them."

"But *do* you have a boyfriend?" Emily presses, eyes wide.

"That—that's none of your business."

Wrong thing to say. Emily loosens her seat belt and edges closer toward me, despite my protests.

"It is so my business," she says, drawing herself up to look taller, more important. "I'm your sister. You have to tell me."

"You're only a kid."

She shoots me an indignant look. "I'm ten years old."

I snort despite myself. "My point stands. And also, you're *nine*."

"I'll be turning ten in less than half a year," she argues, her voice bordering on a whine. "It's the same thing."

"Still doesn't change the fact that I'm older than you."

She goes silent at that, but I know the conversation isn't over. She's just taking her time to think up a good counterargument; we're both like Ma in that way.

I'm thinking too—thinking about how I should handle this, what story I should feed her. The good news is that Emily isn't allowed to use social media until she turns thirteen, so she can't know the *details* of my essay. But people at school will continue to talk . . .

I lean back against the soft leather seat and close my eyes. I can feel a stress migraine forming.

When I open my eyes again, Emily is taking out a packet of matcha-flavored Pocky from her schoolbag, a very triumphant expression on her face.

"What?" I say.

"Nothing." But she's smiling now. A dangerous sign. "It's just that . . . you might not have to tell *me*, but you'd have to tell Ma and Ba, right?"

My pulse jumps. "Emily—don't you *dare* . . ."

"Then just answer my question," she insists, ripping the packet open. "I'll keep it a secret. Cross my heart."

I clench my jaw, weighing out my next move. I essentially have two choices: bribery or blackmail. Then my gaze lands on the Pocky sticks in her hand.

Perfect.

"I'll explain when I'm ready," I say. She opens her mouth to argue, but I continue, louder. "Until then, you have to promise not to speak a word about this at home. I'll buy you ten packets of Pocky if you do."

She falters, mouth still half-open. If there's anything Emily's willing to make a compromise for, it's food.

"Fine," she bites out eventually, and I let loose a small, silent sigh of relief. At least that's one less thing to worry about for now. Then Emily crosses her arms over her chest, jutting her chin forward. "But I want fifteen packets, and I want the cookies-and-cream-flavored ones too."

I frown. "You're getting thirteen. Cookies-and-cream only if they're available, plain chocolate if not. And that's final."

It's not until I see the happy gleam in her eyes that I realize she was planning this all along—that she probably only wanted twelve or thirteen packets in the first place. I'm going to have to be more careful around her when she gets older. She's already picking up on some of Ma's negotiation tactics.

Unsure whether to be annoyed or impressed, I hold out my palm.

"Um, are you going for a handshake?" Emily asks.

"No. I'm asking for a Pocky; I barely had lunch." On cue, my stomach grumbles. As good as the roujiamos were, I only had a few bites in the end. After I received Sarah Diaz's email, I was too busy freaking out to eat anything else. I mean, the opportunity could change the course of my whole career—my whole *life*. Just thinking about it now makes me a little dizzy.

"That's not my fault," Emily protests, holding the snack packet close to her chest. But after a beat, she grudgingly hands me three Pocky sticks.

"Thanks, kid." I grin, and she pulls a face at me. She hates it when people call her that.

We're both quiet for the rest of the drive, Emily because she's eating, and me because I'm trying to draft a reply to Craneswift. After about a dozen attempts, I end up sliding my phone back into my pocket, email unsent.

I don't know what to say. That's the problem. I don't even know what the internship itself would entail, what the consequences will be if my story is anything but airtight.

All I know is that I need a proper plan—and soon.

I spend the rest of the afternoon trying to formulate a plan while completing my math homework, and the only things I end up with are a bunch of most definitely incorrect answers and a worsening headache.

So after dinner, I decide to give myself a break and join my family in the living room.

This is our routine: At around nine o'clock every night, the four of us huddle together on the couch with a bowl of cut fruit or roasted sunflower seeds, and watch one episode of a C-drama.

"So," I say as I get comfortable, draping a thin blanket over my legs. "Whose turn is it to choose?"

Emily beams. "Mine."

Ma sighs from beside me. "You're going to pick something with a xiao xian rou as the lead, aren't you?"

Xiao xian rou is one of those trendy terms I learned only after we moved back to Beijing. It literally means "little fresh meat," which I realize sounds somewhat carnivorous, but it's used to describe most attractive male celebrities in their teens or early twenties.

"What do you think?" Emily says, her smile widening. Then, seeing Ma's expression of relative despair, she adds, "Don't worry, Ma. You'll get your pick next time."

"When will it be my turn?" Ba grumbles, rubbing his eyes. "You know how I feel about those romance dramas; why do people keep crashing into each other? And why do the female leads keep telling themselves to jiayou? Nobody talks like that."

"It was your turn last time," I remind him. "Remember that torture scene with the blood and guts everywhere? Emily complained about not being able to fall asleep afterward?"

Ba blinks, then sinks back in his seat. "There was hardly any blood—"

Emily and I burst into loud protests at the same time.

"Oh my god, Ba, there was *so much* blood—"

"The floors were bright red—"

"You couldn't even see the actor's face—"

"My eyes were bleeding just watching it—"

"And everyone *died* at the end."

"Okay, okay," Ba says hastily, exchanging a swift, amused look with Ma. "You girls choose."

Emily lifts her chin and sniffs. "As we should."

We have something of a system going, since all our tastes are so different: Ba loves those old war dramas where all anyone ever does is scream "traitor" at the top of their lungs and get hit by an unnecessary amount of bullets in slow motion; Ma prefers her business dramas, even though she spends half the time scoffing and yelling things like *"That's not how CMPs work!"* at the screen; and Emily and I will watch pretty much any idol romance featuring a good-looking lead.

I have a theory that Ma secretly likes her idol romances as much as we do, though. I made everyone watch *The Untamed* when it was my turn, and she seemed more invested in the characters than any of us.

Emily snatches the remote and starts streaming this cute campus romance drama. Ba's eyes glaze over a little, and Ma grumbles something about how all the opening credits look the same these days, but I lean closer to the TV. This is exactly what I need right now: pure, joyful escapism.

We're about two minutes into the first scene (which, predictably, involves the protagonist and love interest crashing into each other in the hallway and getting their phones mixed up) when I realize the male lead looks familiar.

Very familiar.

He has the same sharp jaw, the same dark gaze and perfectly rumpled raven-black hair. The same elegant cheekbones and tall nose. And even though his character's posture is different—for once, he's not slouching or leaning on anything—his expression, the way he's looking at the protagonist with that disarming mixture of exasperation and amusement, is all too familiar as well.

Caz Song.

I'm watching one of Caz Song's dramas.

Well. So much for escapism.

I try to act normal about this revelation—I mean, far more surprising things have happened today—but I can't describe how weird it feels to see one of your classmates flirting with some famous actress on the TV screen in your own living room. It somehow feels like an invasion of privacy, though I'm not sure if it's *his* privacy or mine. Maybe both.

"He's hot," Emily comments as the camera zooms in on Caz's eyes, then on his full, naturally pouted lips.

I almost choke. "Don't—don't say things like that, Emily."

"What? He *is*." Emily turns to Ma for support. "Isn't he good-looking, Ma?"

Ma studies the screen carefully. "Mm. Better than most of the xiao xian rous I've seen." Then, catching Ba's eye across the couch, she adds with emphasis, "But obviously your father is the best-looking guy out there."

"Of course I am," Ba says.

Emily snorts. "Su-ure."

"Well, I don't think he's *that* hot," I grumble, pulling my blanket up to my chin. On-screen Caz is stroking the girl's cheek now with one thumb, and I can feel my own cheeks growing warm. "It's probably just makeup. And filters."

I know for a fact that it isn't makeup or filters, because Caz looks like that every time I see him at school, but there's no way I'm admitting he's attractive out loud, to my family.

"Your standards are way too high, Jie," Emily says.

"She's right," Ma agrees, patting my knee. "You'll never find a boyfriend if you don't even want someone like him."

Emily opens her mouth as if to make a correction, and my heart almost stops. But then she winks at me and mimes zipping her lips shut. I read somewhere that sisters develop their own kind of telepathy, which must be true, because I'm one hundred percent sure I know what silent message Emily is sending me: *Remember the Pocky.*

Of course I remember, I send back with a glare. *Just keep quiet.*

Got it, she replies. *By the way, can you get me some water?*

I roll my eyes, but I get up and pour everyone a glass of warm water from the kettle, then cut up a mango just to be nice. As I sit back down, I can't help reading over Sarah Diaz's email on my phone again. It's still there, still real, tangible evidence that Craneswift wants me to work for them—but also that I can't possibly keep up my lie on my own. My eyes fasten on one of the internship requirements:

It would be wonderful if your posts could share more details about your relationship, and provide photos of you two together . . .

Where the hell am I supposed to get *photos*? Do I hire someone from those dodgy rent-a-boyfriend sites? Photoshop some random guy into a selfie? But no, neither option sounds reliable. And with how fast the internet moves, I'm pretty sure everyone would find out the truth within a day. It has to be somebody I actually know, somebody convincing . . .

"Jie, are you even watching?" Emily calls.

"Huh? Oh—yeah. Of course." I snap my head up just in time to see on-screen Caz Song invite the female lead onto the back of his motorcycle. As I watch the two of them ride through the city, the artificial sunlight moving over them, I'm struck by an idea.

A ridiculous, absolutely laughable idea. An idea that might complicate everything further.

But an idea that might just work.

Later that evening, when everyone's asleep, I turn on my laptop. Suck in a deep breath. Then, feeling weirdly self-conscious and almost *nervous* for some reason, I search "Caz Song" on Baidu.

The results come up at once.

There are even more relevant articles and interviews than I expected, because—to my slight dismay—Caz Song is somehow even more popular than I expected. He has over five million followers on his official Weibo account alone, a ridiculous number of fan pages declaring their undying love for him, and a whole series of professional photo shoots and special campaign shots with sponsored brands. In each one, he's so beautiful he looks fake. It's almost offensive how perfect he is, a teen fantasy made flesh.

There's something bizarre about the idea that this one guy in my class, who I see around the lockers and cafeteria and suffer through math pop quizzes with every day, is known by millions of people across the country. Not only known, but *liked.* Adored to the extent that someone left a six-paragraph comment under a video of him, asking him to sleep well and stay hydrated and take care of his houseplants.

Then I remember that *my* writing has been viewed by millions of people too, that all those people now know me by extension, and my head just about implodes. Which brings me back to why I'm doing this in the first place.

Why I need to do this.

Before I can lose my nerve, I start with the basics: Caz's Baike page.

It's basically the equivalent of Wikipedia, in that it'll give you all the biographical information you want on a famous person, divided up into nice, neat categories.

Some of the stuff I've already been made to know against my will, just from overheard conversations at school. Like how he was born in America but moved to Beijing when he was nine; or how his parents are both doctors, both originally from a tiny town in South China; or how he's professionally trained in martial arts, about ten different instruments, horse riding, and archery.

But there are other details listed too, important things I've definitely missed—

Like the fact that he lives in my compound.

My heart leaps. It's perfect. It's almost *too* perfect, as though designed by fate, or maybe God himself, if God were interested in the petty drama of awkward teenagers.

I scroll further, faster, moving on to the more gossipy, fan-made sites.

The most viewed article dates back to only a couple weeks ago. Apparently, there'd been something of a scandal at a huge awards ceremony, all because Caz Song had failed to help an older, well-respected actress into her seat. The comment section below is, of course, a war zone. Some are so enraged by his behavior one would think he had shoved the actress down the stage and laughed in her face or something. *I'm sorry, but I simply can't stand him any longer*, one user wrote. *I used to imagine he'd be the thoughtful, chivalrous, perfect-boyfriend type, but clearly he doesn't have even the most basic manners. Goodbye, Caz. It was good while it lasted.* Other hard-core fans have jumped out to defend him: *But maybe he didn't see her!* Or: *If he'd helped her, all the antis would've blamed him for not respecting her personal space. There's literally no winning.*

The whole thing's absurd, yet what's wilder is that a massive cosmetics brand actually dropped Caz Song after the backlash, claiming that all their ambassadors ought to be "thoughtful" and "sensitive" and "courteous," and demanding an explanation for his behavior. Someone's even made a video analyzing the situation, which I click on. It's followed by another video, titled "All of Caz Song's Interviews Pt. 1" . . .

I don't notice how deep I've wandered down this particular rabbit hole until I find myself watching a twenty-minute, fan-edited video compilation of Caz Song drinking water.

"This is ridiculous," I mutter to myself, promptly slamming my laptop shut. "I'm being ridiculous."

For a while, I just sit there in my own silence, listening to the apartment breathing around me. The birds singing in the night's distance. The dull tangle of piano chords drifting from some floors down below, by some neighbor I know of but have never met before.

Then I grab my phone. Read over the email I've pretty much etched into my brain by now.

I had the tremendous pleasure of reading your viral essay "Love and Other Small, Sacred Things" last night, and I found myself extremely moved . . .

And resolve hardens inside me. I open my laptop again and pull up a blank PowerPoint, suddenly grateful for all the times Ma asked me to look over her work before delivering a presentation to her company. This shouldn't be too different from that.

In big, bold letters, I type out the first slide: *A Strategic, Mutually Beneficial and Romantically Oriented Alliance to Help Further Our Respective Careers.*

CHAPTER FIVE

The one major downside of my plan, I quickly realize, is having to speak to Caz Song alone.

Because Caz is never alone. Like, *never*.

Early in the morning, I find him surrounded by at least half our year level at the lockers, all of them seemingly fascinated by the way he takes his books out of his bag. Then, during class, people keep sliding into the seat next to him and going up to him for help, despite the fact that he's far from the best student. Even his walks to the school cafeteria are somehow a big group activity, with at least ten people trailing after him, offering to buy him lunch or describe today's specials.

By the end of fifth-period PE class, I'm starting to feel restless.

Desperate.

So when everyone's released early to go change, all stinking of fresh sweat and ancient gym equipment, I throw on my uniform as fast as I can, pack my stuff, and wait outside the boys' locker rooms.

A few guys come out first, hair still dripping wet from the showers (I've never understood how guys can actually shower at school), and start at the sight of me. I give them an awkward wave.

"Nothing to see here," I call cheerily, stepping aside to let them through. "Just chilling . . ."

To my immense relief, Caz is the next person to emerge. His hair is more damp than wet, falling in messy ink-black strands over his face, and for a moment I remember the way he'd looked on my TV screen last night. The way he'd touched that other girl's cheek.

"Hi," I say. My voice comes out higher and louder than I intended, bouncing off the dull tiled walls around us.

He pauses. Stares at me. "Oh, look," he says finally, his mouth curving into something too muted to qualify as a smile. "It's my nonfan."

I suppress a wince and try to go on as if I haven't heard him. "Do you—do you have a minute?"

My pulse speeds up. I've never done this before, never approached a boy out of nowhere, let alone a celebrity. We're standing so close that I can smell his shampoo—a fresh, mildly sweet scent that reminds me of summer. Green apple, maybe.

Caz shrugs, looking somewhat bemused. "Yeah, sure, I guess."

"Perfect."

Without another word, I grab his wrist and drag him into the nearest empty room—

Which happens to be a janitor's closet. Great.

"Uh," Caz says as I shut the door behind us. The sharp stench of bleach and damp cloth instantly rises to my nose, and I'm acutely aware that there's a dirty mop propped up inches away from my hair. "Why are we standing in a janitor's closet?"

"That's an excellent question."

I yank open my schoolbag and fish around for my laptop before setting it up on a shelf of hand sanitizer. To be honest, I'd really been imagining this playing out a different way; there'd be a projector, for one, to bring out the high-res visuals of my slideshow, and enough space for me to make elaborate hand gestures without knocking over a giant mountain of toilet paper.

But whatever. I can be flexible.

"So. I have an idea," I tell Caz as formally as possible while I wait for my PowerPoint to load. "And it's going to sound a little . . . *outlandish*, maybe, but I promise it'll be good. For both of us. Life-changing, even."

Caz arches a dark brow. "Are you trying to recruit me for a cult, Eliza?"

"What? No, I—"

"Because I'm not allowed to join," he continues over me, leaning back against a vacuum cleaner and somehow managing to make it look cool. "Contractually speaking, I mean. My manager doesn't want me to join any group or organization unless it's the next big boy band."

I don't even know how to respond to that.

"No . . ." I finally manage. Shake my head. "No, this isn't about a cult or a—a boy band, for that matter. It's about *this*." I point to my laptop screen, where the first slide is now up and ready, the giant title glowing in the dim light of the closet.

I can sense, rather than see, Caz's surprise.

"Before you say no or get weirded out," I tell him, taking advantage of his silence, "just let me give you more details, okay?"

"Sure." Now he sounds amused, which isn't exactly what I was going for, but it's better than impatience or outright contempt, I guess.

With a click, the PowerPoint changes to the next slide: *A Very Brief Summary of My Current Predicament.* Screenshots of my essay, the BuzzFeed article, and a couple of the most liked Twitter comments are pasted below.

"Are all your slides this wordy?" Caz muses.

I frown at him. "That's obviously not the point."

"Right," he says. Cocks his head. "So enlighten me: What *is* the point here?"

Faint irritation rises inside me, like the just-audible buzzing of a fly or the itch of a new clothing tag against your skin. Still, I force myself to smile. Keep my cool. "Well, you know how I said in my essay that I've been dating this guy since . . ." I trail off when I notice the blank look on Caz's face. "You haven't read my essay?"

He jerks a shoulder. "Honestly? No."

Okay. This is going to be even harder than I thought.

"I can check it out now, if that helps," he offers, reaching for his phone.

The idea of him reading my essay within such close proximity of me while I stand around and wait for his reaction kind of makes me want to bolt out the closet, but I wait silently as he searches for the right link, taking what feels like all the time in the world.

His eyebrows rise when he finally finds it. His lips twitch.

Then, to my absolute horror, he starts reading my essay aloud. *"It was the kind of small, subtle moment they rarely show in the movies or include in the novels. There was no dramatic orchestra playing in the background, no fireworks, nothing but the pale summer sky simmering gently around us, the soft scratch of his sweater against—"*

"Oh my god," I say, mortified.

He keeps reading, louder. *"—my cheek. I missed him. That must sound ridiculous, because he was already standing as close to me as the laws of physics would allow—"*

"I hate this so much," I tell him through gritted teeth. I can physically *feel* myself cringing. "Please stop."

He flashes me a grin, and the rarity of it is enough to make me falter, if only for one second. Then he says, "Are you sure you don't want to hear about how you *let him bury his face in the crook of my neck, almost like a tired child. I tried my best to stay completely still, to just be there for him, the way—*"

"Caz," I snap.

"Eliza," he returns, but thankfully he stops torturing me with my own writing. "You know, I hate to break it to you, but if you can't stand the idea of *me* reading those few sentences, you're *really* not going to like the fact that"—he consults his phone for a second—"over a million people have already read your essay."

"That's fine. I mean, that's not the same thing. Those are strangers."

I can tell he doesn't understand my reasoning, and I'm not sure how to explain it to him, why I'd much rather show my work to random people on the internet than people who know me in real life, so I swiftly move the conversation along to more pressing issues.

"Here's the thing, though," I begin, gesturing back to my PowerPoint slide. "The essay you just read is . . . well, it's fake."

"Fake," Caz repeats. His expression is unreadable. "Which part?"

"Um, pretty much all of it," I say in a rush, as if this might make the situation less embarrassing. "I mean, I was the one who *wrote* it, but . . . there is no boyfriend. There's not even a boy. It's just—the personal essay assignment was due, and I didn't know who to write about, so I kind of panicked and—"

"Made something up?" he finishes for me.

"Yeah," I say awkwardly. "Yes."

He nods once. Looks away. At first I'm scared I've upset him—maybe he's one of those students who's super serious about academic integrity or something, in which case I'm screwed—but then he presses one hand to his mouth, and I realize he's trying not to laugh.

Unbelievable. Absolutely unbelievable.

"It's not funny," I protest, crossing my arms. "This is a—a major . . ."

He points to the slide title. "A predicament?"

"Yes. Now stop finishing my sentences," I tell him, annoyed. "And *stop laughing at me.*"

"All right, all right." He straightens and composes his features with impressive speed, all remaining traces of humor wiped clean from his face. No wonder he's a professional actor. "So let me get this straight: Now everyone's rooting for you and this made-up relationship, and you want me to pretend to be the boyfriend from your essay until everything dies down. Is that it?"

I open my mouth to respond when the warning bell rings, a harsh, shrill sound that cuts through the closed door. Within seconds, loud footsteps and voices and laughter spill out into the halls, about two hundred teenagers talking at once, accompanied by the slamming of lockers, the snap and thud of books. The sound of people drawing closer. *Crap.* I only have ten minutes before the final bell goes off. "Look, whatever. The point is, if you agree to do this with me, you'll be benefiting from it too. I'll help you out with your college essays, for one—"

"Hold up." He raises a hand, very narrowly avoiding knocking over a bottle of cleaning spray. His brows furrow, the first crack in his cavalier demeanor. His voice is careful, controlled, when he asks, "Who said I needed help with my college essays?"

"Um . . . You did. On the phone the other day. During the parent-teacher interviews . . ."

"Right," he says dryly, though there's an undercurrent of tension to it. Frustration. "From that private conversation you weren't listening to."

There's no dignified way to reply to this, so I just give him a small, sheepish smile and pray he'll let this particular detail drop. Of course he does not.

"I don't recall mentioning anything about getting *help,* though," he says, his chin jutting forward, dark eyes flashing. "That doesn't sound like me at all."

"Not, like, explicitly. But it seemed a pretty pressing issue and also—don't take this the wrong way or anything—but I've read your usual essays for English when we've done those peer-evaluation things. And I'm not saying your work isn't, um, *good*, but if you're really hoping to impress the admissions team, some help definitely wouldn't hurt."

His voice is completely aloof when he says, "You know, for someone who claims to not be my fan, you sure know a lot about me."

"Not by choice," I retort. "You're kind of everywhere."

This comes out way more resentful than I meant, and I quickly backpedal, aware of the most basic business principle: Don't insult the person you're trying to loop into a deal. "Look, it's not just the essays you'll be getting. It's also good publicity for you. I mean, if you look at the comments"—I nod toward the last slide—"people are already in love with you, just based on my very flattering descriptions of my supposed boyfriend. And who doesn't love the idea of a famous, swoon-worthy actor dating a non-celebrity writer from his own year level? It's perfect fairy-tale-slash-magazine material. Plus, after your awards ceremony scandal—"

Something flickers over his features. "How . . . did you know about that?"

"This is a thoroughly researched proposal," I explain, though I feel an annoying rush of heat. Now he's probably picturing me googling him, which *can't* be good for his already-inflated ego. "And thanks to my research, I'm confident that this could help clear up the backlash. Everyone will know from my essays that you're *exactly* as sweet and considerate as they'd fantasized about. So?" I stop to take a breath. "What do you think?"

He doesn't say anything at first, just stares at me, his chin still slightly raised as if in self-defense, the lines of his body pulled taut.

Please say yes, I pray inside my head. My heart is thudding so hard against my ribs I'm scared he can hear it. *Please, please say you'll go along with this.*

"Hmm" is all he says, poker face perfectly in place. "So this fake relationship—"

I glance pointedly at the PowerPoint.

"Sorry," Caz says with a little mock bow, and reads off the first slide, "This *Strategic, Mutually Beneficial and Romantically Oriented Alliance to Help Further Our Respective Careers*—"

"S.M.B.R.O.A.H.F.O.R.C. for short," I offer.

"Yeah, uh, I don't think that's shorter," Caz tells me. Clears his throat. "I mean, there are definitely less *letters*, but. You know. Time-wise . . ."

"Fine." I bite my tongue. "Just carry on with what you were saying."

"Well, what would it . . . involve, exactly?"

Hope flutters in my chest. He's considering it, then. Caz Song might actually agree to this.

"Nothing too wild," I reassure him, my heartbeat quickening. Ma always says she feels this physical tug inside her whenever she's about to close a deal. I never understood what she meant until now; every muscle in my body is tensed, on edge. My hands feel shaky with adrenaline.

I quickly pull up the next and final slide. There, I've laid out a basic timeline: six months, covering the period of my internship with Craneswift, and made to coincide perfectly with when his next drama starts airing, for maximum publicity. Then there are all the ground rules, such as no mouth-to-mouth kissing, no physical contact beyond casual shoulder-bumping and occasional hugging (only when absolutely necessary), and no elaborate romantic gestures unless there's a substantial crowd watching. Coming up with this very specific list at around three in the morning was probably one of the lowest points of my existence so far—which is really saying something.

"No *mouth-to-mouth kissing*?" Caz reads, and I can tell he's making a conscious effort not to laugh again. "As opposed to what?"

To my great annoyance, I can feel the back of my neck heating. "You know what I mean. It's just—it's something people say."

"I've literally never heard anyone say those specific words in that order before," he informs me, lips curving. Then, maybe catching the murderous expression on my face, he makes a half-hearted surrendering motion and says, "Okay, okay. Sure."

"Sure?"

"I'll do it."

I blink, my brain lagging a little. "Wait, sorry. You'll do . . . ?"

"This." He nods at the laptop. "S.M.B.R.O.A.H.F.O.R.C. Though I really think we could come up with a better name."

"Really?"

He pauses. Leans closer, until there is nothing between us but the dark, thin air, the green-apple scent of his shampoo. I instinctively take a step backward. "Yes, Eliza," he says, his voice somber. "I really do think we need a better name."

I'm so relieved—so stunned by my own victory—that I don't even mind his joke.

"Then I guess . . . I guess it's final," I say slowly. "We're doing this." I extend my hand for a proper handshake to close the deal, the same time he raises his for a high five.

Wait. Who the hell *high-fives* this kind of thing?

"Okay . . ." I say, when neither of us moves. "Um, I guess we can . . ."

He rolls his eyes at me, but not before amusement dances over his sharp features. Then he takes my hand in his and shakes it. His skin is warm and surprisingly smooth, soft even, save for the few calluses on his palm. And despite his casual stance, his grip is firm. Ma would approve—not that it matters.

I pull away first.

"So. Okay," I repeat, kind of dazed. This is all happening very fast. "Good talk. I—I'll be in touch."

I move to open the door, to run somewhere quiet and collect my thoughts, but Caz holds out an arm in front of me. He looks like he's debating something, but after a beat, he says, "You know you could've chosen a different method, right?"

I blink, uncomprehending.

"You overheard my conversation the other day," he says slowly, like he's surprised he has to even spell this out. "Private details about my life. And you're a writer. A good one, with what's now a substantial audience."

"And . . . ?"

"You could've blackmailed me into working with you. Threatened to write up a huge piece on my struggles with school or my family relationships or whatever unless I agreed to your conditions. You didn't have to make this a *mutually beneficial* arrangement." There's still that faint teasing edge to the way he says it, but his eyes are dark, more serious than I would've expected.

"That . . . never occurred to me," I say in total honesty, surprised both by the idea itself and how fast his mind worked to produce it. Threats and forced deals must be the natural way of the world to him.

"It never occurred to you," he repeats. Then his face smooths out, and he draws closer. "Well, too late to change your mind. We're starting now, right?"

"Huh?"

“This is a good opportunity,” he says, gesturing to us, then to the dim, cramped closet and the stream of noise right outside it. Before I can fully grasp what he’s suggesting, he drags a hand through his already-messy hair, undoes one shirt button, and bites his lips until they look slightly swollen and red. As if . . .

As if we’ve just been making out in here.

“Well?” Caz is watching me, expectant. Completely unfazed. Almost *bored.*

I guess this wouldn’t be a big deal to him. Actors like him must go around pretending to kiss people all the time. In fact, he’s probably filmed scenes way more intense than mere kissing, with professional cameras trained on his lips and a whole room of people watching him too.

But the closest I’ve ever gotten to kissing a boy was that time in seventh grade, when I turned around during a frog dissection the same time my lab partner did, and our lips came about an inch short of touching. He’d freaked out and bolted to the bathroom, spitting and rubbing his mouth the whole way as if he’d been poisoned, while I shriveled up in my seat and prayed for the floor to swallow me whole.

I was pretty glad to leave that school behind a few months after the unfortunate incident.

Anyway, it’s not like I can say any of this to Caz. He’ll probably laugh at me, or worse, *feel sorry* for me. So I take out the tinted lip balm I always keep in my pocket and smear it around my mouth, trying not to think about how ridiculous I must look. I mean, the chances are that I now look more like a clown than someone who's just come out of a hot make-out session. Do people even *come out* of make-out sessions? Or do they *emerge*, maybe, exit gracefully, like some kind of ethereal mermaid from the sea? No, that doesn't sound quite right either . . .

Whatever.

"How's this?" I ask Caz.

He inspects me for a second, his gaze thoughtful, and something shifts over him. *Within* him. Like a camera's clicked on, and he's sliding into a new role, a different character, the change so swift it alarms me.

Then he reaches for my ponytail. "Can I?"

I don't really know what he means, but I smile. Nod. Resist the impulse to run.

And then Caz's long fingers are running through my hair, tugging my ponytail loose, his movements so light and fast I barely register anything except a faint, pleasant tingling sensation over my scalp. It's a small, casual gesture, but in the brief moment when his hands are still in my hair and his eyes are on me, I feel . . . *something*. Something like embarrassment, yet not like it at all.

Then the feeling's gone. Caz moves away and turns toward the door, glancing back at me over his shoulder. "Are you ready?"

No. Not even remotely.

I know I can't trust the boy standing before me—this pretty actor with his perfect hair and practiced charm and hordes of fans, the person everyone either wants or wants to be. But right now, I don't have any better options.

"Of course," I tell him, injecting as much enthusiasm into my voice as possible.

He seems to believe me, though, because he motions me forward and pushes the door wide open.

For one short, blissful second after we emerge from the janitor's closet, no one notices us.

Students continue to pack the school halls, yelling out to their friends from opposite ends of the corridors, shoving aside people's books and bags to get to their next class. Nobody spares our messed-up hair and swollen lips a second glance, and I wonder—foolishly, naively—if maybe this won't be as big a deal as I'd thought.

Then, in the next second, *everyone* notices.

The scene isn't quite as dramatic as it would be in a movie. People don't freeze in place or stumble down the stairs or drop their bags in shock. But there's a noticeable dip in the volume, a pause, like a video buffering.

Whispers start fluttering around us.

Caz, to his credit, looks totally unperturbed. He's wearing the smug, slightly sheepish expression of a guy who's just been caught kissing a girl he likes and doesn't mind the whole world finding out.

I, on the other hand, don't know what to do with myself. My face feels all hot and itchy, and a few wisps of my hair have stuck to my lip balm. Now more than ever, I wish there was some sort of guide on what to do when you're thrust from anonymity to the center of attention within two days' time. It's enough to give anyone whiplash.

"Oh my god," someone standing to my left says, and it works like a trigger, setting off a round of audible reactions:

"Oh my *god.*"

"Are you seeing this? That's Caz Song and—"

"Is *he* the one from that girl's essay?"

"Tell Brenda. She's going to freak, holy shit—"

I can sense more than a dozen pairs of eyes pinned on the back of my head as I walk with Caz to English, our shoulders close enough to touch.

"You good?" Caz whispers to me at the doorway, one hand resting against the frame behind my shoulder. A thousand times, in movies and music videos and real life, I've seen couples stand together like this. But for me, this is completely new.

Not that I can let it show.

"Yeah," I say, doing my best to sound flippant. "Of course. Are you?"

He laughs, and only then do I realize how dumb my question must sound. Why *wouldn't* he be fine? He's an actor, a celebrity. Attention is his version of normal.

The bell rings again—a final warning. Everyone seated is staring at us.

I avert my eyes and hurry to my usual table in the middle, where I always sit alone. To my surprise, however, Caz drops into the empty seat beside me, as if he's done this a million times before.

The staring officially turns into open gawking.

"What are you doing?" I mutter out of the corner of my mouth. Though there aren't any formal rules about it, everyone knows the classrooms are strictly divided into different territories: the overachieving, academically gifted kids at the front, the popular and sporty kids at the back, and everyone else in the middle. Caz moving over here from the back row is like the high school equivalent of someone crossing the North Korean border.

"It's easier this way" is all he says, tipping his chair backward.

Mr. Lee strolls into the classroom, does a small but visible double take at the sight of us sitting together, and starts handing out worksheets. Caz immediately tears off a corner of the reading activity on burial rites, scribbles something down on it, then slides the crumpled note over to me.

He does all this while keeping his eyes straight ahead, his expression bored and blank.

I can be that good an actor too. I pretend to be busy jotting down the date on my worksheet as I smooth out the note, shielding it from view with one hand.

His phone number is written across the center.

Right. I write down my own number in the space below, tear it off, and wait for the teacher to turn his head before sliding the note back.

My first time exchanging numbers with a boy, and it feels like I'm organizing a bank robbery or something. Then again, it's probably for the best. The only way this arrangement will work is if we keep things purely professional.

Back in my room later that afternoon, I reply to Craneswift's email.

It takes me a whole hour just to draft three sentences. Half that time is spent trying to figure out where to put my exclamation marks and how many I should use. In my defense, there's a very delicate balance to strike. If I use two exclamation marks in a row, for example, I'll risk coming across as overeager and needy. But if I use *no* exclamation marks, everything I say will sound strangely flat and cold. In the end, I decide to play it safe and add only one exclamation mark after the *thank you*.

Then I lose another half hour debating which sign-off is most appropriate (one article online recommends *Sincerely*, while another is morally opposed to it).

If this is what being a Working Professional is like, then honestly, no thanks.

Once the email's sent, I change out of my uniform and plop down on my bed, not expecting to hear another word from Craneswift until at least the next morning. But then my phone dings with a new email.

Sarah Diaz wants to call.

Like, right now.

"Oh my god," I say, shooting to my feet. My heart is already racing in a mad staccato. "Oh my god, oh my god, oh my god."

She's attached her number in the email. I enter it carefully into my phone, double-checking every digit, then press the call button with trembling hands. While the call dial plays, I stare at the blank whiteness of my bedroom wall and try to focus on my breathing.

Sarah picks up on the third ring.

"Hello?" My voice sounds way too high and shaky. I sound like a *seven-year-old.* I clear my throat. "Can you hear me?" No, now it's too low.

Before I can remember how to speak properly, Sarah Diaz says, "Hi, Eliza, I can hear you," in this smooth, crisp, super-professional tone I've heard Ma adopt whenever she's speaking to clients.

"Hello," I repeat, for literally no reason. *Get a grip on yourself.* "Ms. Diaz. It's so nice to meet you."

"Oh, you can just call me Sarah." Then, maybe because she can sense my nerves and raw awe through the phone, she lets out a small laugh. "Sorry to schedule a call so soon. I hope you're not too busy—"

"Oh, no, not at all," I hurry to respond. "I had no plans whatsoever. I'm, like, super free. I'm always free."

"Well, that's good to hear," she says, and she sounds like she means it. There's the low hum of a printer in the background and the clack of keyboards, and I imagine her seated behind a sleek black office desk with a clear view of the city below, a steaming cappuccino and glossy magazines spread over a coffee table. What must it be like, to live a life like that? To be someone like her? "I guess I wanted to first tell you how much I enjoyed your essay, and how glad I am that you've agreed to our internship offer. As you might already know, we're really hoping to expand our readership and attract the younger demographic, and we think you'd be the *perfect* person to help us achieve this. Your writing has this really authentic, youthful energy to it that'll be sure to resonate with teens, while also having the depth that appeals to our older, existing readers . . ."

Okay, listen to this, I tell myself, pressing the phone as close to my ear as possible, the screen warm against my skin. *Really* listen. *Memorize every word. You're not going to have the chance to be praised by someone like Sarah Diaz again.*

But I'm so focused on reminding myself to listen to Sarah talk and marveling over how strange it is that I'm on the phone with her that I don't actually process a single thing she says.

Next thing I know, she's asking, "Does that all sound good with you, Eliza?"

"Um . . ." I try not to panic as my own confused silence fills the line with static. Either I just say yes and find out later what I've agreed to, or I ask her to repeat everything she said in the past five minutes and risk looking like an idiot. Crap. What would Ma do? "Sorry, um, could you just clarify that last part? I want to make sure I fully understand everything before deciding to proceed."

"Oh, yes, certainly," Sarah says, still maintaining that same pleasant, professional tone. "So right now we're looking at a weekly blog post on our site, in the Love and Relationships category: Think of it as a sort of follow-up or update on your relationship, what you've been doing together, where you've been going out on dates. The more details the better, really; we want our readers to feel like they're really on this journey *with you*. And it'd be great to cross-post on social media too—preferably on Twitter, since that's where your following seems to be growing the fastest, but it's up to you. Altogether, it shouldn't take more than a time commitment of fifteen hours per week. Oh, and toward the end of the six-month period, we'd *love* for you to write a longer article on any topic of your choosing; we'll print it in our spring edition. What do you think, Eliza?"

"Okay," I agree slowly, as if I could possibly say no to her. "That sounds good."

"Oh, wonderful!" Somehow, I can almost *hear* her beaming. "And you're sure your boyfriend won't mind? I understand that it's a lot of publicity, especially given that you're both still quite young . . ."

From the sound of it, she doesn't know about Caz yet. I'm tempted to tell her right now—she'll probably be ecstatic; after all, what's more newsworthy than dating a semi-celebrity?—but I make myself wait. It's better if she finds out through some secondary source. It'll be more convincing that way.

"I don't think he'll mind at all," I reassure her. "Publicity is, like, his thing."

She laughs out loud, probably thinking I'm joking.

After we confirm the internship contract details and I hang

up in a daze, I check my email, still half-convinced I'm hallucinating about all this. But there it is—the contract she promised, with my name written at the top. *It's real.* Craneswift. My favorite publication wants *me* to work for them.

I stare and stare at the email until my eyes blur and my heart threatens to burst. Then I collapse back onto my bed with a soft, strangled laugh.

"What even is life," I whisper out loud to myself.

CHAPTER SIX

For the second time this week—and two days in a row—I find myself standing inside a janitor's closet with Caz Song.

"We really need to find a better meeting spot," Caz mutters as I lock the door behind us. It's still early in the morning, before classes officially start.

"It's not my fault you're so popular," I tell him, trying and failing to conceal the faint creep of irritation in my voice. A few minutes ago, I had to literally grab him by the elbow and steer him away from a crowd of excited students like some kind of bodyguard. "And anyway, this place isn't *that bad.*" I gesture to the four different brands of disinfectant on the shelves and tray of yellow-green sponges beside my feet. "It's actually pretty, um, well supplied. Very practical. Like, if there were an earthquake or something, we'd do really well in here, you know?"

Caz makes a quiet sound that could either be a laugh or a scoff. "Okay, stop trying to sell me this janitor's closet or whatever it is you're doing and tell me why we're here. Again."

"Well, I just wanted to make sure we're both clear on what we'll be doing today. Dating-wise."

He gives me this look like, *That's it?* "And you couldn't have simply texted me about this?"

"I was busy yesterday," I reason. Which is true—I spent ages going over the details of the contract, and another two hours trying to word a professional-sounding reply to Sarah—but not the full truth. There's just something about directly reaching out to him via phone, outside school, that's mildly terrifying.

Okay, *really* terrifying.

Caz shakes his head. "What even is there to discuss?" Before I can reply, he suddenly stills with fake horror. "Wait, don't tell me you have another PowerPoint ready—"

"No," I say, rolling my eyes, even though I did actually consider the idea for a moment last night. But he doesn't need to know that. "And there is *so much* to discuss; consistency is key to a believable lie. Like, I don't know, are we going to be walking to class together? Are you planning on sitting next to me in every class? Will we be having lunch together? Is having lunch together going to be, like, a permanent thing from now on? Do you introduce me to your friends? Should I know who your friends are, since we're supposed to have been together for months already? If someone asks about your parents or something, do I act as if I've met them? If someone asks me whether or not you have abs, do I say that you do?"

"For the record, yes."

I stare at him. "Yes?"

"If someone asks whether I have a six-pack, tell them yes." He makes a long, leisurely stretching motion with both hands, like a cat in a warm patch of sun. He's so tall that his fingers almost scrape the closet ceiling. "It'll be good for my image."

"Fine. Then *you* better tell everyone I'm a great kisser."

He grins then, slow and wide and teasing, and for the first time, I notice that he has dimples. A useless discovery. And yet . . . "You got yourself a deal."

"Okay. Then . . . great."

"Great."

"Cool."

"Cool," he echoes, and I swear he's just trying to get under my skin now.

"Wonderful," I snap, crossing my arms. "Now, on to more important things . . . So if we are walking to class together—"

"Can I just say something?" he says.

That same feeling of vague annoyance from yesterday spikes inside me. Seriously. Caz Song was a lot more charming when he was only a pretty image on my TV screen. "Aren't you already saying something?"

"Can I say something else, then?" Without waiting for me to agree, Caz spreads his palms out and says, "Look, I appreciate what you're trying to do here with this whole, uh, consistency thing. But maybe . . . just *maybe* . . . you don't have to coordinate every single detail? We could just get into our roles and let the story develop naturally. It'll be more believable."

Develop naturally. As if anything about our current arrangement is or could be natural.

"That sounds like a horrible idea," I tell him. My palms actually feel a little clammy at the thought. Planning things out in detail means there are boundaries, and boundaries mean I'll at least have control over something.

"Why?" he asks, not backing down. "What are you so afraid of?"

I feel myself bristle. "I'm not—afraid." Then, hearing the blatant lie in my own voice, I switch to the offensive. "What do *you* have against following a nice, well-thought-out schedule?"

He breathes out through his teeth. "I don't. It's just—I'm already following a *lot* of nice, well-thought-out schedules, you know? That's kind of the nature of my job."

This is enough to make me falter, if only briefly.

"Humor me," Caz insists. "Just for a day. If it doesn't work, we can try it your way."

No thanks. The words are already poised on the tip of my tongue when the first bell rings. It's always loudest in the morning, an awful, drawn-out screech that can be heard at least three streets away. I think the point is to encourage students to get to class faster, but I know for a fact that some people have turned up to school ten minutes late just to avoid listening to the bell scream.

I wince as the sound echoes down the hall. There's no time to negotiate, so I shoot Caz my firmest no-bullshit look and say:

"Fine. But only for today."

• • •

I regret my words almost immediately.

We're heading out of the old senior building at the far end of campus to first-period math, into the sticky summer heat, and surprisingly, nothing too embarrassing has happened yet. Around us, all our classmates are keeping their distance, watching us only when they think we're looking away. Above us, the sky is so blue it looks fake.

Caz keeps quiet as we walk side by side, which I appreciate. The only thing worse than awkward silence is the kind of meaningless chatter designed solely to fill said silence.

Then, without a word of warning, Caz reaches for my hand, his long, slender fingers brushing against my own, and I honestly can't explain what happens next.

It's like my body goes into defense mode. Without thinking—without even *registering* what I'm doing—I jerk away and slap his wrist.

There's an awful, horrifyingly loud clapping sound. The kind you usually hear in movies during a dramatic showdown.

And then a speechless pause. Followed by—

"What the *hell*," Caz says, looking more confused than angry. He draws his hand back down to his side, but not before I see the irritated red of his skin. "Why did you just hit me?"

"S-sorry," I babble. I can feel my whole face burning, my fingers tingling from where he touched them, however briefly. "I—I don't know. I was just surprised."

"That your *boyfriend* would hold your hand?" he asks, confused.

"Yes. No. I mean . . ." I sigh. Avert my gaze, cursing myself for landing us in this ridiculous situation, and the even more ridiculous, excruciating confession I now have to make. I don't think anyone can hear us, but I keep my voice low in case. "I haven't exactly, um, held hands with a guy before."

"Wait." Caz's footsteps slow. "Never?"

This is already getting way too personal for my liking, but since I still feel bad for basically attacking him, I nod once and say, "Well, yeah. I've never dated anyone before, so . . ."

My words hang in the hot air between us. We're on the school oval now, dark asphalt and bright, artificial grass everywhere. Thankfully, there's enough free space for us to continue our conversation far away from the rest of our classmates, so no one can hear Caz when he repeats, incredulously:

"You've *never* dated anyone before. At all."

"Nope," I mumble, walking faster, as if I can somehow outpace my own embarrassment. I mean, it's not like the notion of having minimal romantic experience at my age is *inherently* embarrassing or anything. It's just . . . Caz Song is the last person I want to be talking to about this. Caz Song, who's the definition of desirable, who has everything a person could ever want, who's never had to worry about rejection or loneliness or being left behind. Who, according to the articles I've read up on him, has been in at least three relationships before, all of them with models or his gorgeous costars.

"Huh" is all he says. I can feel him studying me, as if trying to puzzle something out. My skin heats, and not just because of the scorching sun. "Then . . . how did you manage to write all that about falling in love?"

This question's easy, at least. "Bullshit," I tell him, and I'm glad for the conviction in my voice. "It's all just sentimental bullshit. I only wrote it for the assignment."

Caz doesn't ask anything else after that, or attempt to spontaneously hold my hand again as we approach our class. Good. I tell myself this is good. Great. Much better than him thinking I secretly long for a movie-like romance or care about any of that stuff.

It's not as if I don't believe in love itself, because I've witnessed it. My parents first met in high school, when Ma was class captain and Ba was the quiet, mysterious kid who always came to school in wrinkled shirts and turned in his homework two days late. After they were assigned to the same desk, they started passing handwritten notes and doodles to each under the table. Notes turned into lunches together, which turned into proper dates, which eventually then escalated into a serious, long-term relationship. They ended up going to different universities on opposite ends of the country to study very different things, but they handled the distance just fine.

And now, decades later, at the age where most marriages tend to stagnate and turn sour, they still love each other that much. They don't always remember their anniversary or go out to fancy restaurants for dates, but Ma once spent four hours lining up in the rain just to buy Ba's favorite brand of roasted chestnuts, and Ba has been to every single one of Ma's work events and cocktail parties, even though he hates those kinds of social functions.

I guess my point is that I do believe in love. Really. I'm just not convinced that kind of love could ever happen to me.

CHAPTER SEVEN

"Okay, tell me everything."

I'm stretched out over my bed in an old sweatshirt and plaid pajama pants, my laptop balanced precariously on top of a mini pillow mountain. Zoe's face takes up most of my screen, her skin an unnatural shade of white in the lamplight. She's in her bedroom too; I can make out the crammed bookshelf behind her, the Polaroid photos stuck to her wall. Photos of us from years ago.

Just seeing them makes me miss her more, makes nostalgia sneak under my ribs and twist around my heart, even though she's technically right in front of me.

"You go first," I tell her, shifting onto one side. "How did you do on your history exam?"

For as long as I've known her, Zoe has dreamed of studying computer science at Stanford the way I've dreamed of becoming a writer, which means every single test she takes matters. Counts toward something.

"Oh, *that.* I guess it went better than I thought," she says casually, but I know from her small, ill-concealed smile that she must've gotten full marks. She wouldn't be satisfied with anything less.

“We love an intellectual,” I say, and she laughs. I laugh too, happy that she’s happy.

“Okay, okay, but seriously.” She holds up a hand. Straightens suddenly. “My test scores aside—I feel like we really need to revisit the fact that you’ve somehow *become famous* since we last talked? And you’re doing this prestigious internship and shit—which I only found out through a freaking *magazine article*?”

I can guess exactly which one she’s referring to. There was an article published just yesterday featuring a photo of Caz and me walking to class together. Whoever took the photo managed to capture the precise moment Caz reached for my hand—right before I slapped him. In it, my eyes are wide with visible surprise and maybe a trace of embarrassment, my cheeks flushed pink. And Caz is doing that thing with his mouth, one side of it curved up in an almost smile, his gaze intent on me.

“Yeah, I know,” I manage. “It—it’s pretty wild.”

“No, like, seriously. Listen to this.” Her nails clack rapidly on her keyboard, then she clears her throat and starts reading. *“Eliza’s boyfriend is none other than gorgeous up-and-coming Chinese American actor Caz Song. Best known for his roles in* The Legend of Feiyan, Everything Starts with You, *and* Five Lives Five Loves, *the young star has been making some serious waves in Mainland China—”*

“I’ve already read it,” I cut in hastily, making a face.

“And I think you’re being *way* too low-key about this,” Zoe says. “Did you know that you’re trending on Weibo, like, right now?”

"Yeah, Caz's management already told him." Which he then proudly passed on to me, alongside the statistic that interest levels in his next drama have already shot up 300 percent. I'd be happier for him if he weren't so terribly smug about it—or his insistence that *spontaneity* is the best way to go.

"Caz," Zoe repeats, rolling the syllable on her tongue like it means something. "So what exactly is the situation with him?"

By instinct, I open my mouth to lie, but then I remember that Zoe *knows.* She's the only person in the world who knows my essay was fake, which now—ironically—means she's the only person in the world I can tell the truth to. "He's . . . Let's just say he's damage control."

Her brows rise, unsurprised. Zoe is always one step ahead of everyone. "Until when?"

"Until my internship ends and I get my shiny letter of recommendation from Sarah Diaz, and then we can part ways happy and successful and never bother each other again."

"Hmm," Zoe says.

"What?"

She blinks at me, all innocent. "Nothing."

"Come on." I shoot her a look. "We both know what your *hmms* mean. Out with it."

She snorts. Shakes her head. "I just think it's funny, that's all."

"Funny?"

"Yeah. I mean, if you'd just gone and written something *real*, you wouldn't have to go through all this trouble."

"It's too late to say that now," I protest, fighting against the pinch of dread in my stomach. Yet it's sharper now than ever. I still remember the first time Zoe read one of my English pieces in class, before we were even best friends. She'd looked up at the end, eyes wide, and said—and I've memorized every exact word: *Have you ever thought about being a writer? You're so freaking good at this.* She was the first person to really believe in me, and in some ways, this is precisely what she'd wanted for me, for my life. In other ways, this is the total opposite of that. I swallow the lump in my throat and press on, "The essay's already out, and for better or worse, everyone believes it."

"But maybe, if you told the truth—"

I force out a small snort. "Are you kidding? Have you seen those people on Twitter get torn apart just because people suspected they made up a fake funny text exchange? If the truth gets out, I'll probably be fending off hate comments and death threats for the rest of my life—"

Before I can complete my little monologue of doom, an unfamiliar voice calls down the hall on her end:

"Hey, can I grab the salt-and-vinegar chips?"

It's a girl's voice. Someone our age.

"Help yourself," Zoe calls back, twisting around in her chair, and I'm suddenly struck by a memory of us at our last sleepover, me raiding her snack cupboard while she blow-dried her hair and worried aloud about the usual things: that email the teacher hasn't replied to yet, the grades for tomorrow's quiz, the committee she signed up for but wants to quit. "Just don't touch the barbecue ones."

"Got it," the voice responds with a giggle.

"Who is that?" I ask as Zoe turns to me again.

"Oh, that's just Divya," she says. Like she expects me to recognize the name. Then she seems to remember I'm halfway across the world now, an entire ocean away. "Right, sorry, you wouldn't know her; she's new. Her parents are out of town, so she's crashing at my house for a few days."

"Right," I hear myself say. There's a dull, unreasonable stabbing sensation in the pit of my stomach, a sick feeling that tells me nothing except: I should go. "Um, cool."

"Do you want to say hi?" Zoe offers.

"No, no, it's fine," I say quickly, sitting up. "I'll just— You two hang out. Have fun. I need to write up something for my internship anyway, so . . ."

"Okay." She's already nodding, looking elsewhere, distracted. I can hear the pad of footsteps moving closer, the crinkle of the chip packet. "Okay, then. We'll talk soon, yeah? Just text whenever."

"Of course." I do my best to smile, even though the movement strains my lips. "I miss you."

She blows me a quick, perfunctory kiss. "Miss you too."

Then the screen goes black, and it's just me, staring at my own reflection in the following silence. My eyes look dark and heavy. Sad.

I slam my laptop shut.

Since Caz has upheld his end of the deal so far, it's only fair that I uphold mine as well.

Which is why I agree to meet with him the following Saturday afternoon at Chaoyang Park to help him write his essays. We both decided that a casual public setting would be best, since going over to each other's apartments would raise far too many questions from our families.

Still, as I finalize the time and location with Caz, I can't shake the odd, jittery feeling that I'm preparing to go on a date.

It's the kind of rare, blue-skied day that draws all the families out of their apartments, eager for a chance to breathe in some fresh air. On my way there, I pass at least a dozen smiling couples and young parents, toddlers waddling behind them on stumpy legs and stony-faced tweens texting as they walk feet ahead, squinting down at their screens in the bright, natural light.

The sun is everywhere, a hot palm on the back of my bare neck. I'm wearing a thin cotton dress with cherry blossom patterns printed over the front. It's not until I reach the park and catch sight of my reflection in a tinted shop window that I realize how ridiculously short my dress is; every time a breeze blows past me, the skirt flutters high up my thighs.

"You've got to be kidding me," I mutter, slowing to a stop. Using the window as a mirror, I attempt to pull the dress down to a more conservative length, but that only makes the *top* part way too revealing instead.

Desperate, I snap a quick photo of my reflection and text it to Zoe.

on a scale of Victorian-era-housewife to business-magnate's-fifth-wife, how suggestive does this dress look? be honest.

business magnate's second wife before the first wife's divorce papers are finalized. why?? are u planning on seducing that actor boy?

I almost drop my phone. *ABSOLUTELY NOT,* I start to type—just as I notice Caz's reflection behind me.

"Ohmygod," I blurt out. Spin around, half my thoughts still tangled up in my unsent message. "I'm not here to seduce you."

His dark brows crinkle. "What?"

"No—no, wait. Um, please forget I just said that—" Resisting the urge to bury my burning face in my hands, I clear my throat. Try for a normal greeting. "Hi."

His mouth twitches, but to my great relief, he goes along with it. "Hey."

"Hi," I repeat awkwardly.

Then I bring my gaze down. I'm so used to seeing Caz in school uniform that it takes me a second to register his full appearance: a plain fitted shirt under a leather jacket, black jeans, and those white Nike kicks so many guys are into for reasons that elude me. He looks different. Good.

But of course, he always looks good.

It takes me another second to notice that something's missing.

"You . . . you didn't bring your laptop?" I ask, incredulous, scanning him up and down. He isn't holding anything. In fact, if it weren't for the clothes, I'd think he'd rolled out of bed and wandered straight over here. "Not even a notebook? A sheet of paper? A—a pen? *Nothing?*"

He shrugs. "No."

I stare at him. "You do know what we're meant to be doing today, right? Like, I didn't hallucinate the part where you begged me to write your college essays for you . . ."

"Okay, first, I never *begged*," he says, rolling his eyes. "You offered; I never beg anyone for anything. And second, I figured you'd come well prepared, so there was no point bringing any of that stuff on my own."

"Wow." I shake my head. "That's very presumptuous of you."

"Well, you *did* bring the stuff we need, didn't you?" He gestures to the bag slung over my shoulders, a smile forming on his lips, like he's already won the argument. "So I was right to presume."

"But what if I didn't?"

"But you did," he points out.

"That's really not the . . ." I trail off, distracted by a sudden, strikingly vivid vision of us standing around and bickering like this for the rest of the afternoon until the sky goes dark. I sigh. Give my dress one last, futile tug. "Fine, whatever. Let's just go and get this over with."

He grins at me, his teeth white enough to blind. "That's the spirit."

The last time I visited Chaoyang Park, I was about four years old. Young enough that most of my memories from back then are blurred now, closer to something from a long-buried dream or a faded family photo than an actual recollection of events. All I can really remember now is the taste of cotton candy melting on my tongue, a bright streak in the sky—a balloon, maybe, or a painted kite—and Ma's loud, easy laughter, spilling over the glittering green lakes.

Still, as I walk through the front entrance with Caz beside me, I'm struck by this overwhelming sense of déjà vu, of *nostalgia*, akin to coming back home after a long holiday away.

Everything here looks so familiar: the rusted yellow-and-blue exercise equipment mostly occupied by old yeyes and nainais; the paddleboats skimming over the murky lotus pond waters; the table tennis tables set up in tidy rows over the courtyard. Even the scent in the air—that odd, distinct mix of moss and fresh-blooming flowers and fried sausages—makes me miss something I can't name.

All I know is that it makes my chest ache.

"You been here before?"

I turn to find Caz studying me. His tone and expression are casual enough, but there's this sharp, observant look in his eyes that leaves me feeling more exposed than my dress does.

"A long time ago," I say, staring straight ahead. A little boy is devouring a stick of tanghulu by the lawn, the candy shell crunching loudly between his teeth. "Before we moved, I mean. I haven't come back since."

"Well, I doubt it's changed much."

"Yeah," I say, though there is something different about the place I can't quite put my finger on. Or maybe I'm the one who's changed.

"So where exactly have you visited?"

I blink. "Huh?"

"Around Beijing. For fun." His eyebrows shoot up at my lost expression. "Wait, don't tell me you haven't been *anywhere* in all your time here. You've been back for what, like, two months already?"

Four months, actually. But that wouldn't help my case, so I don't correct him.

"It's not like I'm a tourist," I grumble, hitching my bag higher up my shoulder. "Am I supposed to go visit the Great Wall or something?"

"No," he says. "But there are plenty of places besides the Great Wall—and better than the Great Wall too. No offense to Qin Shi Huang. You know, snack stalls, shopping malls, Wangfujing . . ."

"I've been busy," I protest, my voice taking on a defensive edge. "And my parents have been working practically every day since we got here and . . ."

"What if I took you?"

Caz says this so casually that I'm unsure if I've misheard him.

He must catch the look of disbelief on my face, because he slows his steps and explains, "I've actually been thinking about it. And you raised a pretty fair point the other day."

This time, I'm *certain* I've misheard him. I slow down too. "Are you . . . are you admitting I'm right?"

"Not about the strict scheduling," he says with a decisive jerk of his head. "But about you hitting me when I attempted to hold your hand."

I suppress the urge to cringe. "We, um, really don't need to revisit that—"

"No, but we do. Nobody's going to believe we're together if you act like I'm about to kidnap you each time I make a move."

"Have you considered . . . *not* making any moves?" But as soon as I say it, I can hear how naive I sound. How inexperienced. Most of the couples at our school can barely keep their hands off each other. "Fine," I mutter hastily, before he can jump at the opportunity to tease me. "So what are you suggesting?"

"Chemistry training," he says, like this is a real term used by real people.

"Chemistry—what?"

"I've done it with all my co-actors. It's basically a series of activities we do together to get comfortable with each other fast; it helps build chemistry and make our interactions look more natural on-screen. Plus, we'll need to learn each other's backstories so we don't get caught for not knowing something obvious."

I pause. I *have* vaguely heard of something like that before. Still, my voice comes out wary. "What . . . kind of activities?"

"Depends." He shrugs. "Sometimes we'll hang out at the mall, or do a couple's photo shoot, or go on a private spa retreat for a weekend. Obviously the two of us won't have the same resources and flexibility, but I could show you around Beijing. And you need more material for your blog thing anyway, right?"

"Right," I say slowly, coming to a complete standstill in the shade of a wide oak, as if thinking and walking are mutually exclusive activities. "Right. That sounds . . . I mean, no offense, but that sounds like we'd be spending a lot of time together outside school. Is there really no quicker way to do the chemistry-building thing—"

Without looking at me, he says, "Sometimes the directors will throw us into a small, dark room and get us to make out for ten minutes. We're usually pretty familiar with each other after that."

Despite the shade, I feel the sun's heat all over my cheeks. "Okay, trips around Beijing it is," I say quickly, and I swear I see the twitch of his lips. Because of course he's delighting in my discomfort.

I duck my reddened face from view and focus on my phone. Seconds later, Caz's notifications dings.

"Invitation from Eliza Lin: New calendar event," he reads out loud from his screen, eyebrows raised. *"Chemistry training at five p.m. every Saturday."* Then, in the same breath, he says, "Yeah, that's not going to work."

"Excuse me?"

"This schedule isn't going to work," he repeats simply, and starts walking again, one hand in his pocket, weaving past the passing family bikes and cotton candy vendors with infuriating grace.

I have to run to catch up. "What? Why?"

"I know you don't have much experience with the entertainment industry, Eliza," he says, with enough arrogance that I have to physically grit my teeth to restrain myself, "but I am—as they say—*booked and busy.* I'll probably be shooting or on the road for half these times. Unless you want to wrestle my manager for control over my schedule."

I chew my tongue and walk faster. "Okay. Okay, that's fair. I get it. Then how about this—we'll make it this time *for now*, but if something comes up, you just give me a forty-eight-hour notice and we'll reschedule."

"Forty-eight hours?" He shakes his head. "Too long. Make it an hour."

"Twenty-four hours," I insist. "And you have to text me the location beforehand."

"Wow." Caz lets out a half laugh and runs a hand through his hair so that it looks perfectly windswept: a move I've seen captured in slow motion and thirsted over on every fan forum out there. "I feel like I'm dating my manager."

I scoff out loud at that, but my gut tightens. *Well, here it is*, I think grimly, willing the hot, sharp pang to dull. *Proof that I'd suck in a real relationship. I can't even be an appealing fake girlfriend.*

Yet as if he's heard my thoughts, Caz turns around, and his eyes are darker, his mouth softer at the corners, almost gentle. "I'm kidding, by the way," he says evenly. "You're still way hotter than my manager." Before I can even react, he twists back to face the paved path and adds, like an afterthought, "Fine. I'll send you the location. But I'm in charge of transport."

"Can you—can you even drive?"

He snorts. "Don't worry, I have alternate means of transportation."

"Oh," I say, immediately picturing him showing up outside my apartment in a massive horse-drawn pumpkin carriage for some reason. I give myself a mental shake before I can do something horribly inappropriate, like laugh. "Okay, fine. But we'll be splitting all costs fifty-fifty. Don't try to be a gentleman and pay for me; money will only complicate things."

"Fine," he echoes.

"Great."

"Great," he repeats again, and it's kind of incredible that he can piss me off even when he's technically agreeing with me.

"Wonderful," I bite out, marching right past him. Still, I can almost *sense* him smiling his insufferable look-at-me-I'm-a-superstar smile behind me.

And his smile turns out to be scarily effective. We've only just rounded the corner, where the crowds are denser and the paths are lined with food stalls, when these two teenage girls come into view. They both stop walking when they see us.

Or rather, see *him*.

"Oh my god," one of them murmurs in Mandarin. She's wearing a cute floral bucket hat that looks close to sliding over her eyes at any second. She nudges her friend in the ribs. "Oh my *god*."

Oh my god, I think too, but with pure dread. I'm really not here to watch strangers fangirl over Caz Song's very existence. I just want to write his essays and go home and curl up on the couch with some dramas. Though he's kind of already ruined that particular experience for me; I can't even watch a drama now without realizing that *this* actor once shot a variety program with Caz, or *that* actress once filmed a kiss scene with him.

"You don't think . . . ?" Hat Girl is saying.

"It's him," her friend answers. "It's definitely him."

They're both trying to sneak looks at Caz's face in the most conspicuous way possible. If I weren't searching for a quick escape route (would it look weird if I ducked behind that bush?), I'd probably laugh.

The first girl clears her throat, adjusts her hat with visibly trembling fingers, and approaches Caz. She looks like she might start crying. "Um, hello? Caz Song?"

It must be weird to have a complete stranger call out your name in a park like you're classmates or something. But as weird as it is, Caz must also be used to it, because he straightens, his charm dialed up, immediately reverting to my initial boy-from-the-magazine impression of him. Perfect. *Too* perfect.

I can only imagine how I must look in comparison.

"Hey," he says, smiling at them both. "How are you?"

"I'm just—I'm a huge fan," Hat Girl says, her voice trembling too, her words tumbling out in a great rush. "I've watched every drama you've starred in. My favorite has to be *The Legend of Feiyan* . . . It was, like, the *perfect* adaptation of Hero's novel—you're exactly how I pictured the male lead when I first read it . . ."

The other girl has whipped out her phone and started filming the exchange, and panic flashes through me. I do not need every Chinese netizen to see a video of me looking like this. My dress is still too short, and I'm suddenly *very* conscious of the pimple on my forehead.

But Caz has started chatting with them in earnest: about his next drama, his castmates, his diet and workout routine, each answer so smooth I wonder if he's reading off an invisible script. I linger behind him, feeling somehow both invisible and way too exposed, when Hat Girl turns her attention to me and her eyes widen.

"Oh, holy crap—are you Eliza Lin?"

I blink. "Yeah . . ."

To my surprise, her face splits into a broad beam. "I *love* your essay. Your writing's amazing."

My pulse skips, and heat, good heat, rushes to my face. "Wow," I say, sounding as shy as I feel. *This random girl actually likes my writing.* I mean, I've gotten more than enough compliments from people online by now, but this is different. This is actually happening in real life, and it's happening to *me.* "Um, thank you. That means a lot."

"No, for real," she says. "I think it might be one of my favorite pieces ever."

The heat spreads all the way through my body like sunshine, and I decide that maybe I don't mind the attention. Maybe I even crave it a little.

"You look a lot better in real life than your school photo," she adds with complete sincerity, and nudges her friend, who's still filming. "Don't you think?"

Her friend lowers her phone at last and meets my eyes, and all the warmth seeps out of me. Her gaze is ice-cold, and her tone no friendlier. "You're Caz's girlfriend?" The question sounds almost like a threat.

"Um . . ." I lick my dry lips. "I—"

"Yeah, she is," Caz answers for me, and—to everyone's shock—slides a casual hand around my waist. Distantly, through the sensation of his skin against my dress, I remember the slide from my PowerPoint: *No physical contact beyond casual shoulder-bumping and occasional hugging.* "We're actually on a date right now."

Hat Girl claps a hand to her mouth. "Oh my god," she says again. "That's so adorable. I'm, like, such a fan of your relationship."

Meanwhile, her friend looks like she's experiencing something of an extreme facial spasm. If Caz weren't still holding me, I'd bolt in the opposite direction.

"Please ignore her," Hat Girl tells me, following my gaze. "She's been a solo stan of you for ages, Caz. I think she just needs a bit of—time to adjust to the news. It's *great news*, though. Really."

Caz just smiles and nods, and I try to smile and nod too, as if it's perfectly normal that this girl I've never spoken a word to hates my guts.

As soon as the two of them leave—and only after Caz has signed her bucket hat with a Sharpie he apparently just carries around everywhere with him—he lets his arm drop and we make our way deeper into the park.

We're silent for a few minutes, both thinking, before he turns to me. "Hey, are you okay? I know my fans can be a bit . . . protective—"

"No, it's fine," I reassure him quickly.

He tilts his head a few degrees, like he's struggling to figure me out. "Are you sure?"

"Yeah." When he looks doubtful, I add, "*Seriously.* I'm not that sensitive."

"Okay, well, in that case . . ." He takes a deep, somber breath, and just when I think he's about to say something profound, he blurts out: "Did my hair look okay just now?"

I blink. "What?"

"My hair." He clears his throat. Rubs the back of his neck. "When I was taking photos with them. Did it look good?"

"Your vanity is astounding," I inform him, spinning around. To think I was actually finding Caz Song agreeable—*thoughtful*, even. At the end of the day, all he really cares about is maintaining his perfect, plastic image.

"Okay, sure, whatever," he says. "But seriously, I just want a second opinion—"

"It looked good," I say irritably. "You always look good. You know that." I hold up a hand before he can gloat. "But if you ever use my words against me, I will personally cut all your hair off myself. Got it?"

His smug, infuriating smile falters, but only for a second. In the sort of exaggerated, too-deep voice you only ever hear in the theaters, he replies, "Whatever you say, my love."

CHAPTER EIGHT

It's close to noon before we find a space quiet enough to work: an empty picnic table surrounded by nothing but wild grass. Caz hops onto the wooden seat and leans back, his head tilted lazily toward the sun, eyes closed, his sharp, lovely features awash in hazy gold.

For one dumb moment, I can't help but think, *No wonder why he's so vain.* If I were that beautiful, I would be vain too.

I ignore him and lift my laptop onto my knees, then open up a blank Word document, privately grateful for a reason to focus on something other than him.

"So I'm going to assume that you haven't written anything at all for your applications yet," I say, pulling up a new Google window beside the page. "Would that be correct?"

"Yeah," Caz says, without an ounce of shame. "Absolutely."

Well, at least he's honest. "Then we'll start from the very beginning. Find the prompts and start brainstorming." I flex my fingers over the keyboard. "What schools are you applying to again?"

"Just the usual," he says tonelessly, the same way one might talk about booking a dentist appointment or filing taxes. "My mom found a couple decent universities in America that accept late applications. The Univeristy of Michigan is one, I'm pretty sure."

I raise my brows. "Whoa there, no need to sound so enthusiastic."

He laughs, but even that lacks his usual wry humor. "Yeah, well . . ." For one second he looks like he's going to make a confession, tell me a secret, and an unbidden spark of anticipation shoots up my spine. But then he kind of shrugs and shakes his head. "It is what it is."

"Again. Your enthusiasm is overwhelming."

We both lapse into silence as I search around for the right college application topics. The prompt this year is pretty typical, if not disappointing in its lack of originality: *Tell us about a particular experience where you struggled. What did you learn from it?*

"Yeah, sounds good," Caz says when I show him, giving the prompt the most cursory of glances.

I stare at him. "That's it?"

"What else do you want me to say? Excellent identification of prompt? Exemplary organizational skills?"

"No—" I huff out a sigh, trying my best to keep my frustration at bay. "That's not what I mean. If I'm going to help you write this essay about your struggles, you need to actually give me some source material. Tell me about a time where you, you know. Struggled."

Caz merely lifts a hand over his face, blocking out the sun, his knife-cut jaw and cheekbones cast in sudden shadow. "Why can't you just make it up?" He turns back to me, a gleam in his eyes. Which just seems wrong, scientifically. How can his eyes *gleam like that* if there's no light? "Isn't that kind of your area of expertise?"

I choose to ignore the jibe. "It's not that simple."

"Why not?"

"Because," I say, exasperated. "My essay only worked because I still included real-life details—like searching for apartments in my compound, or the grocery store near our school. I still had my main personality traits, my voice, my—my defining characteristics. So anyone who's read it would believe it was written by me. Right now I don't know *nearly* enough about you to create an entire essay out of nothing, especially if it needs to be factually accurate."

Writing is simply a form of lying; I've always known this to be true. But to tell a *good* lie, a *convincing* lie, one that is both logically constructed and consistent and emotionally resonant—that takes time and effort. Attention to detail. And in this particular case, it also takes cooperation.

"Look, Caz," I say as diplomatically as possible. "I can't write this essay if you won't give me one solid, realistic example—and please don't tell me you haven't, because literally everyone struggles in some way at some point—"

"What a profound statement," he says dryly. "Did you get that from a musical?"

"Don't change the subject."

But he elects to stay silent instead, and with every second that passes, I can feel my already-threadbare patience wearing thinner and thinner.

"This is *your* college essay," I remind him. "And it shouldn't even be that hard to write in the first place. It's hardly rocket science."

"Not for you, maybe," he shoots back.

"Well, maybe if you tried—or cared even the slightest—"

"I *am* trying." He sighs. Rakes his fingers through his hair, but it's less his famous, calculated, heartthrob gesture and more genuine agitation. "See, this is why I don't like—" He stops himself.

"What?"

"Nothing."

"No, tell me," I insist. "Why you don't like—what? Studying? Planning for the future? Doing things you're bad at?"

He doesn't answer, but a muscle works in his jaw at my last guess.

I almost laugh, torn between sheer frustration and amusement. "Caz," I say. "I know there are people who'll literally worship you for drinking water, but you realize you don't *actually* have to be perfect all the time. I mean, I'd probably like you a lot more if you weren't so perfect. You'd be way more—I don't know, *human*. Not just some shiny product of the entertainment industry."

Surprise flashes over his face, though it's quickly clouded by something like wariness. "Is that how you see me right now? As a . . . shiny product?"

"No," I say, then pause. "Well. Sort of, yeah."

He falls quiet, his eyes trained on a splash of color in the cloudless sky. A kite. It's shaped like a dragon, with golden bells for eyes and painted Peking opera masks making up the rest of its body, its long, flared tail undulating in the breeze.

"I guess . . . that's fair," Caz says, yanking my attention back to him. He huffs out a small laugh. "It's funny, because after I landed my first role, I promised myself I wouldn't become one of those bland celebrities who only give corporate answers and sidestep any meaningful questions about themselves."

"But?"

"But, like, for instance: In an old interview, I mentioned this singer I was really loving. And then the next month, he was exposed for doing drugs—which I had *no idea* about, I just thought he was a creative lyricist. But somehow the story turned into me encouraging teenagers to do drugs, and I had to issue a public apology, and it took weeks for all that to die down—mostly because this other actor made the headlines for misquoting a classic novel."

As he speaks, I get a startling glimpse of the boy behind the glossy magazine cover. Someone a little afraid. That part I can relate to, at least.

So it's with full, gentle sincerity that I say, "Well, you're safe with me. I'll only write the story you want to tell for this essay; I won't twist your words or anything like that. Promise."

A long pause. A soft breeze brushes through the grass, past my cheek.

When Caz glances up again, he looks different. Or he's

looking at me differently, his eyes less black than brown, the rich shade of freshly upturned earth.

"Fine," he says at last. "I'll talk."

Caz Song broke his arm when he was thirteen.

But *break* is too gentle a word. What he really did was fracture it and dislocate it at once, splitting the bone down the center. In certain places the bone had been shattered so completely that tiny white shards had poked up against his skin, threatening to pierce straight through. The pain, according to him, was manageable. Nothing more than a brief flash of agony, a crushing sensation, fire spreading up from his fingers—followed by numbness.

The pain, I imagine, was unbearable.

He had injured himself performing a stunt for a historical C-drama. It was his first time playing a fairly important role—the crown prince's spy—and he wanted to prove he was up for the job. If he didn't, there were at least four other actors his age with more connections who could replace him at a moment's notice.

The stunt required that he leap over two sloping palace roofs (with the help of wires, of course) and do a double flip in the air before launching directly into a fight scene. He managed to make the jump over one roof before one of the wires accidentally went slack. He stumbled, landed hard at the wrong angle. By instinct, he'd lifted his right arm to protect himself. A mistake.

"I knew pretty much straightaway that I'd broken it," he says, rolling back his sleeve to show me. The ghost of a jagged white line trails from his elbow down to his wrist, cutting its way into lean cords of muscle. I have to fight this strange, abrupt urge to trace my fingers over the scar, just to see if it still hurts. To see if he would let me. "I mean, I *heard* it."

A jolt of imaginary pain lances through my own arm at the thought.

"But you kept going," I guess, tearing my eyes away from his scar before I can do something foolish.

"The cameras were still rolling." He shrugs. "Everyone was waiting. I figured I could afford to finish the scene."

And so he did. He finished that scene, and the next, and the one after that. For two whole hours he said nothing, just kept his head up and stayed in character and pulled off all the remaining stunts himself. It wasn't until his scenes were done for the day and the director was completely satisfied with everything that Caz asked, quite calmly, whether he could go see a doctor, as he couldn't feel his fingers. The staff member assigned to bring him there had taken one look at his arm—now no longer hidden by the thick, layered sleeves of his costume—and almost screamed.

The doctor had been horrified as well. Shocked that Caz hadn't passed out from the pain at that point. Caz had simply smiled his famous, crooked white smile—the smile that made all his costars and viewers fall at least a little bit in love with him—and said, *Come on, it's barely a scratch.*

"And what did the doctor say to that?" I ask.

He runs a hand through his perpetually messy hair. "Honestly? The drugs kind of kicked in at that point, so I can't be sure."

"Nice." I snort.

"Though I *imagine* he shook his head in admiration and murmured to the nurse beside him, *What a brave young man.* Maybe even a few tears were shed."

"And then everyone in the operating room burst into loud applause?" I say sarcastically.

He stares at me in fake shock. "How did you know?"

A small, involuntary giggle rises up my throat, though I quickly squash it down again. Still—a *giggle.* It doesn't make any sense for me to feel that way now.

No. I need to clear my head. Refocus. I'm not here to make friends, to get my hopes up about people only to be let down over and over again. *Especially* not when it comes to Caz Song, who makes a literal living off pretending to feel things he doesn't.

Nothing else.

"Go on," I tell Caz, sitting back, a safer distance away from him. "What happens next?"

He hesitates, as if sensing the change in my tone, however subtle. But after another beat, he nods and picks up where he left off.

After the operation, the doctor advised Caz to rest for at least a month. The next week, he went back on set again. He worked with the director to devise a way to hide his cast under his costume and refused to restrict his movements in any of his scenes. Even when he went back to the hospital for further treatment or was forced by his parents to rest, he secretly studied his script under the covers of his bed, repeating lines to himself over and over again.

By the time they wrapped up shooting, his arm still wasn't fully healed yet. But his performance, according to the director and his cast members, was phenomenal. Far beyond their highest expectations.

Except the drama never actually ended up airing. The main lead got involved in a huge scandal concerning an underground strip club, and the higher-ups decided it was best to cancel the drama altogether.

"It was still worth it, though," Caz says, picking up a long blade of grass and wrapping it around one finger like a ring. Caz can never seem to keep still. "I learned a lot."

And while this does sound like typical corporate bullshit, I'm surprised to find myself actually believing him.

Even after I have all my material for the essay, it takes me longer than usual to get into the writing zone. I'd blame the good weather or the squeals and cheers of children in the distance, but if I'm honest, it's mostly because of Caz. Even when he isn't talking or looking my way, I can sense his presence keenly, as if every molecule in the air is oriented toward him. I'm almost tempted to ask him to move to another table, though I know that isn't fair.

But once I *do* manage to tune out all unwanted distractions, the words come in a flood. My mind sharpens. My fingers find a natural rhythm over the keys. Because I might be clueless about dating and hand holding and dancing for fun in a crowded classroom, but *this*—this right here, stringing words together to mean something—is my element. This, I could do all day for the rest of my life.

It feels like the closest thing I know to home.

When I reach the final paragraph, Caz disappears for a few minutes and comes back with two tanghulus, the jewel-like fruits glistening in the light. One of them is the traditional flavor, the type I used to have as a kid: a string of bright red hawthorns pierced through with a wooden skewer. The other is crowded by giant, ripe strawberries and green grapes and fat slices of kiwi, all sprinkled with a generous layer of white sesame.

"I saw you eyeing that little boy's food earlier," he says by way of explanation. He holds the skewers up before me like he's about to perform a magic trick. "Take your pick."

I blink at him and push my laptop slowly aside, surprised that he noticed. Or maybe he's only acting this way in case someone else is watching, just to make it look more like a date. And to make himself look more considerate. "Um . . ."

"I understand it's an incredibly difficult decision to make," Caz teases when I continue *um*ing for a solid minute. "A lot at stake here. Would you like to talk it over with your lawyer first? Consult a third party?"

"That *probably* won't be necessary," I say, playing along. "Though it might be wise for me to evaluate the pros and cons of both options. Really think this one through."

"Yes, of course."

I snort out a laugh and take the traditional hawthorn tanghulu from him. "Thanks."

He waves his free hand. "Anything for my fake girlfriend."

A brief, inexplicable pain fills my chest, like my heart has snagged on a stray piece of barbed wire. Unsure what else to do or say, I bring the tanghulu to my lips, letting the thin paper cover dissolve on my tongue first. Then I bite down. The inside is so sour it makes my eyes water, but the smooth, sugary exterior helps balance it out. It tastes just like I remembered.

For a while neither of us says anything, content to simply chew and enjoy the silence while the summer breeze blows around us, pleasantly cool against my skin. Then I lick the sticky skewer clean, toss it into a nearby bin, and get back to work, savoring the sweet aftertaste of the fruit.

"Done," I say a few minutes later, clapping my hands together.

"Done already?" Caz looks up in surprise, then down at my laptop screen. He's only just finished eating his tanghulu. "Damn. That's impressive."

I try not to let his words go to my head, though a flush of pleasure still spreads through me, warming me down to my toes. "I'll email it to you when I get home," I promise, packing up my things. But as I prepare to shut my laptop, I notice three new messages from Zoe, and beside those, an email notification from Sarah Diaz.

I immediately open it, my heart thudding, half-convinced as I always am these days that Sarah will message me out of the blue going, *Hey, I just found out that you're a complete fraud and your essay is a lie! You've now been blacklisted from every magazine and publisher in the world, and everyone hates you. Bye!*

To my relief, the new email doesn't say anything along those lines. Not yet, anyway.

Eliza!

Just wanted to check in and see how you're going with your blog post for tonight. I was looking around at the comments on your Twitter, and it's pretty clear everyone is dying to see another (ideally less blurry) photo of you and Caz together. Even just a couple selfie would be amazing—

"Eliza? You good?"

I slam my laptop shut and spin around to face Caz. "Yeah," I say, as cheerily as possible.

I'm cringing before the words are even out of my mouth. "Could we—would it be okay if we took a selfie together? Right now? For my internship?" Wow, I could not have chosen a more awkward way to ask that.

A ridiculous, self-satisfied smile spreads slow over his lips like honey. "Of course. *Anything* for my nonfan."

My face heats. "When are you going to let that go?"

"When you join my fan club."

"So: never," I say flatly.

"Don't sound so certain" is all he says as he adjusts the screen.

And I don't know what compels me to do it, what gives me the nerve—whether it's because I'm still riding the adrenaline high of having just written an essay that I know is really good, or because the persistent heat has subdued the impulse-control section of my brain, or because I want to startle that smug smile off his face—but just when he's about to take the photo, I stand up tall on my tiptoes and kiss his cheek.

Click.

The camera flashes once, capturing the kiss for eternity, and I pull back. Suddenly uncertain what to do with my mouth, my face, my hands. The aftermath of my one moment of impulsivity.

"And you say you don't have any experience with this stuff," Caz remarks after a pause, his tone casual.

"Well, you're not the only one who can be spontaneous."

One corner of his crooked mouth lifts higher. "Clearly."

It should all be over then: the selfie, the essay-writing session, the strange electricity in the air. But as he hands the phone back to me, our wrists brush, bare skin against skin. Immediately, every nerve end in my body ignites as if struck by a match, and I freeze, stunned by my own response.

I expect Caz to move away, but instead he slides his long fingers around my wrist. Runs a thumb over the frayed string bracelet there.

"You always wear this," he says.

I nod. Swallow. "Yeah. I know."

He waits for me to say more, but I'm too busy trying to act normal, like I'm not hyperaware of how close we are, how his hand is still moving slowly over my skin, his touch warmer and lighter than the summer air.

CHAPTER NINE

I once heard this theory that when you dread something, time moves faster, as if the universe is determined to conspire against you.

I can now confirm firsthand the theory is true.

It's Monday night, and my family is gathered around the high kitchen counter, bowls of diced vegetables and light brown loaves of store-bought bread spread between us.

Since we had homemade dumplings for dinner yesterday, we're making our special sandwich recipe tonight. Ma and I first came up with the idea when we were living in America; it's like a basic baguette sandwich, except we fry the leftover pork-and-chive dumpling fillings into a golden patty, then add pickled carrots and fresh coriander and red oil chili sauce. The combination tastes so good that sometimes Ma jokes we should sell the idea to one of those modern Asian fusion restaurants in downtown LA.

At least, I *think* she's joking. When it comes to her and potential business opportunities, you never really know.

"So how's school been?" Ma asks as she slices a loaf of bread in two and passes it down. We're seated in a kind of factory-line arrangement, Ma in charge of handling the bread, Ba assigned to the meat patties, and Emily and me left to do everything else.

This sudden pivot in the conversation catches me off guard. Up until a few seconds ago, Ma had been talking in elaborate detail about how she patched up that major Kevin-shaped crisis with SYS; apparently, she'd done some stalking, pulled a few strings, reached out in private to the son of the company head ("a very polite young man, and quite easily flattered too; I do hope he ends up taking over the company") and smoothed the whole situation over.

"Uneventful," Emily says, reacting much faster than I do, then shoots a meaningful glance my way from across the counter. "What about you, Jie? Anything . . . *interesting* going on in your life?"

I chew the inside of my cheek.

This is the part I've been dreading: telling my parents and sister that I'm dating Caz Song. Even though I've already bought Emily the exact amount of Pocky specified in our previous verbal agreement, I know that no amount of snacks or bribery will stop the word about my new relationship status from spreading and inevitably reaching my family. I mean, I've already gained a few thousand more followers from my blog post about our trip around Chaoyang Park: "Let's Cancel All Our Plans and Kiss at the Park Instead." I have two more posts in the works for the Love and Relationships section next week, each as ironic as the next: "When You Know, You Know: It's Love" and "A Little Anecdote on How to Survive Those First-Date Jitters."

So since them finding out *is* inevitable, I'd much rather Ma and Ba hear the story from me than yet another impassioned think piece floating around on the internet, or one of our many aunts who browse the gossip articles on WeChat.

All of which sounds great in theory.

In practice, I'm so nervous I keep dropping the pickled carrots.

"Yes, how *is* school, Eliza?" Ma asks, turning to me. She wiped off her makeup right before we started cooking, and her eyes still have that dark, smudged quality from leftover eye shadow, making them look even sharper than usual. "Have you made any friends?"

My mom's evident concern for my social life aside, this seems as effective a conversation opening as any. I might even be able to put a positive spin on my news. After all, a boyfriend is technically a kind of friend, right? Just with more potential physical contact.

I clear my throat. Attempt to ward off all non-family-friendly thoughts with a quick wave of my hand. "I—um. Yeah. I think so."

"You *think* you've made a friend?" Ma's brows furrow, perplexed.

"I think he counts as a friend," I clarify. I can already feel the heat rushing to my skin. "Depending on . . . on your definition of the word."

Something in my voice must give me away, because everyone looks up. The line between Ma's brows deepens. Ba merely appears surprised and a little lost, though that might be because he's halfway through composing a new poem in his head.

My only source of comfort right now is that we've never had a no-dating policy in our household.

It's strange, really, the kind of things my parents are strict about. Like, they'll freak out if I wear a tank top outside and my bra strap is showing, or if I go to bed with wet hair, but they aren't opposed to the idea of me dating in my final years of high school, and they'll encourage me to attend social gatherings because they consider it a "life skill."

I know a lot of people can't wrap their heads around my parents' logic. My friends at my old schools could never understand why I was allowed to have sleepovers at my place, but not theirs, or why it was such a big deal that I stay off my phone during family dinner times. A lot of them were shocked that we even had proper family dinners, instead of quick bites between school or work.

But if I'm honest, I don't mind it. My parents' rules might not make total sense to others, but they do to Emily and me.

Plus, their highly specific rules mean that no matter what I say next, I at least don't have to worry about my parents disowning me.

"Are you trying to tell us something about a certain boy in your life?" Ma asks slowly, tentatively, as if phrasing the question wrong might scare me away. Though I doubt there is a *right* way to ask about this kind of thing.

Emily, as always, is much more direct. "So you do have a boyfriend?"

"Well . . ." I lick my dry lips. It's even harder than I'd imagined, telling them about Caz when they're all studying me so intently. I pretend to rearrange the slices of carrot on my plate, then answer in Mandarin. "Uh, yes."

A beat.

Panicking, I continue. "There is. I am. I mean, I'm with someone. In, like, a romantic sense—though of course, given our age and the general dating trends in modern-day society—"

"Who is it?" Emily asks, saving me from my rambling.

Neither Ma nor Ba says anything, but Ma is making that poker-face expression she always does when she's trying very hard to absorb a new, significant piece of information: her gaze carefully guarded, her mouth pressed in a thin line.

"Um, you know the male lead from that drama we've been watching?" I begin.

Emily raises her brows. Ma nods once.

Ba stuffs a new patty between the loaves of bread.

The silence tightens around me. I can only hear the kitchen clock ticking like a bomb, counting down the seconds until I force myself to say, "Yeah, so, that's him."

Another beat.

I expect shock. Confusion. Maybe even awe.

What I don't expect is for my family to burst out laughing.

"Tian ya," Ma manages through her sudden fit of hysteria. She's actually wiping at her eyes. "I didn't think you were one of those—those idol chasers, Ai-Ai. And you looked so serious about it too!"

Emily is snorting into her hand. "If you're dating that Caz Song guy, then I'm dating Gong Jun."

"And I'm dating Liu Dehua," Ma adds, shaking her head as she resumes her bread slicing again.

Ba frowns at her. "You're *married*."

"Oh, it's just a joke, Laogong." Ma nudges him playfully with one elbow, and Ba's expression softens at once. "Of course I haven't forgotten about you."

If my face wasn't on fire before, it definitely is now. "I'm not joking," I protest, setting my plate of carrots down. "I *am* dating him. He goes to our school." Desperate, I turn to Emily for help. "You know he goes to our school, right? And he lives close to us?"

"Yeah, I've heard," she allows, still smiling slightly. At least she isn't outright laughing anymore.

Progress. Kind of.

"I'm sure you will find someone, Ai-Ai," Ma says. God, now she's *comforting* me. This is so not how this conversation was supposed to go. "You're a very bright girl, and you're funny, and you can—you can eat spicy food, and you . . ." She trails off with a vague gesture, evidently searching hard for more positive qualities of mine.

"You are very good with those carrots," Ba offers.

"Yeah, yeah, that's really nice of you guys. But I'm literally trying to tell you that I *have* found someone. In fact, you know what?" I snap my fingers together, struck by a lightning bolt of inspiration. "I have proof."

As my parents exchange puzzled, if not somewhat alarmed, glances, I wipe my hands on my shirt, take out my phone, and open up the selfie I took with Caz. The one of me kissing his cheek.

"This is where I was the other day," I explain, spinning it around so they can see. "With him."

I resist the urge to melt into the floor as everyone leans in and inspects the photo closely from every angle, as if it's some rare, endangered specimen never captured on film before.

"Well," Ma says at last, sitting back, her poker face falling into place again.

For a moment, I can't decide what's worse: my parents refusing to believe that I could be dating Caz Song, even with photographic evidence . . . or my parents believing in my lie fully. Trusting me. A needle of guilt pricks my stomach at the thought.

Then Ma clasps her hands together on the counter, all businesslike, the bread now totally forgotten beside her. "I suppose I'm just curious to know . . . How exactly did your . . . this"—she points at the screen—"begin?"

And so I tell them. I tell them the exact same story I wrote about for my essay, because the more consistent your lie is, and the fewer versions of it you come up with, the better. It's easier to keep all your facts straight that way.

When I'm finally done, and most of the bread has likely gone stale, Emily claps a hand to her mouth.

"Oh my god. Are you going to invite him over?" she asks, eyes wide. "We should all meet him. And if we ask him for some autographs, we could sell them—"

"No!" I yelp. Bringing Caz home is one boundary I definitely do not want to cross.

"What do you have against money?" Emily demands.

"I'm not talking about the autographs." Though there's no way I'm letting *that* happen either. "I just want to hold off on the meeting-my-family thing, okay? It—it's too much, too soon. And besides, you'll probably see him around school anyway."

"Your sister's right," Ma tells Emily, coming to my rescue. "We don't want to scare the boy off." Then she turns to me. Smiles, the faint lines of her face softening, her Super-Professional Businesswoman mannerisms melting away. She's just my mother, who always lends me her shoulder as a pillow during long plane rides and boils sweetened mung bean soup for us every summer to help stave off the heat. "You shouldn't wait *too* long either. I remember that I first introduced your father to my parents shortly after we graduated." She winks. "Obviously, it turned out quite well."

There it is again. The needle in my stomach.

But still, I make myself say it: "Yeah. Okay."

Despite what I've told Emily, I don't actually expect her to bump into Caz at school. After all, the primary and senior schools run on different timetables; we're always stuck in class during the primary students' lunchtimes or assemblies, and vice versa. It's why I've only ever seen Emily at the start and end of the school day, when we're waiting for the driver together, or when I deliberately seek her out in her classroom.

But on Friday, in an unfortunate twist of fate, our English class is dismissed twenty minutes early—right when the primary school kids are having their break.

I spot Emily the second I step out into the sun-flooded courtyard, Caz somewhere close behind me. She's playing that traditional Chinese ti jianzi game with at least eight or nine other girls her age. It's a simple game, more speed than strategy, requiring that the players pass a shuttlecock between them using mainly their feet.

I stop to watch them play, my books hugged to my chest.

They're all giggling madly, yelling at one another whenever the shuttlecock looks close to falling, dashing forward and back again every time they see the flash of colored feathers.

It doesn't take long to dissect the group dynamic; years of quietly observing my classmates at new schools have honed my skills.

Even though Emily and her friends are technically all standing in a circle, the prettiest one—the one with the polka-dot hairband and loudest, tinkling laugh—is clearly the leader. She keeps barking out names and instructions at the others, and it's her who takes the shuttlecock from whoever's retrieved it without so much as a thanks.

And Emily, I realize with a small, anxious jolt, is hovering somewhere toward the bottom of the social ladder. None of them seem to bother passing the shuttlecock to her, and when she does manage to kick it, none of them cheer very loud.

I feel myself frown. This isn't supposed to happen. Emily has always been the social butterfly of the family, likable and adaptable in all the ways I'm not.

But then again, maybe all the moving around hasn't been quite as easy for Emily as I believed. Or maybe there's something about this school in particular that has made it harder than usual.

"Is that your sister?" Caz asks, breaking through my thoughts. He's pointing straight at Emily.

I turn to him, surprised. "Yeah. How did you know?"

He shrugs. "You two look alike."

This is so inaccurate I almost burst out laughing. Unlike Emily, I've inherited none of Ma's delicate, sculpted-ice features, her glossy hair and dewy skin. Instead, I take after both my father and no one, my face drawn from a random arrangement of broad, cutting strokes and round lines, like some kind of afterthought. "You're probably the first person in the history of the world to say that."

"It's the smile," he says, eyes flickering to me. "You two have the same smile."

Before I can even think of an adequate response to this, Emily catches sight of me.

"Jie! Jie!" she yells, breaking off from the circle and sprinting across the short length of the courtyard. Her pigtails whip forward as she skids to a stop before me, seconds away from crashing into my stomach, and looks up, breathless and beaming.

Then she sees Caz. And she goes perfectly still.

"Hey," Caz offers.

Emily's eyes are so wide she looks like a cartoon character. "You're . . . Caz Song," she says, voice hushed. "My sister's boyfriend."

"Yeah." Caz bends down slightly until they're the same height. Smiles. It's a different smile from the one he wears on TV, or around people in our year level; it's gentle, kind. "I am."

"Holy shit," my nine-year-old sister whispers.

I elbow her, hard. *"Language."*

"Sorry," she says, sounding not even remotely sorry. "I meant holy *crap*. Happy?"

"Not really," I mutter.

Caz's smile widens until his dimples are visible, and Emily positively melts. Which, under ordinary circumstances, should be a good thing; everyone *wants* their family to like their boyfriend. But all I feel is a faint pang of unease. The more attached Emily gets to Caz, the more it'll hurt when our six-month relationship reaches its end.

Thankfully, this conversation from hell is interrupted by none other than Emily's entire friend group—

"*Emily!* Come on!"

"Dude, what's taking so long?"

"Are you playing or not? Because we can play without you, you know." This, from their leader. She's crossed her arms over her chest, tapping her foot impatiently on the asphalt. I feel an immediate surge of dislike toward her.

"I—I'll be there in a minute!" Emily calls back, then turns back to us with large puppy-dog eyes. "Can you guys join in?"

I expect Caz to make some polite excuse about schoolwork and leave, but instead, he nods and grins widely. "Of course."

Emily squeals and throws her skinny arms high up over her head, looking like a perfect stock-image result for when people google "happy" or "celebration." "For real?"

"Yeah, for real."

I stare at Caz over Emily's shoulder, my mind spinning. All he does is smile back at me. What the hell is he up to? We agreed to keep our families out of this, and I can't imagine him benefiting from this situation in any way. Is he so committed to his role as the perfect fake boyfriend? Or is it just a habit for him by now, to constantly entertain, perform, impress?

"Well, you guys go ahead," I say, backing up against the building wall, books still clutched tight to my body like a shield. "I'll watch from here."

Emily pouts. "You're not coming?"

"I . . . don't think that's necessary."

"*Of course* it's necessary." Caz's smile is evil now, wicked. He extends a hand in invitation, and a third possibility pops into my head: Maybe he just wants to see me make a fool of myself.

"Come on. Who *doesn't* enjoy kicking pieces of glued feathers around?"

I take another step backward; my heel hits cold brick. "No, no. No, I'm basically allergic to it—"

"What, fun?" Caz says, and Emily giggles.

"Intensive exercise," I correct. *As well as embarrassing myself in front of a group of strangers. No matter how tiny they are.*

"You call ti jianzi intensive exercise?" Caz shakes his head like I've just told a bad joke. "Eliza, I've seen eighty-year-olds kick shuttlecocks with minimal difficulty. I think you'll be fine."

Emily nods vigorously and turns her dark, pleading eyes on me. I've always hated those puppy-dog eyes. Hated them, because they're so effective. Because they always make me say and do things I know I'll regret—

Like saying yes to her game of ti jianzi.

A brief, stunned silence falls over the girls as Caz and I make our way toward their circle, though I suspect the silence is directed more at him. I imagine seeing him from their perspective, this famous actor who has appeared without warning like someone from a dream: tall and easy mannered and effortlessly handsome. And he is smiling at only Emily, barely acknowledging the others, saying, "Thanks for inviting me over, Em," with a wink like they're best friends.

Whatever his reasons, an unexpected gust of warmth fills my chest seeing them together like this, blows all the locked doors and windows inside me wide open.

But apprehension soon comes creeping in on its heels.

Interacting with siblings is murky territory. No matter how hard I try to control our arrangement, to keep it strictly scheduled and organized and professional, things like this pop up and threaten to tangle everything irrevocably.

"You go first," the girl with the polka-dot headband instructs Caz, her eyes hard, hands firm on her hips. She has the high, ringing voice of someone who is used to having her way, but when Caz raises a cool eyebrow at her, she wilts. Mumbles, "Or—or whatever works best."

"I can go, Meredith," Emily says cheerily. The leader, Meredith, frowns, but she doesn't protest. Not with Caz and me standing here, disrupting the power dynamics.

Emily picks up the shuttlecock and kicks it high into the air, with a sound like rattling coins. The girl beside her catches the object on its way down using the toe of her sneaker, then bounces it over to Meredith, who passes it quickly, roughly, to Caz—who retrieves it with ease.

He bounces the shuttlecock back and forth between two feet, even hits it with the top of his head, which draws in bursts of loud, enthusiastic applause.

And he looks . . . Well, he looks ridiculous. This isn't exactly a graceful, dignified game, and even Caz can't quite manage to make ti jianzi look the way horse riding or archery or boxing does. But he's good at it, insanely coordinated, confident despite the inherent ridiculousness of this game, and that's more than enough to impress.

He's *so* good, in fact, that soon he's drawn a substantial crowd.

I try to keep my attention on the shuttlecock, but my skin tingles with the new, uncomfortable awareness. There are far too many pairs of eyes trained on us. On me. Sweat beads above my brow.

"Go, Caz!" someone cheers from the sidelines, joined by some unnecessarily loud whoops and whistles, as if this is the final round of the Olympics.

Caz just smiles his superstar smile and continues passing the shuttlecock around without any hint of self-consciousness, at ease in all the attention.

But when the shuttlecock comes flying toward me, I fumble and drop it. And then I hear it: a low but audible snort from one of the watchers. There are too many people around to tell where it came from, but it doesn't matter. My whole face burns as if struck by a match.

Shakily, I pick the shuttlecock up again and attempt to kick, but it flops pathetically to the side, and Emily has to retrieve it instead. This time, the snort isn't even muffled. Nor their voice, dripping with obvious disbelief:

"*That's* the girl who's dating Caz Song?"

It feels like someone's reached into my stomach and squeezed my insides into a ball. This sort of first-degree humiliation is exactly what I wanted to avoid. And even though it's irrational and petty, I feel an abrupt stab of anger toward Caz. Caz, who's still smiling, playing to the audience, the sun's molten-gold light falling around him like a halo.

Of course *he* enjoys doing things on a whim. Nothing is ever embarrassing for *him*.

"I—I'm going to rest for a bit," I call out, stepping back into the shade, my blood pounding hot and thick. Everyone is staring. "You guys keep playing without me."

Caz shoots me a quick look like, *Are you sure?* Emily and her friends don't even glance up.

"Really. It's fine," I say.

But they've already started up again anyway.

"I like him."

It's later that afternoon, and Emily and I are balanced on the low metal railings outside the school library, feet dangling inches off the ground, while we wait for Li Shushu to pick us up. Our bags have been dropped on the lawn, bloated and brimming with textbooks, dirty Tupperware, laptop chargers, and more useless yet mandatory things.

My shoulders hurt.

I massage them with one hand, slide back on the poles, look ahead. Cars have already started pulling into the outside parking lot, tinted glass and polished metal gleaming, fumes rising off the pavement in waves, like heat.

"Who?" I finally ask, though I can guess.

"Your *boyfriend*," Emily says, tearing the head off a gummy worm with her teeth. One of her friends gave her an entire packet after lunch. "Caz. My friends really like him too."

"I'm not surprised. Everyone loves him." An embarrassing, residual note of bitterness from the ti jianzi game tinges my voice. It's not like it's *Caz*'s fault that he's so universally adored.

That whatever it is I'm deficient in—charm, looks, the ability to draw people in, to make them stay—he has in excess.

Not his fault at all.

And yet the bitterness lingers, like the herbal medicines Ma always brews for us when we have a cold.

"Do you think he'll play with us again tomorrow? Or the day after?"

Emily's face is open, hopeful, eager. I have to look away, ignoring the sharp stone in my stomach. The last thing I need is for her to get attached to Caz. Especially when I don't know how he really feels—if he was so nice because he really likes her, or just likes kids in general, or if it was a onetime thing. Either way, I should really talk to him about leaving my sister out of this.

More cars crawl past us, spitting out smoke.

"I don't know," I say slowly. "But just don't get your hopes up, okay? Caz is really busy with his shooting schedule and endorsements and things and . . . and there are a lot of people who want to spend time with him."

And when my internship ends and his drama premieres, he won't have any reason to spend time with either of us.

"Oh. Okay, then." Emily nods, disappointed but already accepting it.

Then she grins and licks the rest of the purple gummy until it's a shiny, transparent color, the sugary tail sticking to her fingers.

I wrinkle my nose. "That's low-key very gross."

She sticks her purple-stained tongue out at me. I pretend to push her off the railing, and she shrieks, laughing.

The parking lot is starting to empty instead of fill now, students tossing their bags into back seats and trunks, doors clicking shut, tearing open packets of chips and Wang Wang rice crackers to savor on the ride home. And still, no familiar car shows up.

It's not the first time Li Shushu has been late; his schedule is divided between us, Ma, and Ba, and of course Ma is his first priority. The chances are that she had to run off to an emergency meeting with a client, or one of her conferences got pushed back.

But as the minutes drag by and Emily's supply of gummy worms runs low, I can feel her patience waning.

"So. Tell me about your friends," I say—to distract her, but also because I'm curious. Because I can't help wondering how things would've turned out if Caz and I hadn't intervened, if she'd still be left on the perimeter of her friendship circle. It's a feeling I'm quite used to but that I don't want Emily to ever experience.

Emily snorts. "You sound like Ma."

"Yeah, but I'm part of *your* generation. I can understand these things. Give you advice."

"That's what all old people say."

I really do shove her this time—lightly, of course—and she teeters for a moment, arms flailing everywhere, before hooking a foot around the rails and regaining her balance.

"Fine," she huffs out. "What do you want to know?"

"I don't know. You just haven't talked about them a lot. And this is my first time seeing you at lunch."

She kicks a leg out, swinging it into the blue air, toes touching the clouds. "Well, I only started hanging out with them recently."

"Why only recently?"

"They didn't know what to think of me." The way she says it, I realize she's repeating something one of her friends told her. Probably that Meredith girl. And I know I probably shouldn't be hating on a nine-year-old, but it still makes me angry.

"How come?" I ask, my voice neutral.

"They . . . weren't sure where I was from." Emily's voice is neutral too, but it grows quieter the more she talks. "Like, there are these girls in my class who only speak Cantonese to one another, and all their families have been friends since kindergarten. And then there's this other group that's predominantly American and Canadian, and they're not really close to any of the local Chinese kids. They're *friendly*, but not close. And I'm not . . ." She scratches at some invisible itch on her elbow. "I guess I'm not like any of them."

We fall into silence. The parking lot is almost empty now, one long, blank stretch of gray. Still no driver, no familiar face.

"That's a hard word," I say after a while. *"Predominantly."*

"We're meant to learn ten new vocabulary words every week. For English. I also learned the word *dichotomy*."

"Nice, nice."

"Yeah. I'm not sure what it actually means, though."

"You'll get it when you're older," I reassure her. "Or . . . or at least you'll get better at pretending you do."

She blows a stray wisp of hair out of her face. "I hope so. Maybe I'll find my Zoe."

I pause. "What?"

"You know, like a best friend who'll always be there for me, and stick by me no matter what happens. Like you and Zoe."

"Oh. Um, yeah. Right." But a sliver of doubt creeps through my voice, and it's this—the doubt itself, the immediate squeeze in my chest—that worries me almost as much as the unusually brief texts we've exchanged recently, or how all her latest Instagram posts feature her and that new Divya girl hanging out together, or how she's started tagging other classmates in those Facebook memes instead of me. I've been through this enough times with old friends from old schools to know how this tends to go. How those daily texts turn into weekly updates turn into sporadic once-a-month catch-ups turn into nothing.

But this is *Zoe*. The one who's stuck around longest. The one who knows me better than anybody. Since when did I start questioning the strength of our friendship?

Before my thoughts can spiral further, I get back to the point. "Hey, you will . . . tell me, won't you? If anyone in your class excludes you, or says something mean to you."

"If I did, what could you do about it?"

She doesn't say this in a mean way, as a challenge; more in this very offhand, matter-of-fact manner that twists my heart into knots.

"I'd punch them," I decide firmly.

"Really?" Emily eyes me with faint disbelief. "No offense, Jie, but you can't even hit a cockroach without screaming."

"Well, I mean, first of all—cockroaches are disgusting, and they have no right to make those crunching sounds when they die. And second, *yes, really*. I could do it." And I would. For her.

She considers this, then hops onto the ground, dusting sugar off her palms. "Okay, then. I guess."

Our conversation is cut short by the rumble of an engine drawing closer, the school gates creaking open to let our driver's car in. He slows the vehicle when he reaches us—the only two students left on campus—his front windows rolled down, the blast of cold air and a snippet from some Chinese radio talk show escaping through the gaps.

"Sorry," Li Shushu calls, sticking his bald head out. "I had to pick up your mother from a convention. Got stuck in traffic."

"It's fine," I call back. As Emily runs over to heave our schoolbags off the grass, the canvas bottoms now stained with damp green patches and mud spots, I hold the car door open. Hold out my other hand.

"Come on." I nod at her. "Let's go home."

CHAPTER TEN

Even though it's the last thing I want to do after the ti jianzi game, I show up on time for our first official chemistry training session the next day. And as it turns out, Caz wasn't kidding about his *alternate means of transportation.*

"You ride *this* everywhere?" I demand, staring at the horse-sized motorcycle propped up by the compound gates. It looks like something someone in the Mafia would ride, or something a forty-seven-year-old billionaire might buy to keep up with the times. Most of the vehicle is coated a pure, glossy black, from the wheels to the leather seats, but with fire-red streaks running down the sides. Hardly the kind of transportation I expected to see first thing on a Saturday morning, or that I had in mind when Caz texted me about visiting his favorite jianbing stall.

"Beautiful, don't you think?" Caz asks—a rhetorical question, clearly. I mean, he's stroking the seats with more affection than I've seen him show anybody, including his costars in super-intimate scenes.

I stare at him, his winning smile, his casual stance. Unlike me, he doesn't seem to remember the humiliating game at all. Which is just typical of him, really—of *us.* Him, going about his day without a care in the world, while *I* get to sit around and overthink my every exchange with him and wonder why things don't ever come so easily to me.

"Wow," I say flatly as I take a tentative step closer to the leathery, monstrous thing. It's somehow even taller than I originally thought.

"What?"

"You're . . . not the kind of guy who names his motorcycles, right? And refers to it as *she*?" When Caz doesn't reply right away, just laughs and rolls his eyes, I fold my arms across my chest. My horror is exaggerated, but not fake. "You *are*, aren't you?"

He climbs swiftly, easily onto the seat, brows raised at me. "Would that be a huge deal breaker for you?"

"Yes, I'm afraid that alone would be solid grounds for me to break up with you. *Especially* if the name is something like Black Beauty. Or Rebecca."

"You wouldn't," he teases, chucking me one of the two motorcycle helmets dangling from the handlebars. "You like me too much."

I don't know what annoys me more: the arrogant assumption of it, or the way my face bursts into flames, to keep my feelings in check. *Strictly business, remember?* I squeeze on the helmet as fast as my fumbling fingers will allow, if only to avoid his gaze.

I move behind Caz and hoist myself onto the seat in what must be the least graceful way possible, all but kneeing him in the back as I force my legs down on both sides. "Thanks for the tip about wearing pants," I tell him, my voice coming out slightly muffled through the face shield. "I thought you were just traumatized by the length of my dress last time."

His head turns a fraction toward me. "Eliza. If it weren't for the matter of practicality, you could literally come dressed in a trash bag and I wouldn't care."

"Are you sure your reputation could withstand that?" I try to play it off as a joke, but an old note of bitterness edges my voice. Already, fans have started sharing photos of us together and analyzing both his dress style and mine. The nicer ones have labeled my outfits "down-to-earth" and "comfortable" and "youth casual." The not-so-nice ones have urged me to consult Caz Song's stylist.

Maybe Caz saw those comments too, or maybe he hears the ice in my voice, because instead of answering, he's quiet for a moment.

Then he starts the engine, and a thousand loud, violent tremors roll through the steel frame, almost bouncing me off.

"Hold tight," he warns.

I do at once, wrapping my arms in a viselike grip around his stomach and pressing my face between the sharp blades of his shoulders. This close, I can feel the heat of his skin through his T-shirt, the way his muscles contract beneath my fingertips.

He makes a choking sound. "*Holy* sh—not *that* tight—"

"I don't want to fall off," I protest, but I loosen my hold just a little, enough to let him breathe.

"You won't fall," he says, like the notion itself is ridiculous. "I won't let you."

Amazingly, he keeps his word.

We start off at a slow, steady crawl across the street, my hands still clasped tight over Caz's front, our shadows trailing behind us, growing larger, sharper as we leave the shade of the compound gates. Twice, Caz turns around, checking whether or not I'm okay.

When I nod, he shifts gears, and we start speeding up, the landscape rising to greet us—

And it's beautiful.

All of it.

Since Caz has to shoot this afternoon, the hour is still fairly early, the sky the pale blue of a rough watercolor painting. Beijing looks different at this time. More peaceful, somehow. The clean-paved streets and lanes are empty save for a couple of rusted old rickshaws and a few elderly men swinging birds in bamboo cages, humming into the hazy air.

We fly past them down the road, the green of trees and gleam of cars bleeding all around us, shapes and backlit silhouettes melting together.

So this is what it feels like, I marvel as I tilt my face toward the sun, letting the gold-honey light wash soft over me, and catch sight of my own reflection in the side-view mirror. My face is bright with open-mouthed laughter, my eyes creased, shirt rippling in the wind. I look young. Deliriously happy. I almost don't recognize myself.

This is how it feels to be an ordinary teenager.

To be unafraid.

Suddenly, my anger from before feels like a small and distant thing.

We're somewhere deep in the city when Caz slows the vehicle to a stop and lets it rest on the side of a narrow street. He jumps down first, freeing his windswept, movie-star hair from his helmet, then helps me to the ground.

I wobble for a moment, still shaky from leftover adrenaline, knees weak from gripping on to the seat too tightly, before steadying myself against a nearby streetlight. It's a relief to take the crushing weight of the helmet off, to feel the fresh air fanning my cheeks—

Caz takes one look at me and bursts out laughing.

I freeze, self-conscious and a little stunned, because I can't recall seeing Caz laugh like this before: head thrown back and dimples so deep they look carved-in.

Then he says, "Eliza. Your hair."

"What?"

My hands reach instinctively for the top of my head, and I'm horrified to find my hair sticking . . . up. *All the way up*, as if I've been shocked with electricity.

Perfect. Just perfect.

I scowl to hide my embarrassment and quickly smooth my hair back down in a few vigorous pats, then glare at him. "Don't say another word."

"Come on, it didn't look that bad. It's actually quite stylish—"

"Don't."

He bites down on another laugh and mimes zipping his lips, throwing away the key, the full charade, and starts leading me down the street.

"So," I say after a moment, all the awe and adrenaline from the motorcycle ride gone, and the words that have been brewing inside me the past twenty-four hours finally bubbling up to my tongue. "We should probably talk about yesterday."

"What about yesterday?"

He sounds genuinely confused, which only proves my worst suspicions correct. He doesn't care about these things the way I do. He doesn't have to worry about getting hurt, about the consequences of his actions, how one careless smile and a few fake nice words from him could bring someone else to total emotional ruin.

"My *sister*," I grit out. "You playing with her and her friends. What was that?"

He skids to a halt. "Whoa, hold up. Is *that* why you've been grumpy all morning? Because I was being nice to your little sister?"

The way he phrases it—the judgment in his tone, as if I'm being difficult on purpose—makes my blood boil. "I'm not grumpy," I snap, walking right past him.

He catches up to me in a heartbeat. "Yeah, no, of course. Because right now your tone and expression are so gentle. Very peaceful. Not at all like you're fantasizing about strangling me."

Not strangling, I'm tempted to correct him. *Just throwing my fist into your face.*

"I just—" I release a loud puff of air through my teeth. "We shouldn't get our families involved, okay? It's too messy. I don't want my own sister to become collateral damage when we break up."

I wait for some snarky remark, but when he looks at me, his expression is uncharacteristically serious. Even a little sheepish. "Sorry," he says, surprising me. "I guess I wasn't thinking about it like that."

"Of course you weren't," I mutter.

"Hey, listen. If it matters that much to you—I won't do it again, okay?"

My anger weakens slightly, though my distrust toward him holds. "You better not," I warn, jabbing a finger at him.

He stares down at my outstretched finger, then back up at me, and a much more familiar—and kickable—look of amusement sprawls itself across his features. "Has anyone ever told you that you can be pretty scary sometimes?"

I make a point of walking straight ahead without replying.

The jianbing place is nestled between a local kindergarten, a half-empty parking lot, and what looks like an out-of-business textbook store. Two scrawny, sunburnt men in their late twenties are manning the stall, their foreheads shiny with sweat from some combination of the summer heat, the burning grill, and their uniforms: Both have on aprons and plastic sleeves over their loose white tank tops.

They're just finishing up with a young mother's order when we approach from the sidewalk.

"Two jianbings, please," Caz orders in perfect, local Chinese, then glances over at me and switches to English. "Do you want a drink? Soybean milk? Water? Iced tea?"

I'm still busy trying to get my hair to stay flat. I pause at the question, a little flustered, and reply, "Uh, soybean milk would be good. Thanks."

"Sure." Caz turns around and eases smoothly into Chinese again. "Then we'll just have one medium cup of soybean milk, sweetened."

The two men shoot us curious looks, but they don't say anything. They just nod and get to work.

Most of the ingredients have already been laid out over the stand, ready for use at any moment: a carton half filled with eggs; giant jars of black bean sauce and red bean curd and chili oil; a plastic bowl of dough and containers brimming with fresh vegetables.

I watch as one of the chefs spreads the sticky dough over the circular grill in one smooth, rolling motion, until it's been stretched out paper-thin all the way to the edges. He repeats the process with two cracked eggs, the whites sizzling instantly upon contact with the hot metal, the two yolks sliding to the center like twin suns.

Within seconds, the dough turns a baked, crisp gold. Scallions and cut coriander are scattered onto the surface next, followed by pork floss and a thick bean curd paste and fat, fried dough sticks. The savory scent wafts into the air, mingles with the smoke from the grill.

The other man takes over with the packaging, cutting the cooked jianbing into two and sliding them into a small disposable bag, the steam quickly fogging up the clear plastic. Then, without a word, he extends the bag toward us.

Caz nods at me. "You first."

If Ma or Ba were here, they'd probably insist that I do the back-and-forth *you-first-no-*you-*first* thing until one of us runs out of breath or dies from over-politeness. But since the chef's still holding out the bag, and the jianbing really does smell insanely good, I just say, "You sure?"

Caz somehow manages to smile and roll his eyes at the same time. "Eliza. Just take it."

So I do. The bag is so hot it hurts my fingers, and I end up doing that laughable little dance where I pass it between both hands really fast to avoid getting burned.

"Um, xiexie," I tell the chef, who's still looking at me funny.

He exchanges a glance with the other chef, and both of them shake their heads and laugh. Then he says something back, but his regional accent is so strong—or, more accurately speaking, my Chinese skills are so limited—that I can't make out a single word beyond *can*. Which sounds the exact same as *meeting, bribery, clever*, and about fifty other words in Chinese.

So basically he could be saying anything.

I turn to Caz for help.

His expression is unreadable, but he translates right away. "He says he's surprised you know how to say thank you."

"Oh." I glance back at the chefs, unsure what to make of the comment. It's hardly a compliment, but maybe I'm just being oversensitive. Maybe they didn't mean it in a *bad* way . . .

Then the other chef crosses his arms and asks, "Ni haishi zhongguoren ma?"

This time, I understand the full sentence: *Are you even Chinese?*

My face burns. Suddenly I'm not so hungry anymore.

Caz clears his throat beside me. "He said—"

"Yeah, I—I know what he said." There's an embarrassing crack in my voice, the edge of something raw, and I have to look away from everyone. Stare down at a piece of old chewing gum stuck to the road instead. It doesn't even make sense for me to get so worked up about this one offhand question . . .

Except I've heard it before, so many times. Every possible version of it: *Are you American? British? Are you from around here? Are you* actually *Chinese?*

I don't know. Sometimes it just gets really exhausting having to explain your identity to everyone.

After we've picked up both our orders, Caz and I walk in silence for a while, heading to nowhere. I know we're supposed to be spending this time learning about each other, but neither of us seems to know what to say. Willow trees reach out from one side of the street and a breeze sings its soft song through the dripping leaves. The sun has edged higher up the sky now, and it's all blue, everywhere, stark blue and the quiet between us.

Caz breaks it first. "I doubt he meant it that way—"

“It’s fine, Caz,” I say, with a sad attempt at a laugh. “We really don’t have to talk about this. I mean, there’s not even anything to talk about.”

“Well, you’re clearly upset.”

“I’m not—”

“You are. You’re making that face again.” And he actually stops halfway down the street, juts his chin out and bites his lower lip in an impression of me that’s as aggravating as it is freakishly accurate.

I hold up a hand to block him from view. “I don’t look like that at all,” I lie. Then, when it becomes apparent he isn’t buying it: “Whatever. You wouldn’t understand anyway.”

“Why not?” he challenges.

I stop in my tracks too. “*Why not?* Are you serious?”

“Of course,” he says evenly, his dark eyes steady on me.

“Caz. This isn’t— You don’t have these types of problems, okay?” The words come out too quick, too honest, a bitter, breathless rush. “You belong everywhere. You’re welcome anywhere. Whether it’s on the red carpet or in a silly children’s game or in the school cafeteria. You always fit in perfectly, without trying, and—it’s just not like that with me.”

I sense his surprise, and I immediately wish I hadn’t said anything at all. What is it about Caz Song that makes me both want to open up and draw a ten-foot-thick barrier around me?

“Maybe that’s true at school,” he says finally, jaw tight. “But sometimes, in my own home . . .” And he stops. It’s like that moment in the park again: He seems to be battling himself on something, like a boy teetering on the edge of a vast pool, unsure if it's safe enough to dive in. All this time, and he still reveals so little of himself willingly. "Sometimes I feel that way too" is what he settles on in the end. A half answer; a compromise; one foot suspended in midair, the other set firm on the ground. A suggestion that there might be more to him than I've given him credit for.

The precarious truce stretches between us.

I take a bite of my jianbing and I don't taste anything at first, just scalding, tongue-numbing heat, but then the savory bean curd flavor fills my mouth and the scent of fried oil brings back some of my appetite. Something in me softens.

"It's good," I tell him reluctantly.

"Good," he says.

We both sit down on the curb and eat our breakfast and watch the city come to life. It *is* good, I guess, despite everything. Living here. Being here with Caz. Even if Beijing doesn't fully feel like mine yet, moments like this still give me hope that one day, it could be.

I'm pulled from my thoughts as Caz dissolves into a loud coughing fit.

And the melodramatic part of my brain programmed to assume the worst of everything instantly thinks: *Oh god. This is it. He's going to tell me he's suffering from some kind of chronic condition and he's been keeping it a secret this whole time because he doesn't want anyone to worry but he only has two months left to live. We're going to end up in a depressing movie montage of his last days with me and there's going to be a bunch of blood-colored sunsets and slow walks by the beach and one day he'll just collapse before my eyes and—*

"Sorry," Caz says, wincing slightly. He holds up his jianbing. "It's—they don't usually put chili in this—"

My heart slows down, and my panic fades.

"Wait. You can't eat anything spicy?"

"Of course I can," he grumbles, but his cheeks are a few shades too red, and he doesn't make any move to touch his food again.

"Oh my god." It's so unexpected that the last of my anger from earlier dissipates, and I laugh. Once I start, I can't stop. My whole body shakes with ill-suppressed giggles until I'm nearly doubled over on the curb. "Oh my god. This is amazing."

"How?" he says flatly. "What could possibly be amazing about this?"

"Just—out of *all* things," I choke out through my hysteria. "I mean, you were able to complete a bunch of stunts with a broken arm and bear the pain but you can't handle a bit of *spice*?"

He scowls at me, though I can tell he doesn't really mean it. "There was a lot in there, okay? At least two whole chilies—"

"Oh my god, stop—" I clutch at my stomach, laughing harder. "Stop—sorry. I can't. I seriously can't."

"I'm glad you find my sensitive taste buds so hilarious."

"Okay, okay, I'll— Let me just get a grip . . ." I take a deep breath like I'm about to meditate while Caz watches me, unimpressed, but that only sets me off again. I don't even know what's so funny about this. Or maybe it's not that funny—maybe I'm just happy, even though that makes no sense. When I've finally calmed down enough to form full sentences, I hold out my own jianbing in offering. "We can swap, if you want. I promise there's zero chili in mine."

The weeping willow above our heads sways as I talk, its leaves scratching my cheek.

Caz bats the branches away from me and tilts his head, assessing. "You sure this isn't some kind of setup? You haven't poisoned it or anything?"

"I swear. Though, I mean, I've already taken a few bites out of it, if you don't mind . . ." And suddenly it's awkward; I can feel it in the air. *I've* made things awkward. Like I always do.

But Caz recovers quickly. He grabs my jianbing from me like it's no big deal and smiles a little and tells me, "We'll go somewhere that serves milder food next time."

"Next time," I repeat, surprised to find that the idea of these chemistry training sessions doesn't fill me with *quite* as much dread as it did before.

CHAPTER ELEVEN

School is different now.

Better, in a way. I don't find myself dreading the car rides to school so much I feel physically sick anymore, don't have to hover awkwardly at the doorway of classrooms as much as before. It's not like I'm super popular all of a sudden—I still eat all my lunches alone on the rooftop—but people seem to have finally accepted my presence.

I'm not naive enough to imagine this isn't partly because I'm with Caz Song. But another part of it also has to do with my Craneswift blog posts.

My followers have been growing rapidly, climbing by an extra few thousand almost every day, the number of likes and shares rising with them. It's as exhilarating as it is terrifying.

The kind of love I'm praying for, girls have commented under one of my recent posts, "We Dance beneath the Streetlights, Kiss beneath the Moonlight," where the fictional-boyfriend version of Caz Song and I stay out together in our compound at midnight.

This is proof that love exists, others have gushed over another post about us riding through the city together, about seeing Beijing from the back of Caz Song's motorcycle, titled simply "He Swears He Won't Let Me Fall."

And when I'm not describing our dates, our fake cute

interactions, or slyly making references to Caz Song's upcoming drama to help drum up interest, I find myself in the very undeserved position of dishing out love advice. *It's important to be emotionally honest*, I write in one article, tasting the sharp irony of my own words. *Don't be afraid of vulnerability.* Or, in another article for the Love and Relationships column: *I know there's this popular mindset of "I'm strong and independent and I don't need anyone," but the truth is: We do need people. People who'll laugh with us and cry with us and make the bad days bearable and the good days better; people who'll remember what we forget and listen even when they don't completely understand; people who'll need us back. It has nothing to do with strength at all, and everything to do with being human.*

Of course, Sarah Diaz is completely ecstatic about how things are going.

"People love it," she gushes over our fortnightly catch-up call. "People are *invested.* That's a big deal, you know? Your last blog post about those snack stalls you and Caz visited—*so cute*, by the way, and the photos had me drooling—just hit forty thousand views."

"I know," I say, then flush, because it sounds ridiculously cocky, which isn't what I meant at all. "I mean, um. Thank you."

She dismisses my awkwardness with an easy laugh. "Oh, that reminds me, Eliza—how do you feel about doing an interview?"

"An . . . interview?"

"Yes. An interview." Sarah is far more patient with me than I deserve. "I know you've probably received a few invitations already, but this one was sent straight to us at Craneswift. It's with this pretty big Beijing-based media company aimed at Western audiences, so the location and language shouldn't be a problem. And they were *very* complimentary in their email. I can tell they're highly interested in your background, and they'd love for you and Caz to make an appearance together."

"Really," I say vaguely, my mind still catching up to everything she just said.

"So what do you think?" she prompts. Before I can respond, she hurries on. "I know it's a bit of a lot. But think of the *exposure.* This will do wonders for your career, Eliza, I can just feel it."

That's an understatement. It's *a lot* of a lot. And sometimes, at times like this, when I become painfully aware of the sheer magnitude of my lie, the speed at which everything is happening, hurtling forward without brakes, my lungs seem to shrink and I have a vivid, half-hysterical image of being thrown into jail and getting kicked out of school and put on some permanent literary blacklist for making my essay up—

But no—*breathe.* Breathe. I try to breathe.

No one has suspected anything about my love story with Caz yet. I mean, we've had a handful of chemistry training sessions so far and they seem to be working pretty well, and I haven't accidentally slapped him again or anything.

Still . . .

"That sounds . . . interesting," I say, fumbling around for a safe route out of this conversation. "I can—yeah, no, I can probably do that."

Something crashes in the background on Sarah's end.

"Sorry." Sarah's voice sounds smaller, muffled, like she's holding the phone between her ear and shoulder. I think I hear the clatter of wood and a very quietly uttered expletive. "A—a painting of Jesus just fell to the ground for some reason. Weird."

If I were even *kind of* religious, I'd definitely see this as a bad omen.

"Anyway, what were you saying about the interview?" Her voice grows louder again, reverting to its normal cheery tone.

"No, it's just that . . . I—I'll have to ask Caz," I tell her, knowing that I won't. "And really . . . think about it more. Would it be okay to give you an answer some time later?"

"Sure, Eliza." But I can hear her disappointment, however well disguised. "I don't want you to commit to anything you're not comfortable with."

A little too late for that is all I can think as I hang up, my stomach heavy as stone.

Pretty soon it becomes clear that the interview is the least pressing of my concerns.

Because three days before Caz Song's eighteenth birthday, I realize I still have no idea what to get him. I mean, I'm sure there's plenty of advice out there on appropriate gifts to buy at different stages in a relationship, but no online magazines come with a guide for what to give your boyfriend when you're only fake-dating.

It doesn't help that this is *the* Caz Song we're talking about. What are you supposed to give a boy who already has the whole world?

I'm so desperate for answers that I end up consulting Emily later that night—then regret it almost instantly.

"You have come to the right place," Emily reassures me, but it sounds more like *These will be the most painful minutes of your life.*

We're both sitting around the dining table, a giant bowl of bright yellow diced mangoes and sliced strawberries set between us, two fruit forks laid to the side. Ma's off in the other room calling Kevin from marketing again (every now and then, you can hear her sigh and say something like *No, a pool party would most definitely not be appropriate—yes, even if we were to print the company logo on all the beach balls, Kevin!*) and Ba's busy preparing his notes for a poetry reading at some prestigious university tomorrow.

"I will make sure you create the greatest gift of all time," Emily continues dramatically, slamming one tiny fist down on the table. "Anyone who has ever had a boyfriend before will weep in shame. They will have no choice but to bow before you and—"

"Yeah, uh, that won't be necessary." I clear my throat. "I just need, like, a passable idea. It doesn't have to be that good."

"Wow." Emily's been using sarcasm a lot these days. I think she's starting to enter her teenage phase. "Caz is *so lucky* to be dating you."

I roll my eyes and stab my fork into a cube of mango. "Yeah, whatever. Just give me some ideas."

In response, she steals the mango from me with the other fork.

"Hey—"

"I'm *thinking*," she tells me between loud chews. It's not often that I ask for her advice on anything, and she's obviously enjoying this a little too much.

"Can you think faster? I only have three days to sort this out."

"Well, that's on you," she says, which is annoying but unfortunately true.

I've never been the type to procrastinate on schoolwork or whatever, but I do have a bad tendency to avoid anything I find uncomfortable. When we had to leave my old school in London, I meant to personally tell my English teacher that we were moving. But I knew that she really liked me, and that she'd cry at the news right in front of me and deliver a dramatic farewell speech, and the whole imaginary scenario made me feel so awkward I ended up putting it off until we'd boarded the plane, by which point it was of course too late to say anything. She probably thinks I'm dead now, having just stopped going to school one day. Or maybe in a coma.

If awkwardness could be a fatal flaw, it would most definitely be mine.

"Hey, what about a love letter?" Emily suggests, her eyes lighting up. "It'd be so sweet, just like in the olden days—you know, like the early 2000s! And you could write about—"

"No." I shake my head before she can even finish the sentence.

"Nope. No way." The mere memory of Caz reading my essay out loud in the janitor's closet still makes me cringe so hard my back muscles spasm. A letter addressed to him would be even more intimate, and a thousand times more embarrassing. Besides, what would I even write? *Dearest Caz, roses are red, violets are blue, we're not actually dating, but happy birthday to you . . .*

"Well, how about a scrapbook, then? Of all your cutest moments together?" Emily says, undeterred, popping two more pieces of mango into her mouth. "Or a photo collage, with romantic quotes?"

I grimace. "Do you have any gift ideas that aren't so, um . . . personal?"

"But that's the whole point of birthday gifts," she protests.

It's hard to argue with that, so I go for a half lie instead. "I just feel like we're not at that stage in the relationship yet."

"No, you're right," she agrees seriously. "You should save those ideas for your one-year anniversary. Or your wedding."

I almost choke. Even though I know—at least I hope—she's half kidding, it's still a little worrying that she'd even entertain the possibility of us staying together that long. Caz should hold no place in my future, and most certainly not my family's.

Yet another reason why this whole fake love story thing is a mess.

"Wait, I've got it!" Emily jabs her fork high into the air, then at me, which feels vaguely threatening. "You should give him paper cranes."

"Like, origami?"

"Mhm." She nods fast, her pigtails bouncing all over the place.

"I saw a YouTube video about a girl who made them for her boyfriend. She folded a crane for every day they'd been together, and she included a compliment inside each one for him to read."

"I see . . ." It doesn't actually sound like a bad idea. Except for one thing. "I'm not writing down compliments for Caz, though. His confidence doesn't need any more boosting." But maybe I can write him something else.

Emily shrugs. "Well, just remember you'd need to fold a *lot* of cranes."

"Yeah." I do a rough calculation in my head of all the days we've been together. "Around eighty."

She pauses. Frowns at me. "Hang on. Haven't you guys been going out since, like, June?"

Crap.

"Oh, I mean . . ." *Think fast.* I force my features to remain neutral, free of the panic buzzing in my veins. "It's been eighty days since we, like, officially got together. In public."

I search out of the corner of my eye for any sign that she doesn't buy this explanation, but she nods, trusting me. Of course she trusts me, and somehow that makes me feel worse.

Still. No point dwelling on that now.

I spend the rest of the evening watching paper crane tutorials on YouTube and trying to follow them step-by-step. It takes a few dozen tries, and I have to steal some colored paper from Emily's desk, but by midnight, I get the hang of it.

There's something almost therapeutic about the simple, repetitive motions, working alone in the peace of my room at night, smoothing out the thin squares of paper again and again under my palms, my Spotify playlist on loop in the background, the playlist Zoe and I made together before I left, with all our favorite artists: Taylor Swift and Jay Chou and BTS.

As I do, I think about Caz. Smug, vain, infuriating Caz, who somehow keeps managing to surprise me. Who agreed to my bizarre proposal, and is the only reason I've made it this far without getting caught in my lie. Who's funnier than most people realize, and sweeter than I could've ever given him credit for. And despite my best intentions to hold him at arm's length, despite knowing all this will end in a matter of months, I can't help feeling . . . lucky. After all, how many people in this world can say they've seen what Caz Song is really like behind the scenes?

So when I've finished folding, I write a small, quiet wish on each delicate paper crane:

I hope you always catch your train in time.

I hope your birthday always falls on a weekend or holiday.

I hope you land every role you audition for.

I hope you have an umbrella with you whenever it rains.

I hope you always snatch up the last bag of your favorite snack.

I hope you always get the window seat.

By the time I get to the last crane, my alarm clock is flashing. Six a.m. I'm exhausted and nearly out of ideas, and maybe it's because of this that I let the truth slip out onto the page.

I hope you remember to miss me when all this is over.

• • •

On the morning of Caz's birthday, I get up a few hours early to bake him a cake.

This turns out to be much harder than I expected. Somehow, even though I've followed every single instruction written on this random mother's baking blog—which I find only after a three-paragraph-long introduction about her son being a picky eater—the cake comes out all weird and mushy and distinctly orange. I wait awhile in the dim, quiet kitchen, hoping it might look better once it's cooled, but it only starts shrinking and wrinkling at the edges like a sad piece of dried fruit.

Zoe isn't much help either.

"Is it . . . meant to be that color?" she asks, squinting through the screen. I've propped my phone up on the counter beside the dirty whisks and leftover bowls of batter to give her a clear view of the finished product. She was originally going to call before she had lunch and offer advice *while* I baked, but she got held up by a last-minute assignment due at midday.

"Maybe it's because of the lighting," I say hopefully.

"Maybe," she plays along.

We both study the withering cake for a beat. Then I sigh, wipe my flour-covered hands against my apron, and yank open the fridge door again. "Never mind. I'll just—I'll try again. Wouldn't want to give him food poisoning for his birthday."

"Right, right. Chinese ingredients and all that."

My fingers freeze over the egg carton. My head jerks up. "Wait. What?"

"What?" she says back, equally confused.

But I understand faster than she does. "I was talking about my *baking skills*, not the local ingredients," I say, and the sharp, defensive edge in my own voice catches me off guard.

"Oh." Zoe clears her throat, looking uncomfortable. "Well, I only meant . . . I mean, I was reading this article the other day about how they use gutter oil to cook food in Beijing, which low-key seems horrifying and kind of unhygienic, and . . ."

"And you immediately assumed there's gutter oil in everything we eat here?" I ask.

"No, I—I don't—" Zoe shakes her head. Stares at me. "I'm confused. Why are you getting so upset?"

I open my mouth, then close it. Because I don't know how to explain to her what I'm mad about, why I feel so . . . territorial. Only the other week, *I* had asked Ma if the fried dough sticks we bought off the side of the street were safe to eat, and I myself have *definitely* heard rumors of places using already-used oil to cook, even been warned about it by locals. Maybe that makes me a hypocrite.

But maybe it's the same irrational logic that applies when someone insults your family; I can complain about Emily stealing my food or hogging the bathroom all I like, for instance, but I'd fight anyone who says a single bad word about her. Maybe listening to Zoe talk about Beijing like that feels painfully personal because it is. Because the city isn't hers to insult.

Which, of course, begs the question: When did Beijing become mine to defend?

"Eliza?" Zoe prompts, the uncertainty in her features enlarged on my phone screen. "Are you okay?"

Some of my initial anger loosens. Enough for me to think clearly. It's possible I'm being too harsh on her, and either way, there's no reason to get into a massive fight over this one thing, especially when we haven't had a chance to talk in so long. Right?

I release a long breath. Refocus. Touch the frayed friendship bracelet on my wrist. "I'm fine," I tell her, and my voice cooperates, steadies itself before things can escalate.

"Well, if you're sure . . ."

"I am."

"I really—I didn't mean to assume," she says, her voice smaller as she draws the phone closer to her face. "I'm really sorry. I just realized how shitty that sounded—I genuinely didn't mean for it to come out like that."

I crack open another egg, but I apply too much pressure; the shell collapses between my fingers with a soft crunch, little shards of it falling into the bowl. *Crap.* "Um, don't worry about it," I say, distracted, frustration rising inside me. "I need to just . . . just do this thing . . ." With a spoon, I try to scoop all the shell bits back out, but the process takes forever, and requires far too much concentration for me to continue the conversation.

"Can I call you later?" I say at last, biting back a grimace.

"What time?"

After school, I start to tell her, but then I remember the time difference issue. "Like, this time tomorrow?"

"Can't. I have a meeting with Divya and the other student council kids."

"Thursday?"

Some shuffling on her end, like she's looking through a planner. "No. No, sorry. There's this really important chem test . . . Um, what about Friday morning my time?"

"I have a call set up with Sarah—you know, from Craneswift."

"Right."

"Okay, then . . ." I pause and set the spoon down. Suddenly, I can't remember what we used to do, how we'd go about planning these calls. Yet I'm almost certain that it never used to be this hard. "Then . . . bye for now?"

"Mhm. Bye."

And then she's gone, leaving me with a blank phone screen and my eggshell batter and the faint, nagging feeling that something's gone wrong—and not just my baking. But I don't have time to psychoanalyze it.

As the sun creeps slowly over the kitchen window, I mix and stir and pour as if my life depends on it until I've made a hideous but distinctly less orange cake. I pack it into one of those plastic restaurant takeout containers Ma always insists on saving.

I guess it's the thought that counts.

I decide to give Caz his presents before lunch.

He's recently started shooting some big-budget xianxia drama based on a super-popular web novel, so he doesn't show up at school in the mornings anymore—making this the earliest possible time I can get it all over with. I'll hand him the gifts and forget about it for the rest of the day.

But as I draw closer to Caz's locker, the jar of paper cranes in my hands, the candles and birthday cake tucked deep in my schoolbag, I feel two things snake past the sharp of my ribs.

Hope.

Dumb, dangerous hope.

And dread.

It should be physically impossible for them to coexist inside me—this silly lightness in my chest, buoying me up, and this heavy sinking sensation in my gut. But now, in broad daylight, with Caz standing right there, as unfortunately beautiful as ever, I'm forced to admit that what I wrote on those paper cranes wasn't just my exhaustion talking.

I might actually be crushing on Caz Song. Like a total sucker.

Even though our arrangement is already messy enough. Even though this makes yet another starry-eyed, rosy-cheeked fangirl with her heart on her sleeve.

As if to prove my point, in that very moment, Caz's usual gang of friends come spilling through the locker area and swarm around him.

"Happy birthday, my man," Daiki calls, slapping Caz's shoulder while the others echo the sentiment with loud whoops, and Savannah, grinning widely, pulls out one of the most beautiful cakes I've ever seen.

My heart sinks.

It's the kind of creamy white, multitiered, elaborately decorated cake that wouldn't look out of place at a fancy wedding, with delicate blue flowers frosted over the sides and glistening bubble tea pearls placed at the very top. A few random onlookers gasp, some inching closer in hopes of getting a slice.

Suddenly, my own cake feels ridiculous.

It was an absurd idea to make it in the first place. Absurd to hope.

I'm already walking away, debating whether or not to just give my cake to Emily for lunch, when I hear someone call my name.

"Eliza! Eliza—wait up."

I turn around, surprised. Caz is pushing his way through the crowd, past his adoring fans. Moving straight toward me. And I realize abruptly that the only thing worse than having a crush on a star is being made aware of it. My pulse speeds up, and if this were one of Caz's campus dramas, there'd definitely be slow, romantic music playing in the background right now.

Oh god.

This is everything I was afraid of.

"Damn, you walk fast." He shakes his head. Behind him, all his friends are nudging one another and watching us the way you'd watch a particularly fascinating episode of a drama, eyes wide and mouths half-open. Savannah is still holding the giant cake.

"Yeah, well, I have, um, plans already so . . ." I force myself to smile, but all of a sudden I can't remember if I used to smile at him before. Or smile this wide. I'm terrified there's a neon sign projecting my feelings from my forehead. Under no circumstances can Caz Song find out that I like him; the consequences are almost too mortifying to imagine.

He gives me a funny look. "Are you okay?"

"Yeah." I nod hard. *Please, Eliza, get your shit together and act normal.* "Yeah, perfect. Wh-why?"

"No reason," he says slowly. Then his gaze cuts to the glass jar of folded cranes in my hands. "What's that?"

"Nothing." I quickly hide the jar behind me—but I'm still a beat too slow.

"It looks like a present," he says, stepping forward.

"Well, it's not."

He arches a brow. "Are you sure?"

"Absolutely. One hundred percent."

For the briefest moment, something like uncertainty flashes over his face. Like he might actually be disappointed—like I might have the power to disappoint him.

It's a ridiculous idea, delusional really, but I feel myself waver. "I mean, okay, it is, but . . . Just. Don't make a big deal out of it, okay?"

And then I kind of throw the jar at him.

He catches it easily with one hand and turns it over, studies it. He doesn't seem to understand what it is at first until he sees the words written on the cranes. I'm too nervous to look at his face as he goes through some of the wishes, afraid to see the possible scorn in his expression, or boredom, or worse: nothing at all. He probably gets gifts like this all the time at fan meetings. It probably doesn't even matter to him.

But then he calls my name once, soft, and I lift my head in surprise. He looks so obviously, genuinely moved, all his gratitude just lying wide open in his gaze, that I can't stand it. This intimacy. The way it makes my chest heat.

Act normal, remember?

"There's a cake too," I grumble, reaching back into my bag.

The look vanishes; laughter bursts from his lips. "Why do you sound so angry about it?"

"Because. It's really ugly."

"I'm sure you're exaggerating . . ." he starts to say—then I hold out the half-burnt, half-crumbling yellow mess of a cake. We both stare at it for a few seconds. Somewhere in the distance, I swear I can hear a hundred pastry chefs collectively weeping. "Okay," Caz admits. "It is a little ugly."

I snort. "Thanks for being honest."

"Anytime." Then he pauses. "So. Did you want to share the cake?" I can tell he doesn't really expect me to say yes. I've turned down all his invitations before, preferring to eat alone instead of forcing awkward small talk with his many, much more popular friends. Luckily, if people think it's suspicious that we don't eat lunch together, they've never mentioned it.

But while I hesitate, Daiki and the others—who have blatantly and unashamedly been listening to our every word—make their way over.

"We can all share," Savannah says, voice bright, and Nadia and Stephanie nod in fast agreement.

Then, to my surprise, Nadia hooks her slender arm around mine as if we've known each other all our lives. "Come on. We're all *dying* to get to know you better. I mean, Caz has been so secretive about you."

"Oh. Thanks," I say, then realize how unintelligent that must sound. Flustered, I continue. "But, um, you already have a cake and I'd hate to intrude . . ."

"One can never have too much cake," Stephanie says, adopting the deep, dramatic voice of some ancient sage.

"Wise words," Nadia agrees. "Plus, they're different flavors. Like, ours is a brown-sugar bubble tea cake, and yours is . . ."

There's a humiliating moment of silence as Caz's friends all lean in and attempt to classify the lumpy pastry in my hands.

"Yours is . . . of the homemade variety," Savannah puts in politely.

Caz releases an audible puff of laughter. I turn to glare at him, but when our gazes meet, he only laughs harder.

Then Daiki steps between us. "Okay, lovebirds, stop flirting for a second—"

"We weren't flirting," I protest, wondering if one of us has a fundamental misconception of the term. "I don't— We didn't even *say anything*."

"Yeah, but we can see it in your eyes," he says. "And that shit's even more obvious than direct pickup lines."

As if my face isn't already on fire, the others all nod along.

"On second thought, are we sure we want to spend a whole lunchtime around these two?" Savannah jokes.

"Well, it's Caz's birthday," Nadia reasons, drawing my arm closer to hers, our elbows bumping. "He's going to want his girlfriend there." They all turn to me, expectant, Caz included, and though the idea of having to act like we're dating before his group of intimidatingly gorgeous, charismatic friends—and leaving a good impression, no less—makes me want to break out into stress hives and flee the country under a new identity, Nadia's right: It *is* his birthday.

And maybe some small, foolish part of me does want to spend more time with him.

Before I can chicken out, I force myself to nod. "Yeah, okay. Let's go."

But as we approach Caz's regular corner table in the cafeteria, I realize there's a small problem: We're a chair short. Just when I'm scanning the area for a seat, Caz nudges his normal chair over in my direction and makes an elaborate gesture for me to sit.

I shake my head quickly, aware that some students have already started staring.

"Um, you don't have to do that. I can find something . . ."

"No, I've got it," he reassures me. No sooner than the words have left his lips, a blushing girl from year eight or nine hurries forward and shyly pushes a spare chair toward him.

"H-happy birthday," she squeaks out.

He smiles at her politely. "Thank you."

It's a simple response, but the girl's face turns bright red, and she stumbles twice on her short trip back to her giggling, whispering friends.

"You know," Daiki remarks from the other end of the table, where Savannah is already snuggled up against his broad chest, "one day someone's going to crash their car just because you glanced in their direction, and you're going to have to take full legal responsibility."

Caz just rolls his eyes and sits down, tipping his chair back a few degrees.

I feel like *I* should say something—something cool and confident and witty—but my mind's blank. And Savannah's current proximity to Daiki isn't helping. Is this how all couples are meant to behave when eating together? Am I expected to curl up like that against Caz too? Or would it look too deliberate, like I'm copying them?

Then I'm imagining how it'd feel to be that close to him, to rest my cheek over the place his heart beats, let him wrap one strong arm around me—

"Hey." Caz nudges my knee under the table, and I jump, my face flushing.

"Hmm?"

He raises an eyebrow while the others stare over at us with obvious curiosity. "What were you thinking about?"

"N-nothing. Just . . ." I panic and blurt out the first thing that comes to mind. "Just—global warming."

I'm met with a series of blank stares. *Great*, I think with rising despair as the silence stretches on. *This is exactly why you don't hang out with Caz's friends. Now they're going to wonder why he's dating someone with the social skills of a potted plant or a potential kink for a severe climate crisis—*

Then Daiki nods solemnly. “It’s a pressing issue, for sure.”

And somehow, the conversation turns to the latest environmental documentary Savannah watched and the new eco-friendly garbage-sorting system they’ve introduced in China and the fundraiser Caz took part in last spring, which then sends them on a tangent about Caz’s best partnerships (“I’m so glad you’re working with that big cosmetics brand again—they give out the *best* free lipstick”). They’re all so charming, so *nice* and fun, that it’s hard not to get a little swept up, like a peasant at a ball. To wonder if maybe things could be different at this school, with these people. If Caz’s friends might someday become my friends too.

Don’t be naive. I kill that thought before it can take root. I’ve hoped for similar things in the past, and it’s never worked out. My problem isn’t making friends, it’s keeping them. There’s no reason for that to change this time around.

“Eliza!” Savannah whips around toward me, her sharp eyeliner creasing as she smiles. “Should we get a photo of you and Caz together?”

I blink. “For . . . for what?”

But this must be one of those things all real couples just know to do, because she says, like the answer is obvious in the statement itself, “Well, for his birthday.”

“Oh! We should get that cake you made him in there too,” Nadia chimes in, dragging my very sad-looking birthday cake to the table’s center.

“That’s— You really don’t have to . . .”

But my awkward protests are lost in their loud, persistent enthusiasm, and next thing I know Savannah's standing up on her chair in her tall platform boots ("Anything for the angle") with her phone out and waving frantically for me and Caz to sit closer together.

I scoot my chair clumsily over, and after a moment's deliberation, prop my elbow up on Caz's shoulder.

Savannah lowers the phone a fraction and stares.

Nadia cackles into her palm. "Haven't you two been going out for months already? Why are you acting like it's your first date?"

They're only teasing now, but with a creeping sense of foreboding, I realize that it could very well turn into suspicion if I don't do something soon. Desperate, I climb out of my seat and perch myself on Caz's knee instead, pulling his arms around my waist.

Even though I make an active effort not to feel or think anything during this whole mortifying, far-too-intimate process, the taut muscles of his stomach seem to tense for a second before he cooperates, draws me in closer, his chin resting gently against my shoulder.

"That's better," Savannah approves, holding up her phone again.

But I barely register the moment when our photo is taken; all I can focus on is my own thudding heartbeat and pray Caz Song can't tell it has nothing to do with the performance itself, and everything to do with him.

This was never part of the plan.

No. I haven't spent half my life carefully building up ten-foot-tall barricades around myself only for this vain, untrustworthy pretty-boy actor to come in and tear them all down. I need to get rid of this dumb crush—and fast.

CHAPTER TWELVE

Back home, hidden away in my bedroom, I create a brand-new PowerPoint titled *A Step-by-Step Guide on Getting Over an Unwanted Crush.*

I've spent the remaining school day compiling articles and advice columns and every resource out there on how to do this, scrapping all the bullshit tips like "just give it time" or "accept your feelings" and tailoring the information to my own situation. All I really need now is to follow through with it.

So, Step One: Look for Things to Hate about Him.

This should be easy enough. I crack my knuckles and spread my fingers over my keyboard. *Things to hate* . . . There are a number of anti-fan forums up and running, populated by people who absolutely loathe Caz Song: a perfect place to find inspiration. Still, I feel weirdly guilty going on them, as if I'm somehow engaging in an act of treason.

Then I read a few of the hate comments:

@fionaxia: *Caz Song is so fake it creeps me out. You just know that it's all a persona created by his company to win over brainless teenage girls. Does he even have an actual personality?*

@phoebe_bear: *let's be real: if Caz Song weren't born with a pretty face, he'd be a nobody. His acting is just okay. So many people are 1000x more deserving of what he has.*

@stanxiaozhaninstead: *A former fan here (don't judge). Used to love him until he changed his hair. Wish he'd dye it again; now he looks too feminine.*

@cazno1hater: *I have this theory that Caz has hooked up with at least two major players in the entertainment industry. There's literally no other explanation why he'd keep getting these big drama opportunities.*

Next thing I know, I'm clenching my teeth so hard they hurt and creating an account under a fake name and replying: *Caz Song is FAR more talented than you'll ever be. You have no idea how hard he's worked, you pathetic little—*

Okay, so maybe the first step wasn't as effective as I'd hoped. Whatever. I turn my attention to Step Two instead: Develop a Crush on Someone Else.

Over the next couple weeks, I force myself to admire photos of other celebrities every morning. Gong Jun. Deng Lun. Yi Yang Qian Xi. Jungkook. They're all very attractive. I know this objectively. Yet my pulse stays the same no matter how long I stare at them, willing myself to just *feel something.* But I feel nothing, not until I get to school and catch sight of Caz laughing with his friends, where my pulse promptly skyrockets and my stomach somersaults ten times over.

Desperate by this point, I move on to Step Three: Observe Him More Closely. The apparent logic behind this is that crushes are like mirages; they don't hold well under intense scrutiny. So I observe Caz Song, searching for flaws, a crack in the fantasy. At school, and during our chemistry training sessions while we explore the city and memorize as much of each other's backgrounds as possible. In late November and early December, when Caz takes me out to eat lamb kebabs, sweet potatoes in foil, sugar-roasted chestnuts fragrant enough to make your mouth water from yards away. On the first day of winter, when Caz brings me to this place that sells thick sesame-coated bings the size of my face.

The whole time, I watch him—

And I notice all the wrong things.

Like how he's always the first to clean up and throw our trash away without saying a word. How he gets cold easily, his cheeks flushing in the faintest breeze, but refuses to wear extra layers if he doesn't think it looks good, which somehow isn't nearly as irritating as it should be. How he never loses his patience when I can't decide on my order, and never laughs at me when I ask silly questions about how the food is cooked.

Today, he introduces me to a handmade noodle stall near Houhai Lake, and the feeling is still there, curled up snugly against my ribs. The cursed, stubborn crush I can't get rid of.

It's supposed to snow later. This is what I'm thinking about on our ride back. How it'll snow, and how secretly excited I am to see it, to feel it on my skin. I've forgotten what Beijing in the snow looks like. I hope it's beautiful.

We've almost reached our compound when I notice that my right wrist is bare. It takes me another few seconds to realize why, exactly, the sight is so odd—

The bracelet.

The bracelet is gone.

"No," I whisper, my voice buried beneath the rumble of the engine.

The motorcycle is moving too fast for me to stop and search for a short piece of string, but I try anyway, scanning my jean pockets, my sleeves, hoping against threadbare hope that it might've only gotten tangled in the fabric, in the wind, in my hair.

But there's nothing.

Which means it must've fallen off somewhere along the ride, anywhere between the noodle stall and here. Maybe even earlier than that, when we were eating by the frozen lake banks, blowing warm air into our hands—

"Is something wrong?" Caz calls back to me, catching my eye in the side-view mirror.

"I—" The thought of brushing it aside, of simply acting like everything is fine and going home and grieving this loss alone, flits through my mind. *It's only an old bracelet anyway.* And though I've kept mine ever since Zoe gave it to me, if I really think about it, I haven't seen her wear hers in a while. Months, even. But what I say is "Can you let me down? There—there's something I need to find."

Caz doesn't question me; he presses down on the brakes at once, easing us into a smooth stop by the sidewalk. As soon as the motorcycle starts to tilt dangerously, no longer suspended by its former momentum, he leaps off and straightens the vehicle and helps me to my feet.

When I'm safe on the ground, he asks, "What do you need to find?"

"My bracelet. It's blue and kind of thin and—" I fumble around for a more specific description. My mind feels both numb and too full, crowded with a thousand different competing thoughts, none of them helpful. Deep down, I'm already starting to suspect that I might never see my bracelet again. "I—I wear it a lot—"

"I know which one it is." Caz is looking past me now, in the direction of the city we just rode back from. Then his gaze locks on mine, and I expect to see some hint of impatience, or at least confusion over why I'm making such a big deal over a small thing. But he simply asks, "How long has it been missing?"

My throat tightens. "I only noticed a few moments ago, but . . . it could be hours since I lost it. It could be anywhere."

"I doubt it." His expression is thoughtful now. "I saw you wearing it when we were ordering the noodles, so you probably just dropped it on the way home. It can't be too far."

As he speaks, he's already sliding one leg back over the motorcycle seat and gesturing for me to climb on after him.

I hesitate.

"What are you doing?"

"We can retrace our route back to the stall," he says, raising his voice to be heard as he restarts the engine, the now-familiar hum sending small tremors through the pavement. "I'll go slow, so just keep your eyes out for it, okay?"

I feel a frisson of panic, and not just over the bracelet. He's being too kind, too thoughtful. Too *likable.* If I let him help me, trust him with this, then my crush will surely grow malignant.

No amount of well-researched PowerPoints and pretty photos of Gong Jun's face will ever let me get rid of it.

But it's getting colder, and he's waiting for me still, and even I'm not so unrealistic as to imagine I could track down the bracelet by myself on foot.

"Okay," I say slowly, climbing on and wrapping my arms around his waist. The second I do, something inside me snaps into place, as if this one small action has already sealed my fate.

"Hold on tighter," he warns. "It's dangerous, riding around in the snow."

Tentatively, I lean closer, until I can feel the heat of his skin despite the cold.

"Tighter."

"What?" My face flushes. "I'm already—"

He makes a small sound like a sigh and grabs my wrists, pulling them higher so they're locked just over his taut stomach, my entire upper body pressed snugly against his. "I don't want to be legally responsible for any accidents," he says over the hum of the engine.

The search begins. I scan the roads up and down, squint through the wind, staring at every gutter and crack in the pavement and upturned leaf we pass until my vision starts to blur.

Still nothing.

Above us, the sky is a pure, hushed white, a blank canvas, stretching on and on for every inch of ground we cover, until the first snowflake breaks free from the nothingness and tumbles down to earth. More follow. Soft, fat flakes of cold. I thought I'd forgotten this, but the sensation of the ice catching in my lashes and melting on the plastic of my black puffer jacket is oddly familiar, like an old friend.

No bracelet, though.

The snow adds a ticking clock; it'll be impossible to find anything once the ground is lost in white. And we're running out of time.

But just when I'm about to give up and ask for Caz to turn back around—I see it.

A glimpse of blue in my peripheral vision, lying just off the side of the road.

My breath catches, hope inflating my lungs.

"Stop!" I call. "It's there—I think it's there."

As soon as Caz cuts the engine, I'm running. The street is more ice than concrete by now, and twice my feet slip, my weight tipping precariously forward before I steady myself, run faster. My fingers close over the thin string just as it's pulled upward by a faint breeze.

Relief floods through my veins like morphine, dulling the edges of my panic until my heartbeat returns to normal again. I breathe out, grip the slightly damp bracelet to my chest. It's there. Still there.

"You found it?"

Caz walks over to me, and I nod once, embarrassed now that the immediacy of the situation has melted away. I mean, what kind of person makes such a fuss over a piece of string?

He's probably thinking that exact question, because he stares at the bracelet, then up at me, and says, “You wear that a lot.”

I nod again, knowing he’s searching for an explanation and unsure whether I should give it to him. How much of my heart I can afford to reveal. But what he’s done—without hesitation, seemingly without expectation of anything in return—I feel myself sway. Maybe it’s okay. Maybe I can trust him, just a little. “It’s a friendship bracelet. From Zoe.” *My best friend* is what I mean to add, but something glues my jaw shut, freezes the familiar words in my throat.

Just the other night, when I was drafting a blog post, I’d gone to listen to our Spotify playlist, only to find that the name had been changed from “zoe + eliza g8 hits” to “recs for divya.” Which, rationally speaking, is a small thing. Insignificant. But aren’t small things exactly what friendships are made up of? Frayed string bracelets and late-night texts and compilations of your favorite songs?

When you take those things away, what do you have left?

I don’t say any of this, of course, but Caz must see the hurt all over my face, because he asks quietly, “Do you miss her?”

I wrap my arms around my body. Exhale into the frigid air. “I miss a lot of people.”

And this, I think, is my ultimate fatal flaw. Missing people who don’t miss me back. Clinging on to strands of string that shouldn’t mean half as much as they do. It takes so little for me to love someone, yet so long for me to move on.

The snow has thickened by the time Caz parks his motorcycle outside the compound gates.

"Jie! Caz!"

I twist around, helmet still on, wobbling a little as my feet hit the ice-slicked pavement, and spot Emily moving toward us through the white haze. Her round cheeks are flushed pink from the cold, her messy braids tucked inside a polka-dot wool beanie, one umbrella raised over her head while another hangs from her swinging elbow.

"Hey, kid," Caz calls as she draws closer. "What are you doing here?"

I expect Emily to tell him off for calling her *kid*, the way she always does with me, but instead her face breaks into a wide grin. Then, even more surprisingly, she reaches out and does this complex handshake-slash-high-five thing with him in complete sync.

"What . . . what was that?" I manage, rubbing a stray flake of snow from my eyes.

"Our secret handshake," Emily says, then points behind her to our apartment in the background. "Also, we saw you guys riding back just now, so Ma told me to bring you an umbrella. You're very welcome."

But I don't reach for the umbrella. "Since when do you two have a secret handshake?"

"I was invited over to her drama class a few times the other week to give them acting tips," Caz explains while my little sister nods along fast and gazes up at him with clear adoration. "We came up with it during the breaks."

"What?" I repeat, much sharper than I intended. Didn't I *tell* him to leave my sister out of this?

Emily blinks at me, startled. "Why? What's wrong?"

"I just— You're not supposed to . . ." But before I can figure out how to tell her off without telling her everything, Caz's voice cuts through my thoughts.

"Eliza." He's holding his hand out to me, waiting, and for an embarrassing second, I think he's about to show me a secret handshake too, or even pull me into a hug. But then he gestures to the helmet on my head.

"Oh. Sorry." I fumble with the clasps, but my fingers are so numb from the cold that even after three tries, I still can't get the helmet off.

Emily shoots Caz a pointed look. "Well? Aren't you going to help her? Like, isn't that what boyfriends are for?"

My skin heats. "Oh, no, that's really not—"

"No, she's right," Caz offers, stepping forward, amusement tugging at one corner of his lips. Already slipping into his model-boyfriend role. I stay very still as he bends down so that we're at eye level, his cool, slender fingers finding the straps beneath my chin, our breaths pluming the frozen gray air between us, flecks of snow caught in his oil-black lashes.

But it takes him too long, or maybe it's simply too quiet here, with the compound's paths empty save for the security guards, because my heart starts racing as though we ran all the way back home.

And suddenly it's too real for me. His nearness, his gaze, his secret handshake with my little sister when they aren't even meant to *know* each other. *I* might have accepted that I can't help how I feel about him, that it might even be fine, so long as I never act on my feelings. But it's no longer just my heart at stake. It's Emily's too.

I reel back so fast my hair catches on the clasp. I yank it off myself, ignoring the fresh sting of pain and Caz's surprise.

"Thanks for the ride," I babble, eager to escape. "And for—you know, all your help finding the bracelet. We should probably go home now—"

"Home?" Emily repeats. "What about Caz? Can he come with us?"

Panic jolts through me. "That's—"

"*Please?* Pretty please?" she asks, turning her puppy-dog eyes on me. Damn it. The kid really knows what she's doing. "We could introduce him to Ma; I bet she's going to love him too. And we could even watch his dramas together. Oh my god—how cool would that be?"

No. Absolutely not. But the words are stuck in my throat, and to my horror, a scene unfurls in my mind of everything Emily is describing, tinted a soft gold at the edges like a dream sequence. Caz greeting my mother in the kitchen and sitting down on our couch, his arm draped around me while we turn on the TV—

To my surprise, Caz speaks up. "I'd really love that, kid, but . . . I actually have to head back to set this afternoon." Even though he's talking to Emily, his gaze is on me, a meaningful look in his eyes. *He remembers*, I realize. He remembers our conversation after the ti jianzi game: my worries, my warnings. "Maybe another time, okay?"

"Oh," Emily says, wilting. And even though I shouldn't, I feel an echo of disappointment too.

"Well, thanks again," I tell Caz, taking Emily's small, cold hand in mine and giving him an awkward wave with the other one. "And, uh, good luck with your shooting." Then, instead of lingering like I want to, I take Emily back home, realizing as I do that it's getting harder and harder to turn my back on Caz Song.

CHAPTER THIRTEEN

The days start speeding up the closer we get to the Lunar New Year holidays, as they tend to. More tedious classes pass. More tests, pointless homework assignments, lunches on the roof. More comments to wake up to, so many that I don't have time to reply to them all.

Things with Craneswift have only gotten busier too. Now that I have a substantial following, Sarah's pretty insistent on giving the masses what they want—which, in this case, happens overwhelmingly to be more blog posts about Caz's job.

is that ok?? I text Caz the next time he's away shooting, feeling as always that odd lurch, half anticipation and half guilt, that comes whenever my internship demands something from the two of us. *can I visit you on set?*

There's a pause before three small dots appear over the chat screen. Typing. Then they vanish. Appear again.

At last, Caz sends back a message:

Ok. But promise you won't laugh.

"Oh my god," I say as I step out of the car an hour later.

I've never been to a proper drama set before, but it's almost exactly the way I pictured it: giant green screens propped up over the grass, blocking out patches of sky; camera crew and makeup artists dashing in and out of makeshift tents; and props like swords and guzhengs lying about everywhere, all left to freeze in the outdoor chill. I take a quick mental snapshot of the scene, already brainstorming ways to introduce the set in my post.

They're in the middle of shooting a fight sequence, and my jaw practically unhinges when I spot Caz a few yards away.

I almost don't recognize him.

For one, he's wearing a robe. Not like a bathrobe kind of robe, but an actual, semi-historically-accurate set of robes with dragons embroidered down the sides and broad, flowing sleeves. It looks like it's made out of real silk too; every time he shifts position, the black fabric ripples and gleams under the sunlight. I can't stop staring. The outfit somehow has the effect of making him look taller, older, more intimidating, even though it's covering up most of his body.

Then there's the hair—or, well, the wig. Half of it has been tied up and pinned into place with an elaborate crown, but the rest of it spills down his back in a river of shining ink.

"Again!" a stocky, middle-aged woman who I assume is the director calls from behind the camera monitors. She makes an impatient motion with one hand. "Caz—make sure you turn your head this way when . . ." The rest of her directions are lost on me in a blur of accented, rapid-fire Chinese.

But Caz seems to get it right away. He gives her a thumbs-up motion and adjusts his position immediately, lifting the very real-looking sword in his hand with a look of unwavering focus. His jaw is tensed, his gaze sharp, his usual casual demeanor gone.

Five men dressed as assassins rush toward him, and he spins. Strikes. Ducks.

His movements are lightning quick, strong. His blade slices through the air in perfect sync with the other actors, like some sort of violent dance, elegant and epic all at once. When he swings the sword again, two men fall.

A triumphant grin flashes across his face.

"Oh my god," I repeat to myself, my voice kind of hoarse.

Because even though I've found Caz Song attractive on a physical level for a while now, my biggest turn-on has always been competence.

And as it appears, Caz is unbelievably competent at his job.

He carries out the rest of his fight sequence with the same enviable degree of control and precision, his hands becoming blurs as he moves seamlessly between stances, and only when the director yells "Cut!" does he finally slow down. Lower his sword.

His brow is damp with sweat and he's breathing a little fast, strands of dark hair fall loose from their knot, but his whole face is aglow. Euphoric, even. He looks like he would gladly run through that last scene twenty more times.

Then he sees me.

Before I have time to compose my expression, the corner of his mouth tugs up in that crooked smile I secretly love so much, dimples and straight white teeth flashing. It's almost too much—I want to believe the smile is real, that it's meant only for me. But I just witnessed seconds ago how good he is at acting.

"You're really not laughing," he says as he draws closer, his robes swishing behind him. "I'm surprised."

"Yes, well. There's nothing to laugh about," I say, aiming for casual and missing it by about ten thousand miles.

I've forgotten how to talk like a normal person, it seems.

"Mhm." Suddenly he leans in, a glint in his eyes. "Wait—don't tell me. This." He gestures to himself, his costume, and I want to die. "*This* works for you?"

"No." But I can feel my cheeks flushing. "Don't be ridiculous—"

"I'm learning so much about you, Eliza—"

"Oh my god—"

"This is a significant moment in our relationship," he continues, barely managing to keep a straight face. "Really. If I had known earlier that you were into this—"

"I beg you to not finish that sentence."

Thankfully, just as I'm contemplating moving to the Gobi Desert or someplace farther, someone shouts Caz's name in the distance.

"Come on," Caz says, holding his hand out. "I'll show you around."

I take it, knowing that it's all for show yet feeling my pulse race all the same, and he leads me across set. As we walk, I watch him straighten, his smile widen, easing into a different version of himself. He greets all the makeup artists and extras by name, laughing at jokes I swear he wouldn't usually find funny, and stops and poses with some of the supporting actors, his chin tipped up at the perfect angle, his hair carefully brushed. Farther ahead, he points out the equipment to me, explaining in detail how the props work and how certain scenes are shot and how the wires here are old and should've been replaced months ago but still hold up well enough for flying stunts.

It's useful material, all things I can work into my blog post later, but I'm acutely aware that I'm not the only one watching him. Wherever we go, countless pairs of eyes follow, the weight and intensity of it all like a blazing spotlight. Directors, camera crew, the other members of the cast. I've always known in theory that Caz was under a lot of pressure, but it's another story to be here with him, to witness how hard he has to work just to make sure he doesn't slip up in front of all these people.

I can't ruin that for him, a small voice whispers in my head. I can't complicate his already-complicated career by revealing that I have a crush on him, knowing he can't possibly like me back. The best thing I can do to help him is to continue our arrangement without causing any unnecessary drama.

We come to a stop at a set designed to look like the exterior of a palace—half blue screen and half completely realistic-looking, ornate stone pillars—where they're just wrapping up another scene.

"That's Mingri," Caz murmurs to me, pointing at one of the two actors standing before us. "He's playing the young, orphaned general. Unfortunately, he swears an oath of brotherhood with Kaige over there"—he motions to the other actor—"who turns out to be the crown prince of the enemy realm, and his father's murderer."

"Tragic," I comment, which earns me a faint, familiar twitch of his lips.

Mingri looks twenty years old at most, but he has the kind of face that seems young no matter his age, with naturally crescent-shaped eyes and dimples that show even when he's not smiling.

Next to him, Kaige seems to be his complete opposite in every way. He's around nineteen or twenty years old too, but the somber expression carved into his features and the hard, rigid lines of his face look more suited for someone who's been alive for decades. He also looks strangely familiar, though I'm certain I've never met him before.

As soon as the director calls cut, the two guys walk over to us. Well, *Mingri* walks; Kaige kind of just follows, eyes down and poker-faced, dragging his heels the whole way.

"Well, well, the star himself has come to visit us," Mingri sings in Chinese, doing that weird one-arm-hug thing guys all know how to do. Then he beams at me. "And he's brought the famous writer with him!"

Kaige merely nods in my direction.

"Come on, Kaige." Mingri turns to the other actor, nudging him once in the ribs. "The first ever time Caz brings his girlfriend on set, and you're not even going to say hi?"

Kaige's eyes widen briefly, flickering to the spot where Mingri's elbow bumped his shirt, and his ears redden. Then he scowls.

Interesting.

"Hi," Kaige greets me, though there's a hard, wary note in his voice. Or am I only imagining it? Before I can figure him out, he glances past me at Caz, and they exchange some sort of look I can't quite parse. A reference to an old conversation I never witnessed.

Caz shakes his head once, and Kaige clears his throat. "Well, if you'll excuse me," he mumbles, and stalks off alone in the opposite direction.

A long silence follows.

It's definitely not my imagination, then. "Um," I venture. "Did I . . . do something to offend him, or—"

"No," Mingri says quickly, flashing me a sheepish grin. "Don't worry about him. He's just naturally a bit skeptical of any relationship between actors like us and people from outside the industry."

I frown. "What? Why?"

"Well, it's just a lot to handle, isn't it?" Mingri says, looking surprised I'd even have to ask. Beside me, Caz has gone very quiet, his jaw tensed. "We're always out shooting, and our schedule's intense, and we're either getting too much or too little attention, and the fans can be lovely in some cases, and pretty . . . *extreme* in others. And the thing about celebrities, you know, is that you're only ever getting a piece of them—often not even the biggest piece. Most people aren't satisfied with that."

"Oh." Now I remember where I'd last seen Kaige's face—though it wasn't really *his* face, but his sister's. Kailin, a well-known C-drama actress. There'd been a huge news story last year about her dating an accountant. The details are blurry now, but their breakup had been very messy, and very public.

"But don't worry," Mingri repeats, his grin broadening. "There are always exceptions to the rule, and whatever it is you guys are doing, it's clearly working."

I force out a weak laugh, and a few beats too late, Caz joins in.

Once Caz is finished shooting for the day, I find myself in a corner booth at a bubble tea shop with him and Mingri. Everything here has been painted in shades of teal and pink, and the chic interior decorations appear to have been chosen solely for the purpose of luring in wanghongs to take pretty pictures. It must be working: All the customers here are at well-above-standard levels of attractiveness, and a table of girls dressed in full designer clothes have been unabashedly ogling Caz ever since we walked in here. I try to ignore them and focus on mentally outlining my blog post for the day. Maybe I'll start by describing the costumes, their texture up close, how it feels to see your boyfriend moving around in historical robes—

Mingri heaves a loud sigh.

I look up. This is maybe the tenth time he's sighed since his mango milk tea came, which was only five minutes and two giggling groups of wanghongs ago.

Caz raises a brow. "Something wrong?"

"No."

"Okay, then." Caz shrugs and returns to staring at his drink menu.

Mingri's mouth falls open, then snaps shut into a pout. Half a minute passes before he bursts out: "Fine, *fine.* If you *really* must know, I suppose I'll do you a favor and just come out with it—and if you ever tell anyone about this, I'll vehemently deny it—but . . . I might need some relationship tips from you guys."

"Well. This is rare," Caz remarks, reclining comfortably in his seat. "Historic, even."

Mingri glares at him. "Just hear me out, okay? It's about—there's this . . . this person I've been interested in for some time and I see them around a lot—"

"Kaige?" Caz and I say at the same time.

Mingri's face freezes in an expression of such genuine shock I almost feel bad for stating the obvious. His eyes dart from Caz to me to the other booths, which are all empty. "H-how—how did you know—"

"*Everyone* knows," Caz says with some exasperation. "Literally everyone. The makeup artists, that delivery guy who came last Tuesday, our horse-riding instructor . . ." He pauses and jerks his head in the shop owner's direction, who must be twenty years older and has also been unabashedly ogling him. "I'd bet my savings even *she* knows. It's probably the most public secret ever."

"Shit. Am I that obvious?"

"Kaige is a lot worse," I reassure him. "You actually seemed pretty chill when I saw you guys together."

"Wait. You mean . . ." I didn't think it was physically possible for Mingri's eyes to grow any wider, but I guess I was wrong. "You mean there's a chance it's not one-sided or . . ."

"You're so oblivious," Caz says, though not unkindly.

"What did you want our help for, anyway?" I ask before we can get sidetracked.

Mingri manages to get a grip on himself enough to answer, "I wanted to tell him directly. Write a note or something. But all I have is this . . ."

He fumbles around in his pocket for a few seconds before tossing a crumpled piece of paper on the table between us. A letter. I hold it up to the window light. It's written in Chinese, the pen strokes pressed in so deep they're almost visible on the other side, but I can still read it because the only words there are:

Kaige. Hi. I

"Well, that's." I falter, searching for the right description as I set the letter back down. "That's definitely something."

"It's shit, is what it is," Mingri grumbles. "I have no idea what to write."

"Eliza's good at that," Caz says, and at first I don't even realize he's complimented me. Or maybe I'm giving him too much credit, and he's simply tossed all responsibility over to me. When I turn to him, he just smiles.

Then the chair squeaks. Mingri actually stands up from his seat.

"Please." He gazes down at me with large, beseeching eyes, hands pressed together as if in prayer. "*Please* help me. Like, I will actually pay you just for a few lines. And I've read that essay of yours—all I need is something *a quarter* as good as that, and I'm—I'll be set."

"I guess I could offer a few suggestions," I say slowly. "It might not be personalized, since I don't know him that well, so just—change the details accordingly, okay?"

He nods fast. "Anything."

"Okay. So maybe . . ." I pause. Avoid Caz's curious gaze, twisting my fingers together in my lap, where no one can see them. "Maybe you can talk about how . . . I don't know, how his laughter sounds. If it's rougher in the mornings, or lower on the phone, or how he always tips his head back when he finds something funny. How—how you can only see his dimples when he smiles at something real. How you're jealous of everyone who loves him, who knew him before you did.

"And you probably didn't mean to fall for him. At all. You probably had a plan, precautions in place. Maybe you were at peace with your loneliness, but then he sort of barged into your life, uninvited, and you've been reeling ever since, angry at yourself. At him. Now all you can do is sit around and think, like a fool, about the pale, moonlit curve of his neck and measure out potential losses and the weight of his words and prepare remedies in advance for what you're certain will be the most devastating sort of heartbreak. But you continue to like him anyway. Stubbornly. Deliberately. And you . . ." I trail off when I realize how long I've been talking, how much I've been saying. God, what *am* I saying?

Heat rushes to my cheeks.

I can barely bring myself to look up, but it'd be hard to ignore the way Mingri is staring at me—jaw hanging and eyes wide.

And Caz.

If Mingri's gaze is stunned, Caz's gaze is scorching. Searching. He's leaned forward in his seat, and the tender look on his face isn't something I've ever seen before. Then his lips part slightly, as if to speak—

Oh god, I've screwed up. There's *no way* he doesn't know about my crush now. The kindness in his eyes is almost certainly pity. I'm about to get my heart broken by my fake boyfriend, right here in front of five girls who somehow all look similar to Angelababy, and I'm going to carry my humiliation to the grave.

No, I have to undo this. With great effort, I let out a fake, falsetto laugh. "Sorry, um. I don't know what I'm rambling about—it's mostly just dramatic, flowery bullshit. You know how writers can be." I make a point of looking directly at Caz when I say this, hoping he'll believe me. To my relief, the look is gone, replaced by something more guarded. "Did any of it help, at least, or . . . ?"

"Oh, yeah, for sure," Mingri says at once, nodding fast, scribbling something down on the paper. "I mean, that was a *lot* of material. Thank you."

I smile weakly. "Glad I could help."

"Just one thing, though."

"Yeah?"

Mingri sighs, loud and heavy, and asks, "Do you think it'd be too crass if I also mentioned how much I like his ass?"

I blink. "Um . . ." This time, I have nowhere to look but at Caz. But he's looking elsewhere, seemingly lost in thought. "Um . . . no. That—if that's how you truly feel—"

"I do," he reassures me.

"Then yeah, go for it." I clear my throat. "Write from the heart."

CHAPTER FOURTEEN

I'd planned to start writing out my blog post the instant I got home, but instead I end up collapsing onto my bed, my pillow hugged to my chest, reliving every embarrassing second of my little speech at the bubble tea shop.

What had I been *thinking*? This is why I should never be left to improvise anything, ever. I'd basically confessed my feelings to Caz straight to his face. And the way he'd looked at me after, like he was trying to figure out the gentlest way to let me down . . . Sure, he'd still insisted on giving me a ride back, but we'd barely even talked on the way home. At the time, I'd attributed it to my own weird feelings, but now that I really think about it, *he'd* been quieter than usual too. Distant. Withdrawn. He didn't even smile at me when I got off—

I groan and kick out so hard my blankets tumble to the floor.

Just as I'm debating whether to ruin the dramatic moment by picking them back up, or risk a lecture from Ma by leaving them there, my phone buzzes. One new message from Caz. I swallow, my heart galloping in my chest. Oh my god, what if he wants to talk about that Moment today? What if he asks me straight up how I really feel about him? What if he's texting to reject me?

But when I unlock my phone, there's only the sentence:

My parents want to meet you.

Wait, legit? I type, then delete it. It sounds too eager. Like I actually *want* to meet them too. I pause, thinking hard, and try out: *Is this a joke?* Then delete that as well. But by now a significant amount of time has lapsed since I've read his message, and he's probably watching me type and delete over and over again, which is worse than anything I could write. Panicking, I go with: *And what did I do to deserve this great honor?* And hit send. Then instantly regret it. I should've just gone with the first option. That was shorter, at least, and short is casual. Casual is good.

It's possible that I'm overthinking this.

They've wanted to meet you for some time now, he texts back moments later. *Just haven't had the chance to because of work. But they should be home this Saturday, if you're free.*

I frown at the words. He makes it sound like his parents are rarely home at all. And that there's a chance they might cancel even now.

Before I can reply, he adds: *I know we said we wouldn't get our families involved, but mine can be persistent. I promise it's just a quick dinner to get them off my back about this.*

I'll owe you one.

He's right. We *shouldn't* be getting our families involved. It's already bad enough that he and Emily know each other. But then I remember how he'd looked today, the sun in his hair, his lower lip chewed red . . . The terrible thing is that even though I keep embarrassing myself around him, keep putting myself at risk of getting hurt—part of me still wants to see him again.

Fine, I type, feeling like I've failed a self-assigned test. *But only this once.*

Of course, he replies quickly, and I can just imagine his triumphant little grin. *You're the best.*

whatever.

"It'll be okay," I reassure myself out loud, chucking my phone on the bed. I just need to charm my fake boyfriend's parents enough that they approve of me but not so much that they'll actually care when we break up. Easy. Simple. What could possibly go wrong?

So on Saturday, I wait outside Caz Song's door with a box of edible bird's nest in one hand and my heart in my throat.

After checking my warped reflection in the shiny doorknob and confirming that there's nothing embarrassing on my face, other than my face, I draw in a shaky breath and knock.

"Coming."

Footsteps, firm and swift. Then the door creaks opens, and I find myself staring up at Caz. He's in a light gray shirt that hugs his shoulders and Levi's jeans, and he's barefoot. Relaxed. A striped shower towel hangs around his neck, darker in the places where his wet hair has dripped water onto it.

He stares back for a moment, and there's surprise in his eyes and something else.

"Hey," he says. "You're early."

"Oh—sorry." I shift awkwardly between my feet. "I was scared of getting here late. Is it a bad time or—"

He laughs at me. "Why are you being so formal?"

"I'm not," I lie, though I don't dare relax. I'll never forget that pitying look in his eyes back at the bubble tea shop, and I pray to god I'll never have to see it again. If he can act like everything is normal between us, I can too. I won't slip up a second time. I can't.

His gaze goes to the bird's nest. The packaging is bright red, Spring Festival red, with fancy golden edges and an engraving of flying sparrows on the front. I'd bought it only after consulting about twenty different articles along the lines of "The Ten Best Herbal Gift Packages to Win Over Your Boyfriend's Mother."

"This is nice," he says.

"Thanks. It's what the article rec—" I cut myself off. Clear my throat. "Thanks," I repeat awkwardly.

Smiling a little, he takes the box from me, and I do my best to ignore the light brush of his knuckles against mine, and the way he seems to notice it too, his body tensing for the briefest fraction of a second before he turns around.

I can't help but stare as I follow Caz into his apartment.

The whole setup reminds me of a museum, or one of those celebrity home tours where you know the celebrity doesn't actually live there half the time. It's too polished. Too extravagant.

The walls of the wide corridor are lined with framed black-and-white photos and abstract art—the kind that look like someone accidentally spilled a paint bucket onto white canvas but probably sold for hundreds of thousands of dollars and represent the inherent unknowability of the human condition or something—and these gorgeous traditional Chinese landscape paintings, with red-crowned cranes and sloping mountains captured in rich, sweeping ink.

Then there are all the antiques on display: shiny bronzeware raised on tables and slender porcelain vases covered in these lovely floral patterns. There's even a replica—at least I *think* it's a replica—of a life-size terra-cotta warrior just propped up casually in one corner, like this is a totally normal choice of interior decoration.

I have a sudden, horrifying vision of myself tripping on my own feet and knocking over the vases one by one like dominoes, and I instinctively move closer to Caz's side.

"So my father isn't here today," he tells me as we turn the corner, his voice impassive. "The hospital called this morning and said they needed him there for an emergency operation. He wanted to pass along his apologies."

"Of—of course. That's totally understandable," I say quickly. "And I mean, if he really wants to meet me, we could always just reschedule . . ."

Caz shakes his head. "He gets, like, two days off a year."

Soon the corridor opens up into a bright, high-ceilinged living room with huge windows, and a middle-aged woman waiting by the sofas.

Caz's mom pretty much looks exactly how I imagined she would, only more stylish. Her straight, shoulder-length bob is dark against the dewy white of her skin, her thin eyebrows tattooed on. And even though she's standing in the middle of her own living room, she's wearing the kind of satin blouse and ironed pencil skirt that would suit an extravagant company brunch.

I glance down at my own plain white shirt, suddenly afraid I've underdressed. Not that it matters. I shouldn't *want* to impress Caz's mother, who I'll only be seeing this one time in my life. But still. It's the principle of the thing.

"Oh, you must be Eliza!" she greets me, walking up to us.

"Ayi hao," I say politely, and for some reason, I decide to bow. "It's lovely to meet you."

Her pink-painted lips stretch into a wide smile. She has deep dimples, I notice, just like her son.

"Wa, I like your hair," she tells me with an envious kind of sigh. "It's so black and straight. Beautiful."

"Oh. Thank you." I realize it's my turn to pay her a compliment now. An even better compliment than the one she just gave me. "I really like your . . ." *Quick. Think of something, or else it'll sound fake.* My eyes roam over the house, a thousand frantic, half-formed thoughts firing through my brain at once. Do I compliment the decor? Is that a thing mothers like to hear? Or her makeup? Or would it be rude to draw attention to the fact that she's wearing makeup in the first place? Crap. I'm taking too long. *Just say something. Anything.* "I love your . . . nose."

I wince, almost certain she's going to start admonishing Caz for bringing home a weirdo, but she looks genuinely delighted.

"You do?" Her fingers flutter to her nose. "I always worry that my nose bridge isn't high enough—"

"No, no, it's perfect," I reassure her. Then, in a sudden burst of inspiration, I add, "I can really see where your son got his good looks from."

And I didn't think it was possible, but her smile grows even wider, into an expression of such pure motherly affection that I feel a brief pang behind my ribs. Before coming here, part of me had wished she would turn out to be mean and judgmental, one of those evil mothers-in-law from the C-dramas I always watch, someone I could stay wholly indifferent to and forget about the second I left the building.

But now I can't help basking in her approval. Wanting more of it. How am I supposed to hide my feelings from Caz *and* convince his mom I care about him at the same time?

"You're very sweet," she says, then pats Caz's hair down with one hand (he immediately winces and ruffles it back into his usual messy style), and adds in a stage whisper, "I don't think we should feed his ego anymore, though. He has enough people telling him how handsome he is every day. It's probably why he spends so long in front of the mirror before school—"

Caz claps his hands together. Raises his voice. "How about we start preparing for dinner, hmm?"

But Caz's mother goes on like he hasn't spoken. "You know what, I think he's grown even *more* image-conscious in recent months. All that styling with his hair and the expensive skin cream—my god, I swear he uses more than I do—"

"Mom," Caz says, louder, clearly trying and failing to keep his cool. "Mom, that's really not—you're exaggerating—"

"Well, this is very interesting to me," I tell her, ignoring him too. "Skin cream, you say?"

She nods. "And face masks. I've never seen a boy his age care so much about his appearance; did you know, just last Tuesday, he insisted on missing a whole day of classes because he had a tiny blemish on his forehead."

My eyebrows shoot up as I process this, then glance over at Caz's flushed face. He had told me he was busy shooting that day. "Did he *really*."

"So ridiculous, right? Sometimes I worry people at school tease him for it."

"Oh, I don't think anyone at school knows this side of him," I say, marveling at how quickly Caz Song's carefree actor image is unraveling right before my eyes—and how panicked he looks because of it. It's so rare for *him* to be the one discomposed, self-conscious, that I can't help enjoying myself a little. Or a lot.

"Look, I'm starving," Caz tries again, making a sharp turn toward the living room. "Can we start now? *Please?*"

I bite back a smile and walk after him. "Your house is really tidy," I muse aloud as we pass the hall.

"It's always like this," Caz says hastily, at the same time that his mother says:

"Oh, yes, Caz spent *ages* cleaning up before you arrived. Wanted to make sure everything was nice and spotless. He's so thoughtful, isn't he?"

"Yeah," I say despite myself, an unwanted rush of warmth filling my chest. "He is." Caz doesn't look at me, but I notice the color creeping up the back of his neck, all the way to his ears. And I realize I'm in far greater trouble than I'd prepared myself for.

We enter the next room together, where Caz's mother has single-handedly set out a restaurant-standard feast. There are two plates of fish—pan-fried and braised—and shredded pork and crisp lotus and sweet yams dipped in melted sugar, and it's all *so much* that I offer to help right away.

Still, while I set down the plates, I can't stop sneaking curious glances at Caz, watching him as he straightens the chairs, grabs a few spoons to share the main dishes, and wipes his hands fastidiously on a clean kitchen towel.

By the time I'm seated, I've noted a dozen tiny new details, like how Caz helps his mother lift the heavier pots and pans, or how he's the only one in the household with his own designated mug, or how he tries to sneak all the vegetable dishes to the opposite end of the table, as far away from him as possible.

The dinner goes far more smoothly than I expected. In my desperation, I'd prepared a few inoffensive conversation starters to help pass the hours, but Caz's mother ends up doing most of the talking—bragging and complaining about her son in turns, or bragging in the tones of making a complaint.

The latter is a very refined, subtle art, one that most Asian parents seem to perfect by the time their children enter kindergarten.

"It's just so difficult for me," she laments as she sucks the meat off the fish tail. "All these parents keep asking me, *How is your son so brilliant? What's your secret?* And I honestly don't know what to tell them, you know? He's always busy doing his own thing, and he just happens to be very good at it. How do I explain that?"

"That does sound quite difficult," I say cooperatively, while Caz avoids my gaze, his shoulders stiff.

"It's a shame, though," she continues, jabbing her chopsticks at Caz. "It'd be even better if he had the same talent in actually important subjects, like math or English, no? I always tell him—I always say, *Erzi ya, you can't expect to make a living off your looks and acting forever. You should prioritize your studies instead.* But he never listens."

Caz rubs his neck with ill-concealed agitation, the color in his cheeks spreading. Everything about him is unusually tense, though I seem to be the only one who notices.

"Well, he works very hard," I say slowly, unable to press down the surge of defensiveness inside me. "And there are a lot of people who expect different things from him. I mean, I'm just impressed he's managed to juggle everything in the first place."

Caz's mother looks at me with surprise. But just when she's about to say something, Caz leans forward hurriedly. "Mom, were you going to eat the fish head? Because I think we should throw it away—"

"What?" In a flash, Caz's mother has scraped all the remains of the braised fish onto her plate, guarding it protectively with both chopsticks. "Has water gotten into your brain? You baijiazi," she

says. I recognize the term only because it's one of my mother's favorite insults too whenever she catches me wasting food or spending money on anything she deems unnecessary. "The fish head is where the good stuff is—it is the *essence*."

Caz breathes a small sigh of relief, and his diversion tactic does seem to work for a good ten minutes. But when his mother has finished spitting out the fish bones, all of which are scarily clean, she dives right back into the topic.

"Erzi, how are those college essays coming along, by the way? You *know* how important they are. Have you finished them all? I could ask a colleague to read—"

"They're good," he says, his expression working too hard to remain neutral. He's fidgeting with the hem of his shirt. "They're done, actually."

"Really?"

"Yeah. I managed to find . . . help."

We share a small, quiet look over the table, the moment burning inside me like a secret.

"Oh, that's great," his mother says earnestly, and turns to smile at me. "He's always been so stubborn about letting others help him. It's kind of silly, really; why make things unnecessarily hard for yourself?"

"It *is* silly," I agree.

Caz clears his throat, his expression strained with discomfort. "I just—don't like inconveniencing people."

His mother jabs her chopsticks at him again, but it's a gesture performed with exasperated affection. "Sha erzi, what do you know? When you care about someone, you *want* to be inconvenienced—you wouldn't mind being inconvenienced by them every day for the rest of your life. That's what love is. That's all love really is."

When everything's over, Caz and his mother both walk me down to the bottom of the apartment, despite my insistence that I can walk alone. There's a chill in the air but a crispness too, the sweet scent of grass and pine and night-blooming flowers. Of melted snow.

"It was really, *really* nice to meet you, Eliza," Caz's mother tells me, patting the back of my hand, her hair burning orange-brown under the compound's streetlights. "You should come over more often."

"I'll try to," I say vaguely, avoiding any promises I can't keep.

She beams. Pats my hand one last time. "Oh, you must."

After she's instructed Caz to walk me home "like a proper gentleman," she waves at the both of us and disappears back into the building.

And then it's just Caz and me.

"So," I say, all my awkwardness returning. "Um, you don't actually have to walk with me—"

"I want to," Caz says—then, maybe catching the surprise on my face, pauses. "I mean, I should."

We walk in silence for a while through the dark, empty compound, our hands close but never touching, and I can tell that there's as much on his mind as there is on mine. Because the thing is. . . the thing *is* that I should be happy right now, relieved it's all over, eager to drop the act and go home and never entertain another thought about his family again.

But throughout the whole evening, I keep being reminded that these feelings simply aren't going away. Because this isn't just a silly, superficial crush anymore. It's more. It's worse. It's the realization that no matter how hard I try to protect myself, no matter how many barriers I build up and lines I draw between us, I am doomed to get my heart broken by Caz Song. It's only a matter of when and how badly.

And maybe it's already happening. Ever since that moment in the bubble tea shop, he's been acting so—*distant.* So different from his usual self. Maybe this is just his way of rejecting me.

I don't even notice the pressure building in my throat, behind my eyes, until I sniff, and Caz freezes.

"Whoa. Wait." His gaze cuts to mine, black on brown, concern dancing over his features like light over water. "Are you . . . crying?"

"No," I sniff, tilting my head back and blinking furiously at the empty, starless sky, trying to will the wetness in my eyes away. But something warm trickles down my cheek anyway, tracing a trail down to my jaw.

Caz hesitates a second, opens his mouth and closes it again, then reaches out and brushes the tear aside with one gentle thumb.

I snap my head down, stare at him, the tenderness of the gesture breaking open something inside me. I can't remember the last time I felt like this—thawed and vulnerable and exposed and wanting too much, my heart straining at maximum capacity. I can't remember the last time I cried like this either. Not out of anger, or humiliation, or frustration, but because of an unidentifiable ache deep in my chest.

"Sorry," I mumble, voice hoarse and stuffy with emotion. Now that I'm crying, I can't seem to stop. Caz doesn't say anything; he simply wipes away my tears as they fall. "God, I can't believe I'm actually— This is so gross."

Now he laughs, a soft sound that dissolves in the air between us.

"It's not funny," I say, even though I'm laughing a little too, my cheeks damp and my nose running, the sound rattling in my throat. I'm basically the definition of an emotional mess right now.

"Of course it isn't," Caz agrees. He wipes my cheeks again, then brings his other hand gently to the back of my head, consoling me as if I'm still just a kid. "So what's wrong? Was being in my house really that awful?" He says it like a joke, but I can see a trace of genuine worry in his features.

"No, no, no," I rush to say. "No, your house was great—I mean, the terra-cotta warrior was a questionable choice of decoration—"

"My father's choice. My mother and I hate it too. We keep trying to dispose of it when he's not around, but he always finds a way to bring it back."

"Your mother was also very nice," I tell him tearily.

He raises his brows. "You should've seen her stuffing the statue into an actual body bag."

I snort out a laugh despite myself, then continue. "*Everything* is nice. But . . ."

But that's the problem.

If this goes on, I might just die of guilt. But if this ends, I already have too much to grieve. Somehow, despite all my rules and reservations, I'm already in too deep, so far lost in the waves that sinking feels easier than swimming.

"Hey," Caz says softly, lowering himself onto a stone bench and pulling me to his side. "Is this . . . ?" He pauses. I watch him inhale, exhale. "Is this too much for you? Do you want to stop?"

My heart drops, and the night seems to freeze around us.

Do I want to stop?

I should. The smart thing—the selfless thing—to do would be to call it off while I still can, while most of my heart is still intact. There are already too many people involved in this: Emily, his mother, all my readers and his fans. And of course *he* wouldn't have a problem calling it off; for him, it really is just another job, no different from any drama project he's taken up before.

But as I gaze over at his face in the dark, the thought of letting him go *now* sends a spasm of physical pain through me. Because I know all too well how things will turn out after our arrangement is over: We'll go back to being strangers, and I'll be alone again, like I always am. I'll never get to talk to him, to be this close to him, even if it's just pretend.

Because I'm selfish, and I want to live in this dream for as long as I can.

And I know exactly how to ensure it happens.

"We can't stop," I hear myself say, the lie rising fully formed to my lips. How many lies have I told by now? Too many to count. But the only way I managed to rope Caz into this whole arrangement in the first place was by making it about his career; now it's also the only way to keep him here. "Because . . . because we still need to do an interview together."

Caz draws back. "An interview? I don't remember you mentioning it."

"I must've forgotten," I tell him, hoping he can't hear the waver in my breath. "But it's with this huge media company, and I already promised Sarah Diaz we'd be available. It's not scheduled for until after the Spring Festival holidays, though, so if we can keep this up until then . . ."

"I'm willing if you are," he says slowly. It's too dark to make out his expression, but I can feel his gaze on me. As if he's looking for something. "But there's no other reason, beside the interview?"

I tense. The words are there, crowded in the back of my throat. I could tell him. Be honest for once in my life. Be brave. My heart starts drumming louder, so loud I'm certain he'll hear it. I breathe in. *Tell him.* But all that comes out is: "Of course not."

"Of course not," he repeats. For some reason, his voice is strained.

CHAPTER FIFTEEN

The last day before the holidays, Caz rocks up to English class looking how I feel most of the time—

Like shit.

I mean, he's still *Caz Song*, so his features are still aesthetically, geometrically pleasing, but there's a sickly pallor to his skin, a kind of exhausted, bleary look in his eyes. Even his footsteps seem heavy.

"You look kind of tired," I inform him when he plops his stuff down next to mine and slides into his usual seat. We're meant to be answering the reading questions for *Pride and Prejudice*, but what with the prospect of imminent freedom and the dreary winter weather, no one's actually working—including the teacher.

"Really? Because I slept very well last night," Caz says. His voice sounds different as well, raspier than usual and quieter. This is the kind of thing I doubt anybody else would notice, but ever since our conversation in the darkness of the compound, I've been hypersensitive around him, tuned in to his every word and move, trying to decipher how he really feels about me. It's been a long week.

"You're not sick, are you?" I ask.

"Impossible," he says firmly. "I'm never sick."

Unconvinced, I lean over and press my hand to his forehead—and almost gasp. His skin is burning. "You—you're really hot."

Instead of reacting with fear or alarm, like any ordinary person would, the corner of Caz's mouth tugs up. "You just noticed?"

I pull back with a scowl. "Don't be conceited. I obviously meant your temperature; it's way too hot to be normal."

He waves my concerns away. "I'm not sure if you know this, Eliza," he says dryly, "but human skin is *meant* to be warm."

"Yeah, except your skin is literally burning up—"

He sighs. Turns and looks at me with such calm I want to scream. "Maybe my skin is just always this way."

"Are you secretly a werewolf from *Twilight*, Caz?" I snap. "Because it's either that, or your body is in a state of rapid deterioration as we speak."

His lips twitch again, but his voice is firmer, more serious, when he says, "Don't sound so certain. Touching my head with your hand isn't an accurate way to assess temperature anyway."

"Oh, well, sorry for not carrying a professional thermometer in my bag—"

"It'd be more accurate," he continues, undeterred, "if you were to press your forehead to mine. Then you could properly compare the temperatures."

I stare at him.

He stares back, a challenge in the sharp set of his jaw, the dark gleam of his eyes. He thinks this will be enough to get me off his back. He thinks I won't be able to do it.

"Whatever works," I say sweetly, relishing the flash of genuine surprise on his face before I wrap one hand around the nape of his neck and pull him forward.

Our heads touch, and at once I can feel the intense heat rising from his skin, his parted lips, the flutter of his long lashes when he blinks. And then the most wildly inappropriate and unhelpful thought of all time pops into my brain:

This is how it must feel to kiss Caz Song.

I jerk back so fast I almost pull a neck muscle.

"So," Caz says after a pause. "What's the diagnosis?"

"You have a fever," I inform him, feeling somewhat feverish myself. Suddenly, I'm scared I went too far. What if he thinks I was trying to make a move? Or that I'd wanted to kiss him? Is it possible to detect these things?

The shrill ring of the bell cuts through my thoughts. When I look up, flustered, Caz is already rising from his seat.

"Are you going to seek out medical attention?" I ask hopefully.

"No, because I don't need it," he says, walking away before I can even protest, and I decide that I hate him. I will not talk to him, or question him again, or reach out to him. I couldn't care less if he lives or dies.

Seriously. I mean it.

The moment I get home from school, I text Caz:

hey

are u feeling slightly better?

I stare at the message for a good fifteen minutes after it's sent, as if I can somehow will it through the ether to wherever Caz is, but the little blue tick that indicates "read" doesn't show up. *Whatever. He's probably sleeping.* I slam my phone down and try to distract myself with a set of chemistry questions for homework.

It doesn't work.

At 3:52 p.m., cursing Caz Song's name under my breath, I message him again:

just checking to see if you're still alive!!

But that doesn't get a response either.

My imagination starts to run wild with the very worst scenarios: Maybe he fainted on his way home, and no one was around to help him. Maybe his fever was actually a symptom of something far worse, like cancer, or some other chronic condition that only gives him a few more months to live. Maybe he's collapsed inside his own house. Maybe he's *already dead.*

Logically, I know I might just be scaring myself for no reason. He might not even be *that* sick; it's not like I'm a doctor or anything. Maybe he isn't looking at his phone . . . Or maybe he just doesn't feel like texting me.

But logic doesn't stop my stomach from tightening every time I check my phone.

None of my messages have been read.

At 4:15 p.m., I curl up in the corner of my room and stress-send another string of texts:

hi, it's me again

sorry for the spam lol but I'm lowkey really worried about u? Are u at home rn??

Then, realizing I've just admitted in the written word that I'm concerned about his well-being, I quickly add:

obviously it'd look really bad if my supposed bf just died of a fever one cold friday afternoon like some 16th century Victorian housewife . . .

i mean if you're going to be in mortal peril, at least let it be bc of a dramatic horse-riding accident or smth

More time passes without any response. I force myself to help Emily with her English homework and Ba chop up scallions for dinner and outline a new blog post, all the while feeling my brain slowly disintegrating from stress. But I'm not just worried anymore—I'm pissed off. Angry that I'm starting the Spring Festival holidays checking my phone at two-minute intervals because I can't stop thinking about a guy. Angry that even after all this time, he's still too obsessed with putting up a front to ask for help when he needs it. Angry that I've already given him my heart and my trust, only for him to pull away time and time again.

Angry that I even care so much.

When 5:00 p.m. rolls around, I fire one final message of warning to Caz:

ok. look, caz song. if you don't reply within the next ten minutes, i swear i'm going to personally write a 200,000 word enemies-to-lovers fanfic about u and a cactus and post it online and it WILL go viral

Ten minutes later, I grab my coat and march out the door.

• • •

Even though the sun has already disappeared below the horizon, leaving the air comfortably cool, I'm sweating by the time I arrive outside Caz's apartment.

I knock on the door and wait for ages, more sweat trickling from my hairline and beading over my lips.

No one answers, but I can *hear* it: The shuffle of movement. A faint cough.

He's inside.

So of course, I do what any composed, rational, completely nonchalant person would do: I bang both fists against the door and start yelling loud enough to be heard from the next building.

"Caz! Caz? *Caz Song.* I know you're in there—open the door or else I swear—"

Without warning, the door swings open, and I almost fall headfirst into Caz's chest. At the last second, I grab the doorframe to steady myself. I casually brush my hair to the side as if this is the accepted, normal way to show up at somebody's doorstep when they've been ignoring your texts.

"Jesus," Caz says, taking me in. "Eliza. What are you—"

"Are you okay?" I interrupt, then immediately feel like an idiot. He's obviously *not* okay; he looks even weaker than he did at school, his complexion ghostly pale, his eyes pitch-black and feverish. He's also in what appears to be his pajamas—a graphic long-sleeve shirt promoting one of his old dramas and boxer shorts—which is how I know for certain that something's wrong. Under normal circumstances, Caz wouldn't be caught dead in an outfit like this.

He seems to realize how he looks at the same time I do, because he suddenly backs away and starts closing the door again. "Sorry—it's really not a good time right now—"

I grab the handle before he can shut me out. "*What?* You can't be serious."

But he doesn't let go, and for a few absurd seconds, the two of us just stand there, teeth gritted, wrestling the door back and forth between us. It's a testament to how weak he must be feeling that it's actually a pretty even match.

"Oh my god, Caz," I huff out, my knuckles white around the handle. "Just let me in—"

"No."

"What's your deal? You're sick and you need help—"

"I *do not* need help." He says it so vehemently my grip almost falters for a second. I almost turn away. I don't *have* to be here, of course. Whatever this is lies well beyond the realms of our arrangement. But god help me, I care way too much about the stubborn boy on the other side of the door to go.

"Caz. Don't be so unreasonable."

"I'm not. I just think—I appreciate you coming over here to check on me and all, but I really think you should leave." There's a raw edge to his voice, frustration or even anger, though I can't tell if it's directed more at me or himself. "I . . . I don't want you to see me like this."

An incredulous laugh bursts through my lips. "This is not the time to be vain. I couldn't care less if you're in your pajamas—"

"It's not just that. Nobody ever sees me this way."

"*What* way?"

Through the narrow sliver in the doorway, I catch a glimpse of his face. The trace of insecurity there. The shadows under his eyes. Caz is the most image-conscious person I know, and he's a wreck.

"Come on," I say, pulling harder. "Think of it as—as doing me a favor. If you don't let me in, and you end up dying, *I'll* be the one facing charges for negligence as the last person to have seen you. The rest of my life will be ruined."

He rolls his eyes, but I feel the door go slightly slack on his end. "Okay, that's definitely not how that works."

"I'll be consumed by guilt," I go on as if he hasn't spoken. "The police will ask me: How could you just leave him there? And I'll have to explain: I didn't want to, but he basically shut the door in my face—"

His mouth tightens. "Fine. But I want to make it clear that you're here by your own choice. I don't need help or whatever. I'm completely okay." The words have barely left his lips when he dissolves into a violent coughing fit.

I try not to laugh at him as I follow him into the house. At first, I think the situation might not be as bad as I feared. He's walking well enough on his own, his back turned toward me, his every step stiff but deliberate, his shoulders thrown back as if he's in the middle of shooting a scene. He even makes a point of checking his hair in the hallway mirror. But before he's made it into the next room, he sways on his feet and doubles over right afterward, one hand gripping the closest table for support. His breathing uneven, his knuckles bone-white.

My heart lurches.

"Yes, I can definitely see how okay you are," I mutter as I step forward and place one arm around him, trying to hold him up. His weight shifts onto me, and I nearly stumble under it. "You're—you're a lot heavier than you look."

"It's all muscle," he protests, even as he's struggling to stand up.

God, he's ridiculous.

We manage to cross the corridor and enter the living room together—slowly, clumsily, like a pair from one of those three-legged races. But we manage it all the same. As I lower Caz onto the closest couch, one hand rested protectively around the back of his neck, the other around his waist, I scan the room. It's messier than it was when I visited two weeks ago, with jackets strewn over the pillows and annotated scripts lying open on the coffee table, but there's no sign of his parents. Not even a scarf, or an extra pair of slippers.

"They're both on business trips," Caz says, reading my mind. "A medical conference in Shanghai. Left a few days ago."

"Oh." This does answer what I was wondering earlier, but for some reason, I find myself still searching the tables, the marble high counter, even the carpeted floor, as if something else is missing . . . And then it hits me. "Isn't there any water around here?"

He stiffens, confusion flashing over his face. "Sorry, did you want a drink? I'll get you some—"

And he actually makes to get up from the couch.

"No, no, that's not what I mean," I rush to say, pushing him back down. He complies, but I can feel the tension in his arms, the rigidity of his frame. "I meant, haven't *you* had any water since you got home? Or, like, medicine?"

He gives a slight, defensive shake of his head. Looks away.

"Well, have you had dinner, at least?"

"Dinner," he repeats, like it's a foreign word. "Does . . . chewing gum count?" He must see my expression, because he glowers back—though he looks so weak, it's closer to a sulk. "Okay, it's really not that big a deal."

And even though I know he's sick and I'm meant to be extra patient and caring and all that, I throw my hands up in frustration. "I honestly don't know how you've managed to stay alive these past seventeen years. Like, do you just *not eat* or take care of yourself in any way whatsoever and just pray that your body will miraculously pull through enough to—" I stop abruptly when I see him smiling. My hands drop back down. "I'm sorry, is there something *funny* about this?"

"No," he says, but the corners of his lips tug higher, and I can't tell if he's mocking me or not. "Nothing."

I glare at him. "Tell me."

"I don't—"

"Tell me."

"Fine. It's just cute that you're so concerned, that's all," he says with a shrug.

I open my mouth, then snap it shut. For a moment, I'm rendered genuinely speechless. "I'm not concerned," I finally force out, folding my arms tight across my chest. "I'm irritated. And horrified by your total disregard for your own health."

His smile widens. "Clearly."

I twist around, determined to ignore that smile. I've observed Caz Song long enough by now to know that he dials up his charms whenever he feels uncomfortable or at risk of being vulnerable. He'd flirt with a teaspoon if the situation called for it. "I'm going to make some food," I announce, heading for the kitchen. "You just stay here and—I don't know. Rest. Try not to die."

"I'll try my best," he promises, mock solemn.

One of the more useful skills I've picked up from all the moving around is the ability to navigate pretty much any unfamiliar space. Even though I've only been to Caz's place once before, and I've never set foot in his kitchen, it takes me less than a minute to figure out where all the pans and cutlery and ingredients are. Another minute to fill up a pot of water, turn the stove on, and start rinsing a cup of white rice.

Then I open his fridge, blinking into the white-blue artificial light.

There's an alarming shortage of fresh vegetables and meat inside. A half-opened packet of Yakult and that popular

Wanglaoji herbal drink Ma loves. Three canned lychees, two yogurts. An almost-empty jar of extra-mild Laoganma sauce, some withered spring onions, and a few bottles of fish sauce.

Hardly enough to scrape together a meal.

"Are you judging the contents of my refrigerator?" Caz calls from behind me. The couch is lined up with the kitchen entrance so that he has a fairly clear view of everything I'm doing.

"Yes. Very much so," I reply, and glance back at him. "Is it always this empty?"

He lifts a shoulder. "Depends."

"On?"

"How many people are at home. If it's just me . . ."

I can guess at what he was about to say. If it's just him, there's no point in cooking or trying very hard at any of this domestic stuff. And judging from everything I know about him and his career and his family, it's probably *just him* quite often.

"I'm fine with it," he says abruptly, like he can maybe sense the conclusion I'm drawing on my own. "I mean, my mother's home often enough, and my father—he's literally busy *saving lives.* What kind of asshole would I be if I resented that?"

"I . . . don't think it'd make you an asshole," I tell him, picking my words with care. "I think it'd just make you someone's son."

The emotion that crosses his face then—it's not something I can begin to put into words.

But it makes my heart hurt.

My attention is pulled by the sudden, violent boiling of water.

I lift the pot lid before the water has a chance to spill over, and pour the white rice inside, stirring it a few times.

"I thought you couldn't cook," Caz says.

I roll my eyes. "I can't *bake*, but I've been cooking for my family since I was nine. I'm pretty sure I can handle this."

"Since you were nine?" There's a curious edge to his tone, like he genuinely wants to know.

I hesitate. This isn't the sort of thing I'd usually talk about, not even with Zoe, but he still looks so uncomfortable just lying there, so frustrated with himself, that I figure it can't hurt to distract him. "Well, yeah. My mom was always too busy with work or away on a business trip to worry about dinner, and my dad's work schedule was too irregular to allow him to cook at the same time every day, so I guess I kind of just naturally took over." I stir the pot again. "I don't know. The cooking itself has never really interested me, but I liked feeling like I was making a contribution to the family, you know? Proving I could help out in my own way."

Soon, I have the porridge cooking and a bowl of pork floss and scallions prepared to sprinkle on top. When I turn around to check if Caz has fallen asleep, he's watching me, his black gaze inexpressibly soft. Serious.

It makes me nervous.

"What are you staring at?" I ask, trying to sound casual despite the heat rushing to my cheeks.

He tilts his head, but the intensity of his gaze doesn't waver. "Nothing."

• • •

When the porridge is ready, I bring it over to Caz on a fancy tray, crouching down beside him as he sits up carefully, his back resting against the couch cushions.

"You can drink it yourself, right?" I ask, holding the bowl and spoon out to him.

He somehow has the energy to roll his eyes at me. "Don't worry, Eliza, I wasn't going to ask you to feed me."

"Wasn't expecting you to," I mumble, but now I'm wondering if that's what I should've offered. *No*, I decide. He's running a fever—he hasn't lost feeling in his limbs.

"Thank you, by the way," Caz says as he takes the porridge from me, the white steam unfurling between us. "For—for all this." He clears his throat. "I haven't . . . No one's really taken care of me like this in a long time. So. Thank you."

"There's a better way to say thank you, you know," I tell him, hoping to keep things light. To hide the warm, exquisite ache blooming inside me, the forbidden impulse to set the porridge bowl back down and wrap my arms tight around him, hold him, have him hold me too. To offer him the whole world, protect him from everything that could potentially hurt him. "Just three little words."

He stills for a moment, confusion rippling over his features, before he catches on. Huffs out a sigh. "I don't—"

"Come on. You know what they are."

"Eliza—"

"*Caz*."

"Okay, fine." A beat. His eyes lock on mine, a stubborn

muscle twitching in his jaw, and the next three words that leave his mouth sound pried out, strained. "You . . . were right."

I feel my lips split into a broad grin, savoring this small victory, the look of resignation on his face. "In that case, you're *very* welcome."

He pauses. Then adds, "And I'm also sorry, by the way."

I look at him in surprise. "About what?"

"I don't know. Things have just been a bit weird between us recently, and . . ." He looks like he's going to say something else, and my heart lurches—but then he stops himself. "But we're cool now, yeah?"

I swallow. Smile. Try not to dwell too hard on what he means, if I was the one who made things weird in the first place, if he's still thinking about that day in the milk tea store, or maybe my embarrassing breakdown below his apartment. "Yeah. Of course."

Later, he finishes his dinner and compliments my cooking ("It really is much better than the cake"), and I stay by his side until he falls asleep. Until the moon rises higher in the night sky.

And long after that.

As I look at him, so unguarded in sleep, I get this odd feeling in my chest—a kind of twisting sensation, tender as a fresh sore, sharp as the sting of tears. Overwhelmingly so. Like my heart is trying to climb up my throat.

I lurch backward.

Caz's eyes flutter open, his gaze focusing on me, night black and intent. I feel a little shaky under the weight of it.

"Where are you going?" he asks.

"To, um." My voice is failing. "To clean up—"

"Stay," he whispers, the word falling so fast from his lips it could be instinct, a slip of the tongue, a mistake. He looks almost surprised himself, almost shy, though he doesn't take it back. Doesn't run away, the way I would. And it's only when I see the tense, rolling motion in his throat that I realize *just* how hard it is for him to be witnessed in his current raw, weakened state. To ask for anything from anyone.

It makes me want to be braver too, to offer him something in return. Something real, for once.

"I— Okay." Slowly, I kneel back down by the couch. It's so quiet in the room that I can hear my every staggered breath, the low creak of the floorboards as I shift my weight. Everything is shifting. Tilting. Careening wildly off course, and I'm not sure how to make it stop, or if that's what I even want. "Okay. But on one condition."

"What?" he asks, instantly wary.

"If you ever feel sick again, or hurt, or injured, or weak, you *have* to tell me. Don't just keep it to yourself and act tough—"

He starts to protest, but I continue over him, knowing I'm probably crossing some invisible line but not caring.

"Because no matter what happens . . . we're friends now, right? I want to be the person you know you can turn to. The place where you feel safe. I want you to feel like you can just be—*human*, in front of me. Like you don't have to always show your best side. Okay?" I add when he opens his mouth to argue again. "Promise me."

He swallows, hard. Sees something in my face—resolve, maybe, or all the worry I've been trying desperately to conceal—that makes him nod. "Fine."

"Fine," I repeat, letting out a quiet breath of relief.

"Good."

A small smile curves my lips. *"Great."*

And then, since I've crossed the forbidden line already, I reach over impulsively and stroke his hair gently, with one hand.

It's soft. Even softer than I expected. Caz's eyes fall closed again, but not in a tired way; on the contrary, all the muscles in his body seem suddenly tensed.

He only seems to relax when I scoot forward, bring my hand lower down to his arm, and tell him what I've wanted someone to say to me for as long as I can remember. What I'm still waiting for someone to say. "I'm not going anywhere. I promise."

CHAPTER SIXTEEN

After years of celebrating the Lunar Festival in places that focus mostly on Christmas and New Year's, it's nice to finally get an actual public holiday for it.

The two-week break is a blessing in more ways than one. Whatever changed between Caz and me that evening in his apartment—and something did change; I felt it down to my toes on my way home—is put on hold while Caz leaves for Hengdian for the whole length of the holiday. I manage to polish up my first batch of college applications just in time for the approaching deadlines. And Ma manages to organize a long-overdue family reunion at a seafood restaurant; turns out that getting over sixty family members together in the same place at the same time is, in Ma's words, a logistical nightmare.

As soon as we enter through the restaurant's lantern-lit double doors, we're greeted by an open display of fish tanks: crayfish scuttling across the glass and barramundi swimming through the murky waters. I stare at them for a few moments, at their gaping mouths and blank black stares, then tear my eyes away. Knowing how these types of places work, one of them will end up on my plate pretty soon. Better not to get too attached.

A cheery, baby-faced waitress leads us toward a massive private room at the far end of the restaurant, where we hear our relatives long before we see them. My stomach flutters with nerves. I can only pray my mediocre Chinese skills pull through.

And then it begins.

It feels like some elaborate, extended-family version of a meet-and-greet. Ma, Ba, Emily, and I line up on one side of the room, our backs to the floral folding screens, bright smiles arranged on our faces, while our relatives come up one by one to pinch our cheeks and offer gifts: bags of fresh red dates and apricots from their own gardens, and expensive calligraphy sets to help us "get back in touch with our culture." Fat red packets are shoved into our hands (despite Ma's polite protests that we're too old for Chinese New Year money) and many unnecessary, supposedly well-intentioned comments about my weight are made.

There are the sharp-eyed, hard-to-impress uncles asking about my grades and the gossiping aunts who I can distinguish only by the size of their perms. Then there are the relatives I don't know how to address: If it's something-*yi* or something-*yilaolao* or if they're actually our much-older cousins, so Emily and I end up sneaking glances at our phones to search for the right names.

It's all very loud and overwhelming and chaotic and . . . I've missed this. The energy in the air and the warm press of laughter from all sides. The strange sensation of looking out into a crowded room and recognizing variations of my mother's smile, my sister's eyes.

Our laolao—Ma's mom—is the last person to come greet us, and people part for her the way you would for the queen. There *is* something regal about her, even in her late sixties: The hard creases of her face, the steely look in her eyes. The history there. She's wearing the same faded purple blouse she wore in one of the few photos of us together, and her silver-streaked hair has been pinned up in an elegant bun.

"Laolao hao," I say dutifully when she stops before me.

Without a word, she pulls me into a fierce, bone-crushing hug, enveloping me with the sweet scent of herbs and jasmine tea and some kind of laundry powder. I awkwardly pat the back of her shirt, unsure how else to reciprocate.

"I'm so glad you came home," she whispers, her breath warm on my skin, her calloused grip tight around my shoulders, as if she's scared I'll vanish the second she lets go.

When she does let go a few moments later, I'm alarmed to see that her eyes are rimmed red. Yet even more alarming is the faint burning sensation behind my own eyes. I blink hard and pull my lips into a broad smile.

"Of course we came home," I tell her in my clumsy, childish Mandarin. "You're here."

She smiles back at me with so much love that it feels like a tangible weight before moving on to Emily.

But I remain rooted to the spot, thinking. About family. About *home.*

Around five years ago, at a school I can barely remember the name of anymore, our English teacher had asked us to write an essay on the topic of home. Everyone else knew immediately what to write: their childhood house in Ohio, their family farm in Texas, the city they'd lived in their entire lives. Simple. Only I had balked at the idea.

Then, like a complete idiot, I'd actually raised my concerns with the teacher in front of all my classmates.

"What if we don't really know where home is? Or what if—what if we don't have one?" I'd asked.

A few people laughed, as if I was being funny or difficult on purpose.

The teacher just stared at me for a beat. "Don't be ridiculous," he said. "Everyone has a home."

I'd tried to explain what I meant, but by then, the teacher had lost his patience. He said I was lazy, that I was trying to get out of a straightforward assignment by making up nonexistent problems. He didn't understand; none of the other people in my class seemed to either. They hadn't spent half their childhood attending family gatherings and eating Peking duck rolls and flying kites in Beihai Park, only to be whisked away to a country where they couldn't speak the language, couldn't even spell their own name. They hadn't learned to ride a bike on the wide, sunbaked roads of New Zealand, only to have to sell that bike two months later when they moved to Singapore. They hadn't spent their tenth birthday on a plane, and their eleventh birthday crying in the bathroom in England, because they didn't know anybody there and some kid in their new class had made fun of their accent.

Home for them was one piece, one place, not something scattered all around the globe, fragmented into something barely recognizable.

This was what I ended up writing about for my essay, but the teacher had given it back to me, unmarked. Said I didn't understand the point of the assignment. Asked me to do it again.

So the second time around, I made a story up. I chose one of the cities I'd lived in at random and wrote a bunch of bullshit about how I belonged there. In return, I got an A-plus, and the comment: *That wasn't so hard, was it?*

But as I gaze out at the room now, I wonder if maybe the answer to that assignment was as simple as this. Right here. Thinking of all those rooms I walked through at eight, ten, fourteen years old and all the people I met in them . . . if maybe I left a piece of myself in them and took a piece of them with me too; isn't that what homes are made of? A collection of the things that shape you?

My heart feels a little lighter as I take my seat between Second Aunt (the one with the biggest perm) and Third Aunt, waiting for the dishes to come. So far there are only prawn crackers and salted peanuts spread out over the red tablecloth.

". . . I'm telling you, they would be so cute together," Second Aunt is saying as she picks up one peanut after another using only her chopsticks. "I wouldn't be surprised if they were also dating in real life. It's common with actors, you know. Like Tang Yan and Luo Jin. Or Zhao Youting and Gao Yuanyuan. All that time together on set—something's *bound* to happen."

"Yes, yes, and they're both very good-looking," Third Aunt agrees. "Their children would be beautiful—I can just imagine it."

I chew quietly on a prawn cracker and let them gossip in the background. But then Second Aunt says:

"That Caz Song really *is* good-looking, isn't he? His costume designer in *The Legend of Feiyan* must've loved him too; I've never seen someone pull off an ancient costume so well."

And I almost choke on my cracker. *Oh my god.* They're talking about Caz. Not just Caz, but him and his former costar, Angela Fei. The actress who was literally voted one of the Most Stunning Women Alive last year. Even though *I* know they aren't together, a sharp taste fills my mouth. I stop eating.

Across the table, Emily opens her mouth—probably to announce to the entire table who Caz is *really* dating. I shoot her a quick warning look. Luckily, our sister telepathy is as strong as ever, because she pauses, and snaps her mouth shut again.

Neither of my aunts notices.

"No, hang on. I'm pretty sure I heard somewhere that Caz is already in a relationship. With a suren, no less," Second Aunt says, her gold and jade bracelets jangling together as she shakes her head. *Suren*: non-celebrity. She says it the way a noblewoman would say the word *peasant*.

Third Aunt's brows rise. "A suren? Seriously? When he could have had Angela Fei?"

"Maybe she's even prettier than Angela," Second Aunt says, in a tone like she highly doubts it. "Or maybe she has a good personality."

Third Aunt snorts. "Who are you kidding? Young people these days don't date based on personality. Especially not when you're as popular as Caz Song." Then she swivels her head toward me. "What do you think, Ai-Ai?"

"H-huh?" I manage. It's a miracle I can find the strength to speak at all.

"You've been listening, haven't you?" she says, waving a hand in the air. "Can you think of any good reason why a super-attractive, wealthy actor near the peak of his career would choose some random girl over his gorgeous costar?"

"Um, no," I say, swallowing hard, a stone lodged in my gut. "No. I really can't."

I'm lying in bed that night, still wallowing in self-pity from my aunts' conversation earlier, when Caz calls me for the first time.

"Hello?" I say, pressing the phone between my cheek and pillow. "This is Eliza. Uh, did you call the wrong number or something?"

I hear him laugh then, the low sound washing over the speaker like a tide off the shore, and despite myself, I flush.

There's something strangely intimate about calling someone in the dark. It's like listening to your favorite song in the middle of a crowded subway; the world narrows down to just you and this voice in your ear, while everyone else around you goes about their lives, completely oblivious. It feels sacred. Like a secret.

"I know it's you, Eliza," he says simply. "I just wanted to talk to you."

"Oh," I say.

"Yeah." He pauses, and there's a faint rustling sound, the brief creak of springs, like he's sitting down somewhere. "Are you busy now, or—"

"No," I tell him, because it appears I've forgotten how to have a normal conversation consisting of more than one syllable. Then again, I've never had a boy call me at night before, not unless it was for a group project. "Uh, you?"

"I'm back in the hotel," he replies. "We just finished shooting a pretty big scene today." There's a distinct pause. "A kiss scene, actually."

"Oh," I say again. I don't know why he's telling me this, or how the hell I'm meant to respond, or how to block the image out from my brain. Caz. Caz kissing someone else, someone beautiful, with long legs and shiny hair and perfect skin. Someone like Angela Fei. "Um, that's nice. Congrats."

"I . . . wanted to tell you." Maybe it's because of the static from the speaker or the reception on his end, but he sounds almost nervous. "I mean, I feel like I should."

"What?"

"The kiss scene," he says slowly, with meaning, and I kind of wish he'd stop saying that word, because it's inviting all sorts of confusing, forbidden thoughts about him into my head. "It was— I mean, we had to do five different takes, and it was long, and my hands were on her waist, but there wasn't tongue or anything. And our clothes were on. Fully."

"I am . . . so confused right now."

He makes a small, frustrated noise. "Do you seriously not understand what I'm saying?"

"No," I tell him, frustrated too, heat spreading fast over my body, my face. "All I can hear is you describing yourself kissing someone in very rich detail. Which is just lovely—again, really happy for you, but—"

"You're not—you're not jealous?"

Of course I am, I want to say. I want to hang up the phone and go find him in person and shake him. I'm so jealous it's embarrassing. It makes me sick, even though I don't really have a *right* to be jealous in the first place. There's nothing in our agreement that forbids him from kissing other people. Especially considering how it's part of his job.

But maybe, after that night at his place, I've accidentally let something slip again . . . Maybe he's regretting it, opening up to me even a little, or he's worried I've taken it the wrong way, that I think I have some claim on him now. Maybe that's why he's asking.

"Of course I'm not jealous," I tell him, and even manage a little laugh as my nails curl into my sheets. "Why would I be?"

"Okay. Okay, good." A pause. "If you're sure."

"I am sure. *Very*."

"Okay," he repeats slowly.

I pull the phone away from my ear for a second, stare at it, then bring it back. What even *is* this conversation? Why am I doing this to myself? Why do I feel like I have whiplash every time I talk to him? "Okay," I say too, after a pause. "Well, this was—fun. If you were just calling to confirm that . . . Bye? I guess?"

"Sure" comes his eventual reply. I wish I could see him, his expression. Wish I could figure out what he's thinking. "Bye, then."

I hang up first, chucking my phone across the bed and burying my head beneath my pillow with a groan. "What the hell," I mutter out loud, still half-convinced Caz had called me by mistake. And even if he hadn't, there's no way he would want to call me again after this.

But as always, Caz Song manages to surprise me. Because he does call me again the next night, at roughly the same time, and the night after that, and after that. I don't know if it's as a fake boyfriend, to continue our chemistry training sessions while he's away, or as a friend, which I guess is what we are now. I'm too scared to ask. Too scared to ruin another good thing.

At first, the conversations are more awkward than not—at least on my part—and limited to your typical, polite topics: *What did you do today? How was shooting? Did you see this person's latest post?*

Yet the calls get longer and longer, passing the one-hour mark and continuing until the streets outside are perfectly quiet and I can only hear my own breathing in the night. Soon, they become a habit.

Sometimes we talk until my phone runs out of battery. Sometimes I fall asleep with his voice in my ear.

Without meaning to, I start telling him stories about my life overseas. Stories I've never told anyone else before, that I've kept locked up inside me for so long they feel more like a scene from an old film I once watched than something that actually happened to me. I tell him about the last dinner we had with family before we left Beijing, how my laolao had cried and I didn't understand why. I tell him about the classmates I hated, the teachers I loved, if only because they were understanding when I wore the wrong uniform or got lost around campus.

And in exchange, he tells me the things he leaves out of interviews. Like how he secretly searches his own name online every day and very occasionally reads fanfiction about himself. How he hates heights, and is afraid of the dark. How he knows exactly what he dislikes, but doesn't always know what he wants.

"Is that why you're planning to go along with the colleges your mother picked out for you?" I can't help asking.

A pause. "What do you mean?"

"Come on, Caz," I say quietly, staring up at the ceiling and wondering how the ceiling looks from his hotel room. It's probably fancier, taller, chandeliers glittering everywhere. "I was there when I wrote those college essays with you, remember? You couldn't tell me a *single thing* you were looking forward to—I had to make it up for you. But when you talk about acting—you're like a different person. You love it. And you're good at it."

"It's more complicated than that," he protests. "My mother—"

"Seemed fairly reasonable. Maybe it'll take some convincing, but if you really tried to *talk* to her . . ."

"But that's the problem." He swallows, and I imagine him tugging his hair, pacing the room in circles the way he did that day outside the parent-teacher interviews. "If this were just about discipline or making me miserable, I wouldn't feel bad doing whatever I wanted, you know? Except she's not like that. She's just trying to look out for me, help secure a good, stable future—and sometimes . . . *a lot of the time*, I think she has a point.

"Because I have so many friends who wanted to be actors, but never landed a major role, or who worked their asses off and landed the role but completely failed to break out and—I mean, I love acting, but it's *hard* and unpredictable. And besides, how can I even be sure this is what I want to do for the rest of my life? I've only lived, like, a quarter of my life so far. What if I turn down an offer from a great college now only to realize in two years that I'm not interested in acting anymore? What then?"

He stops talking abruptly, his breathing louder than normal, as if he's been running the whole time he was delivering his monologue.

Caz Song isn't only good at hiding physical pain. He's good at hiding the emotional stuff too. Just from looking at him, seeing the way he acts at school, I'd never guess he thought so much about the things he's just said.

"Just consider it," I tell him when his breathing has slowed. "Okay?"

"Okay," he says reluctantly, after a beat. "Okay, I'll think about it."

"Oh, and Caz?"

"Yeah?"

"Thank you for keeping your promise." I clear my throat, hating how awkward I sound. "From that night at your place. I know it's hard for you to talk about all this, but I'm—I'm glad you did."

"It's no big deal," he says, though I can tell it is. Then he pauses. In a voice so soft I barely hear it, he adds, "The same for you."

My heart stutters. "What?"

"That thing about . . . being there for me. I want to be that for you too."

I close my eyes against the words. Of course they're nice to hear. Of course. But this is Caz Song we're talking about; he's uttered a thousand romantic lines just like this on-screen, all with seeming sincerity. I can't trust him to actually *mean* them, can't delude myself into thinking he might reciprocate my feelings, when nobody's ever fallen for me before. When he's Caz the Rising Star, and I'm . . . *me.*

Still, after we hang up, it takes me forever to fall asleep.

I'm so used to seeing Caz's name flashing over my screen that when my phone buzzes on Saturday evening, I pick up without looking.

"Did you finally get to kill the general today?" I ask, referring to the scene he'd last told me he was preparing for. An unexpected benefit of fake-dating a C-drama actor: You get a bunch of spoilers for yet-to-be-released dramas.

There's a long silence.

Then Zoe's voice drifts through the line, confused and oddly distant. Or maybe the connection's just not great today. "Uh . . . what?"

"Oh." I jerk upright on my bed, pushing away the interview notes I'd been looking through earlier for that Beijing media company. For some reason, my muscles tense, as if bracing for something. "Oh, sorry. I thought—I thought you were someone else. Hi."

"Who did you think I was?" she asks. When I don't reply right away, she answers for herself: "Caz."

I make a small, vague sound of assent.

"So you guys are still doing the thing, huh?" Again, there's that weird edge to her voice.

“What thing?”

“The whole dating facade.”

“Well, yeah,” I say, my whole body going rigid now, defensiveness hardening my tone. And then a long, awkward beat passes where we both wait for the other person to say more. I can’t remember when it started being like this, when we weren’t shouting over each other to talk about everything even when nothing had happened. But we’ve been busy.

But we’ve been busy before, back when I was still in America, and it wasn’t this bad.

It’s happening, I think, and as soon as I have the thought, it becomes a permanent stain, seeping through everything and coloring every memory a rotten gray. The changed playlist name. The shortened calls. The unanswered texts. The forgotten bracelet. *Just like all my best friends from the past.* June from London. Eva from Singapore. Lisa from New Zealand. In the end, it’s all just the same.

We’re drifting apart.

No, we’ve *drifted* apart. Whatever is happening now is the aftermath.

My heart seizes in silent despair, but Zoe speaks up again, oblivious to it all. “What are you planning to do about it?”

“*Do* about it?” I repeat, unable to shake the feeling that I’ve lost thread of this conversation.

“Well, I mean, you can’t just keep lying to the world, can you?” she pushes on. “Like, at first, I thought it’d only be this super-temporary thing. A joke. But it’s been entire *months*, and it's just . . . It just seems like the kind of thing destined to blow up in your face."

My jaw clenches, the tension now stretching like a wire all the way down to my toes. One of the reasons I've always admired Zoe is her ability to cut through all the bullshit, get to the very core of things. She's brave like that, braver than I'll ever be.

But that's also precisely why this is the very last topic I want to talk about.

"It'll work out," I say, with all the false calm I can muster while wringing the corner of my pillow between clammy fingers. "Eventually. But I've already promised Sarah—everyone at Craneswift—that I'll do this big interview after the break, and it's meant to be great for my career, and—"

"And I'm all for opening yourself up to opportunities," Zoe says. "Except when your career's founded on a *literal lie*. I mean, how do you expect to retain your readers or earn the respect of any publication out there if they find out—"

"So they *can't* find out," I cut in, gut roiling. "They won't."

"Yeah, well—" She starts to say something else, but a loud notification chimes on her end, and she pauses. "Sorry, the grades for my chem exam just came out . . ."

"Go check it," I tell her.

"You sure?" She lets out a small laugh, but she doesn't mean it. I would know. I used to know everything about her—which laughs she was faking and when she wanted to leave a conversation, a party, a room.

She wants to leave now.

And I don't know how to make people stay; I never have. So I only say, "Yeah, of course. Um, bye."

"Okay. Bye."

But there's a terrible ring of finality in her voice.

CHAPTER SEVENTEEN

The day before school begins again, my life unravels.

Well, it doesn't so much *unravel* as completely implode: starting with the notification that pops up on my phone first thing in the morning.

I kNew You were Lying.

I stare at it for a long time, my heart beating out of control. It's unnerving as hell, and not just because of the arbitrary capitalization.

If I'm being accused of lying, there's only thing I could be lying about . . .

A sick feeling digs into my gut. I sit up fast and unlock my phone, heading straight over to Twitter. And that's when all the other comments come flooding in, so similar to the first. Just as hostile. Just as ominous.

@blondie22: *Liar.*

@abigailsmithh: *Lmao I guess ppl will do ANYTHING for clout these days. Girl bye.*

@user1127: *Caz Song deserves better.*

@MayIsADog: *talk about pathetic??? and here i was thinking we actually had a cute wholesome couple to root for . . . guess not.*

@chengxiaoshi: *I KNEW IT. i TOLD Y'ALL this was a publicity stunt!! I fucking CALLED IT.*

@wenkexing520: *This is why we can't have nice things.*

And it's . . . I mean, I've received hate messages before. It's inevitable for anyone who's ever gone at least a little viral. So-called fans telling me I'm too ugly for Caz, or that I'm holding him back in his career. Random trolls going on about how I'm untalented and overrated. Anonymous users claiming it's anti-feminist of me to fall in love. Racist assholes making the usual stereotypical jokes in the comments.

They've always stung, of course, and hit a little too close to home for comfort, but the obvious strategy was simply to ignore them.

But this. This is different.

My whole body is trembling as I search my own name on Google, and there's a moment when nothing has loaded yet that I can feel my heartbeat thudding furiously in my ears, and I think I might throw up. Or maybe start crying. Then the results appear, and I'm too busy reading about why a bunch of strangers on the internet hate me to even muster the energy for tears.

The source of the problem quickly becomes evident.

Around midnight yesterday, while I was sound asleep, someone posted a long article speculating that my relationship with Caz was only a publicity stunt cooked up by his manager. The article noted some "discrepancies" between my personal essay and Caz's schedule. Like how, on the day we supposedly went out for hot pot, Caz was busy doing promotional activities for his campus drama and couldn't have possibly met up with me then. Or how, in one paragraph, I mentioned the stray cat hair clinging to his sweater, despite the fact that he's allergic to cats. *It's what everyone in the entertainment industry does these days. Has anyone even seen them really kiss, apart from that one peck-on-a-cheek selfie the girl posted?*

Maybe it would've been fine if, by the same strange, unpredictable alchemy of the internet that made my essay go viral in the first place, the article hadn't shot up to number one on trending searches.

And it all fell apart from there.

"Oh my god," I whisper, throwing my phone onto my bed, where it lands with a light, unsatisfying flop. I turn around. Squeeze my eyes shut. "Oh my *god*."

The worst part of all this is that I should've anticipated it. Because it feels like a total end-of-the-world disaster, yes, but it also feels like an inevitability.

Zoe's words from the other day float back to me: *It just seems like the kind of thing destined to blow up in your face . . .*

And suddenly, with an ache so acute it feels like a cavity, I find myself missing Zoe. How I'd walk into a crowded classroom knowing she had saved a seat for me. How she'd always wait for me by the lockers in the morning and after school, an anchor to my day. More than that, I miss the person I always became around her: someone braver and better and stronger, someone who wasn't afraid to crack dumb jokes and embarrass themselves a little and go after what they wanted.

If she were here, she wouldn't know how to fix this either. But she'd know exactly what to say to calm me down, to make me feel okay.

Behind me, my phone chimes again.

No doubt more hate comments. And I know I shouldn't read them, that there's no point torturing myself any further, but it's like telling yourself not to scratch an itch, or press an old bruise: As masochistic as it is, you can't help doing it anyway.

So I grab my phone and brace myself for some variation of *fraud* or *liar* or *I hate your fucking guts*, but instead I see only a name flashing over my screen.

Sarah Diaz.

Weeks from now, when I look back on this particular morning, it'll likely be nothing more a white-noise blur of panic, a gaping black hole in my memory.

I'm barely conscious of the day's events even as they're unfolding. One second I'm on the phone with Sarah, reassuring her that everything's just a misunderstanding and I totally have a plan, when I in fact totally do *not* have a plan, and the next I'm texting Caz, who's only just landed in Beijing and isn't aware of this complete shitstorm yet, but soon will be.

And in between all this, I'm lying facedown on the couch, cursing myself and trying not to pull my hair out.

Still, by lunchtime, I've calmed down enough to start thinking. Hard. Ma has seen PR crises far worse than this—like the rat-in-the-coffee incident, and the toxic-masculinity incident, and the many Kevin-induced accidents—and she's managed to smooth them all over. Sometimes her company's reputation has even improved as a result.

So what would she do?

Issue an apology? A formal statement? No. That's not her style; she never confesses to anything if she can help it. In fact, she'd probably do the opposite. Cover up one major event with another . . .

I close my eyes and think and think and finally, miraculously, like that day I saw Caz Song on my TV screen, an idea comes to me.

If the main issue is that people don't believe Caz Song and I are really together, then I have just the thing to prove them wrong.

My phone lights up.

I flinch by instinct, dreading what I might see, but it's a message from Caz. He's caught up to everything.

What do we do? he asks.

I think I have a solution, I text back. *but you're probably not going to like it. oh, also—what's your manager's number? let me know asap.*

I spend the next day making phone calls and writing frantic emails.

First, I get in touch with Caz's publicity team. This part goes more smoothly than I could dare hope: We track down the IP address of the original poster who wrote up the article, only to find that it's a sisheng fan, a stalker essentially, who's already been given two warnings for lurking around Caz's hotel room. It's perfect. After all, the best way to get rid of an unwanted story is to attack it at its source, erode the credibility of the author. From there, all we have to do is spread the information online and wait for the narrative to write itself. *Jealous fan makes up lies about Caz and his girlfriend. Fan comes up with wild conspiracy theories about her favorite star.*

At the same time, the manager pulls a few strings behind the scenes and accidentally-deliberately leaks some photos from god knows where of a married actor from a rival company leading a brothel worker into his hotel room at night. Within hours, the news blows up and squeezes out the old article on me and Caz from the trending searches, until it's all anyone can talk about.

Then it just comes down to Caz and me, and how well we can pull off the ultimate performance.

"You ready?"

I nod as I move to join Caz on the roof of one of our school buildings. This is my first time seeing him up close since before the holidays, and I'd forgotten how overwhelming it felt just to be in his presence, scandal or not. The buzzing in my stomach, the rush of blood in my veins, every nerve end on edge. His hair is a little longer now, his skin tanner, the lean muscles in his arms flexing as he leans over the glass railings.

He looks good.

Maybe *too* good, in a distracting way. I can't look at him without thinking about those nights with his voice pressed to my ear. It feels like my heart has missed a step.

"Are you?" I ask, quickly stuffing all unnecessary thoughts away. I need to focus. We only get this one chance to fix everything, and it has to be perfectly executed.

"When am I not?" He's making this expression like, *I got it, relax*. I have no idea how he's so chill about this. It's almost irritating. "Let's do this."

I nod again. Exhale slowly and stare past the railings, stamping my feet to keep warm. As expected, the courtyard below and surrounding footpaths are already starting to fill up with students. The roof is the one spot everyone has a clear view of, no matter where they are in the school. The saying goes that people only believe what they see with their own eyes. So I'm just praying that if they see us together, *really together* together, they'll be sufficiently convinced of our relationship.

Okay, it's not the most foolproof plan, and I have no idea if it'll work or not—but it's the best we can do for now.

When enough people have gathered to form a crowd, I twist around and pat Caz's shoulder. "Okay. Start."

He arches a brow, his lips twitching. "You're not even going to let me get into the moment a bit?"

Is he kidding? "You're an *actor*," I hiss. I can feel everyone's eyes on us, watching our exchange. "Be serious."

"Fine," he says, and though I've witnessed it more than a few times by now, it still startles me when he snaps easily into his role, the humor wiped clean from his face, his eyes deepening to black. The color of a moonless sky, charcoal ready to ignite, the earth after a storm. "Like this?"

"Y-yeah," I manage. Swallow. "Yeah, like that." One small step, and I've closed the distance between us. I lift my lips to his ear and whisper, for only him to hear, "Now hurry up and kiss me before people start leaving."

I brace myself. Try to empty my mind. It's supposed to be a professional kiss, if such a thing exists. Neither of us should feel anything other than grim determination to do this well, and maybe a hint of annoyance, impatience at having to do this in the first place.

But this is what happens instead:

Caz cups my face with one steady, slender hand and traces a gentle line down my cheek, and my mind—my mind teeters toward oblivion. My breathing betrays me. His ink-black eyes lock on mine, and I am staring up at him, half in shock and maybe awe. He's unreasonably beautiful and he's so close it makes me ache and I want him closer still. I want him even though I shouldn't. I want him to want me too.

I can't even remember what we were supposed to do.

Then, slowly, he brings his other hand up to my face. His

fingers tremble slightly, and the air between us changes. Solidifies. Overheats. My mouth parts of its own accord, and he sees.

He makes a soft, barely audible sound that could be a sigh or the edge of a laugh or something else, a surrender, and then he leans all the way in, presses his lips to mine like he can't help himself, like he's been waiting forever just to kiss me—

And I kiss him back.

I kiss him with an intensity that shocks me.

Because somehow, I realize I've been yearning for this: the softness of his lips moving against my own, the firmness of his grip, the small, hungry fires spreading from every single point of contact.

Then, just as quick as it started, it's over.

I don't know who pulls away first, but we're suddenly scrambling backward, standing apart, nothing but our uneven breaths touching the space between us. For a split second, Caz looks stunned. Almost drunk.

But in the next second, he is himself again. Confident. Assured. He straightens, runs a bored hand through his hair, and looks out at the students on the school oval.

My blood is pounding so loud in my ears I'd nearly forgotten they were there, but I gaze down too, assessing their expressions. Some are staring at us with open envy and shock. Others . . . Others are frowning, like they're not entirely sure what it is they've just witnessed.

"Do you—do you think it worked?" I ask Caz, my voice way too high to be normal.

"Honestly?" I hear him swallow. "No."

"Wait—*what*?" I demand, twisting around. But before I can even continue, he grabs my wrist and pulls me out of sight, leading me away until we're concealed by jade bamboos and mandarin trees, hidden in a mini garden of our own, soft shadows dancing around us, light bleeding through the gaps in the leaves. "What?" I repeat in a hiss. He still hasn't let go. I'm intimately aware of the warm press of his fingers against my skin, the precise shape and sound of his every breath.

"Yeah, no, these scandals are rarely resolved in a day—or with a single performance. You need to give it a lot more time."

"Then why—" I shake my head. My head is still spinning. I manage to produce exactly one coherent thought—*Caz Song and I just kissed*—before my brain runs into a wall and crashes. *Caz and I kissed*, and for a long moment, from when our lips met, Caz had kissed me like . . . like he really meant it. *No. Stop. Not the point here.* "If you didn't think it would work, why did you agree to the plan?"

Something flickers over his face, but he merely shrugs. "You just seemed like you really wanted to kiss me. And who am I to deny you the pleasure?"

My face bursts into flame. He says it like he's teasing. No, like he's *mocking* me. But of course he is. Of course he hadn't actually meant it—that's how he kisses everyone, all his beautiful costars on set. Who am I kidding? A kiss is just a kiss to him.

"Wow," I say, shifting back, mortification burning through my body like hot oil. "Okay. Well, clearly this was a mistake—and for the record, I absolutely did *not* want to kiss you. At all. It was only for a bigger cause—dire times, and all that—"

"Really?" He moves forward. Cocks his head. "Then what are you thinking right now?"

"I— What?" I flush harder. Through my humiliation, I'm thinking, unforgivably, about what it'd be like to kiss him again, to kiss him and really savor it, even knowing that it'd be more real for me than it could ever be for him.

But it's like the kiss has unlocked every suppressed fear and feeling inside me. Because I'm also thinking about how tens of thousands of people across the world are somehow invested in Caz and me, but only in the fantasy version of our story. I'm thinking about how it would feel to have Caz only to lose him, the way I lose everyone when I leave, the kind of bone-deep, inconsolable pain I would have to suffer as a consequence of my wanting. How easy it would be to revert to that old, familiar loneliness, except this time, the loneliness would hurt more than it ever has before, a loneliness shaped entirely by his absence.

I'm thinking that if I tell him what I really feel, just lay it all out there, there will truly be no going back from this. That it's been hard enough just to get to where we are—from strangers to begrudging allies to actual friends—to demolish every painstaking brick of trust built between us by asking for something more. That I'll have broken every rule I've laid down for myself, just to give Caz—beautiful, unpredictable, guarded Caz—all the ammunition he needs to break my heart.

"I'm . . . not sure what to think," I say.

He takes another step closer. I step back automatically, the bamboo stalks rising up around me, brushing my cheek. He stops. Releases his grip on my wrist, only to bring his hand up to the curve of my jaw, and it's all I can do not to dissolve right there or utter something incredibly dangerous and sincere.

"So you don't have any real feelings for me?" he asks, his voice dipping into a low register I've never heard before. "Not even a little?" He keeps his gaze steady on me, but his fingers trail down to a soft, vulnerable spot at the base of my neck, and I flinch, like an idiot.

I can't speak; I shake my head.

"Really?" he says, one brow raised, looking exactly the way he did that first day I spoke to him, when I claimed to not have overheard his call and he didn't believe me at all.

I hear myself swallow. Try to ignore the sensation of his hands still on my skin. "N-no. None."

Caz responds by leaning in, and for one wild, beautiful, terrifying second, I think he's going to press his lips to mine, and I can't help it—I lean in too. But instead he merely smiles, as if he's just proven something to both of us, and lowers his curved mouth to my ear.

"Liar," he whispers.

And I don't know what to do, how to react, how to process that I've been caught. So I revert to my old habits, my ingrained methods of self-defense: I wrench myself free from his grip. I spin on my heels, twisting away from him. And I run. My feet pound all the way down the stairs, and I shove the door open, bursting into the blinding sunlight. I don't go to class and I don't stop until I'm far enough away and alone in a remote corner of campus. Until it's just me, my racing thoughts, and my violently pounding heartbeat.

CHAPTER EIGHTEEN

I try hard not to think about it.

Really. I try *very*, very hard to block out all thoughts of Caz Song's soft lips brushing mine, his calloused hands cupping my face, the way my insides had sparked and melted as if left too long over red-burning coals.

But the memories keep rushing back, persistent, in such unwanted clarity I might as well have recorded our exchange, analyzed the entire scene over and over like the movies we have to write comparative essays on for English class.

What is the significance of the line "So you don't have any real feelings for me?" What did the look in his eyes symbolize? Discuss, with evidence.

All through the next week, while Caz is away shooting, they continue to spring up on me at random: when I'm half-way through rinsing the dishes (because my parents like to use the dishwasher as a drying rack, and simply don't trust dish-washers anyhow); when I'm changing into my pajamas later at night, half my shirt stuck over my head, long hair tangled up in the buttons—

What are you thinking right now?

"Shit," I mumble out loud, yanking the shirt down with a little too much force and accidentally pulling a few hairs out.

My eyes water. *"Shit,"* I say again, louder, angry at no one but myself.

I refresh my phone—*no new messages since last Friday*—then slam it down. I block him, then unblock him before he can find out. I delete our entire chat history, then instantly regret it.

And it only gets worse from there.

On Sunday morning, Ma—having recently finalized a major project and cleared out some time in her cramped schedule—takes us out to Din Tai Fung for brunch.

I'm finding my way back from the restaurant bathroom, very narrowly avoiding crashing into a waitress carrying a massive stack of prawn dumplings and xiaolongbao, when I see Caz's face.

As in: his face, magnified times ten and airbrushed to above-human levels of perfection and printed over a glossy poster by the table where they're serving tea. It's an advertisement for some kind of lychee-flavored soft drink. He's holding the candy-pink bottle up with one hand and smiling with his mouth closed. It's his fake smile, the one he uses when he's forced to do something he doesn't want.

The tagline below reads, *Get your girl something sweet.*

And it's all so corny and unexpected and ridiculously ill-timed that I can only gape at the poster, at his beautiful, familiar face, the features I've studied in such close proximity in private, blown up for everyone to admire. Something hot and painful wraps around my heart and squeezes.

This poster shouldn't be here. Or maybe I shouldn't be here.

But if nothing else, this proves that my reaction that day was wise, accurate. Not the kiss, but me running away from him. Because one shiny poster in a dim sum restaurant is only the beginning. If Caz's career continues on its current trajectory, if he grows more and more famous, picks up more sponsorships and endorsement opportunities and hit dramas left and right, it won't just be him advertising a cute little drink. It'll be his face on lit-up billboards; his smile on subways; his dark, scorching gaze every time I turn on the TV, remembering how it felt when he used that gaze on me. He will be everywhere, haunting every cursed corner of the country, and I will be left reeling in his wake.

"Are you a fan too?"

I spin around, startled, to find a girl maybe only a year or two younger than I am. She's dressed from head to toe in designer clothes and staring at the poster of Caz as if she's just seen a vision of God himself, both hands clutched tight to her chest, cheeks flushed despite the cool indoor temperature. If we were in a cartoon, her eyes would probably be bright pink heart signs.

"Um . . ." I say, only now translating her question from Mandarin to English inside my head and processing it. "Something like that. I guess."

She releases a small, wistful sigh, eyes still glued to the poster. Then she says, "He's very attractive, isn't he?"

I try not to stab myself with one of the metal chopsticks lying on the table beside me. "Mm," I reply, as noncommittally as possible.

"It's such a shame, though," she continues, clearly oblivious to how little I want to be having this conversation right now, or ever.

"What? What's a shame?"

She raises a perfectly shaped brow, like I'm playing dumb. "Haven't you heard about the whole scandal with him and the writer girl? Some people are saying it's a publicity stunt."

"Ah." With what I hope sounds only like casual curiosity, I ask, "And do you think it is?"

"Not sure." She shrugs. "I'd probably need more evidence. I hear they're doing this big interview together soon, so . . . maybe we'll see then?" She trails off with a shrug.

I quickly excuse myself and make a beeline for my table on the other end of the restaurant. It's not until I'm sitting down between Ma and Emily, my face hidden behind the laminated menu and its many beautifully shot images of steamed buns, that I allow myself to relax.

Then, while my parents are bickering over what type of dumplings to order (Ba launches into a moving, impassioned speech about how pork-and-chive dumplings were a key part of his childhood and eating them always reminds him of home; Ma strikes back with hard statistics—the last time we ordered pork-and-chive dumplings, we only ate 40 percent of them, and plus, can't he see that the *shrimp* ones are on sale?) and Emily is secretly jotting down every dessert option there is on the order form, I slide my phone out from my pocket and search my own name, even though I promised myself I wouldn't.

The comments are, unfortunately, divided too:

@alyssaL: *listen I'm usually pretty cynical about this stuff but did u guys SEE that kiss? the sparks? the intensity?? tHE WAY HE LOOKED AT HER??? like I know Caz is an actor but I don't think he's THAT good an actor lol*

@violetthewen: *I'M SO CONFLICTEDDD now akdfjlala is it real oR NOT*

@clazzy001: *the most unbelievable part for me is why someone like caz song would even be dating this eliza girl???? Angela Fei is way prettier*

@huachengseye: *ok either they're REALLY committed to this publicity stunt or they're REALLY in love w each other and just dgaf*

@chanel.cao: *not everything is for publicity y'all . . .*

I slide my phone away, my stomach churning. As much as I hate to concede he's right, it's just like Caz predicted: My plan was nowhere near as effective as I'd hoped.

Which means neither of us is in the clear yet.

By the time we get back home from the restaurant, I'm determined to find myself a distraction.

Something that will force aside all thoughts of Caz, and the kiss, and the speculation online. Something that will allow me to achieve a state of total, blissful zen. Normally when I'm looking for an escape, I'll just write, but these days all writing does is remind me of Craneswift, and my essay, which leads me right back to Caz again.

So I decide to go running.

Aside from the obvious irony of me literally running away from my problems, this seems like a great idea at first. I dig out the cute two-piece workout set I bought years ago for the aesthetic and haven't touched since, tie my hair back in a high ponytail, and do a few stretches down by the playground. The early spring air is crisp with the scent of an impending storm, the temperature just starting to warm, with the occasional cool breeze. Even better, there aren't too many people crowding the compound's special jogging lanes at this hour.

Everything's perfect.

Then I actually *start running* and come to the rapid conclusion that I hate it.

My body, so used to mild variations of sitting and lying down and slow, unhurried walks between classes, seems to revolt against the sudden change in rhythm. I've barely made it halfway around the lake before my legs start cramping, a tight, wrenching pain that shoots up the muscles in my thighs every time my feet hit the pavement.

Still, I keep running. Forcing my feet forward.

I push on for a couple more yards, gulping down air with increasing difficulty until I sound how I imagine dying walruses must sound, when I see an old man from the corner of my eye. An *old* old man. He's probably in his late seventies or early eighties, judging from the deep wrinkles etched into his skin and the dragon-head walking cane trembling in his grip, and he's shuffling down the lane parallel to mine.

We make eye contact. He flashes me a shaky thumbs-up.

And then—good god—he *outruns* me. Or, well, out*walks*, which is without a doubt much worse. All I can do is stare at his retreating figure until he rounds the corner of an apartment building, his cane's tap-tapping fading into the distance.

Apparently, the humiliation is too much for my body to bear. My knees wobble. My legs give out. I stumble to a stop by the lake pavilion, panting hard, the amount of sweat blurring my vision and trickling down my upper lip wholly disproportionate to the amount of exercise I've just completed.

The only upside of my current state is that Caz Song is definitely off my mind now, because I'm far too preoccupied with my more basic, immediate needs, such as breathing. And not fainting.

I spend an eternity like this, doubled over, clinging to the pavilion pillars and hating everything, before I find the strength to start walking back home.

And then I step into something brown and foul and squishy, which of course turns out to be—

"Crap," I mutter, staring at the literal dog crap now smeared over the heel of my sneakers. *You have got to be kidding me. You have* actually *got to be kidding me.* When no one springs out from a nearby bush to confirm that, indeed, my life is a practical joke, I throw an exasperated hand up in the air. "I mean, wow. Okay. This might as well be happening."

After scanning the surrounding area once—all empty save for two beady-eyed pigeons gliding across the melted fringes of the lake—I squat down awkwardly right there, in the middle of the lane, and attempt to scrape my shoes clean with a twig.

I'm so focused on my task that I don't hear the footsteps approaching until they stop right in front of me.

"Eliza?"

My heart lurches.

That voice. Smooth and low and slightly wry, as though sharing an inside joke with himself. I would know that voice anywhere, but it can't be—it *can't*—

Slowly, I lift my gaze, taking in the details bit by bit. Dark jeans come into view, then a loose white shirt, leaving the arms bared to the cold, the muscles long and lithe, a faint, puckered scar running down the center . . .

Of course it's him.

"Oh. Hi," I say, casually tossing the twig over my shoulder and swaying for a dangerous few seconds before standing up, smile already forced into place. As if this is exactly how I enjoy bumping into people. Covered in sweat. In mid-squat. While wiping animal excrement off my shoes and failing at it, no less.

"Hi?" Caz says, head cocked to one side. It sounds like a question.

You don't have any real feelings for me?

No. Stop. Don't think about it.

"So, um. I stepped in dog poo," I tell him.

"Yeah." His tone is appropriately somber, but the corners of his mouth twitch, like he's making a serious effort to suppress his laughter. "I can see that."

"Right." I nod. My face feels all hot and itchy, and not just because of the sweat. "Well, I was also out on a jog. You know, getting those steps in."

"I can see that too." He gestures to my workout clothes, his eyes lingering.

An awkward silence stretches and strains between us. Or maybe the awkwardness is only me. Caz looks calm, unaffected. Still fighting back a laugh. It's as if our kiss on the roof never happened, as if it hasn't been nine whole days since we last spoke.

I feel a violent rush of anger toward him. This whole time I've been desperately trying to distract myself, fighting off all thoughts of him—so desperate I even resorted to *running* under non-life-threatening circumstances—he's been . . . what? Just living his best life? Studying his scripts? Having a great time forgetting all about me?

My nails dig into my palms.

Caz says something, but I don't hear him, *can't* hear him above the violent buzzing in my ears. Then he repeats himself, louder. "It's going to rain soon."

He's not the kind to make small talk about the weather, so I pause despite myself and follow his gaze up. Sure enough, dark clouds are gathering overhead like a flock of mad ravens, coloring the lake water from green to a deep, depressing gray. That earthy scent in the air is sharper now too, brimming with unshed rain.

"We should probably head inside," Caz says, looking back at me, his eyes almost as black as his lashes. It occurs to me with a jolt that we're standing too close. Again. "I can walk you to your apartment if you'd like."

I fold my arms across my chest, creating a very ineffectual barrier between us. "No. It's fine. My shoes aren't clean yet, and besides, I doubt it'll rain *that* quickly. You can sort of see the sun—"

The words have barely left my mouth when the first few droplets of rain splatter over my top, the cold seeping straight through the polyester sleeves.

Then, as if someone's turned on a giant faucet behind the clouds, it starts pouring.

"Yeah, what were you saying?" Caz asks, his voice almost lost beneath the heavy onrush of water. It's everywhere now, beating down on the pavement in a quickening rhythm, slapping against outstretched leaves, crushing thin stalks of grass flat to the pavement like a heavy boot. The smell of wet dirt and pine rises to my nose.

I glare at him, blinking through the rain. I'm already soaked. "Just—just go. I can walk home myself."

He doesn't leave. Instead, he shoots me a faintly amused look. "Are you sure? Because you look a little . . . winded. Plus, your apartment isn't that far from mine—"

I shake my head quickly, water blurring the edges of my vision. I can't trust myself to be alone with him like this. "I'm fine. I'll be home in no time." But when I try to step back, my leg muscles spasm, and I wobble violently, a hot, tearing pain shooting down my calves. *Great. Just wonderful.* The one time

I decide to engage in voluntary physical activity and my body gives up on me.

In an instant, all the humor falls away from Caz's face, replaced by concern. "You evidently can't."

"I'm just tired from the running, that's all. I'll be okay soon."

He casts me a long, doubtful look. Then: "Let me carry you," he says simply. Readily. His hair has fallen over his forehead in long, wet-ink strands, his shirt plastered to his skin, and despite being drenched from head to toe in freezing rain, I feel all of a sudden like there's water boiling inside me, dangerously close to spilling over.

"What?"

He gestures to his back. "You heard me. I've carried plenty of girls on my back before while shooting. It'll be easy."

As if I need the reminder that big, romantic gestures mean nothing to him. That whatever he's said or done around me, he's done with other girls too: actresses, idols, models. That such close proximity is *easy* for him, when it feels like life-or-death for me.

"I think you're overestimating your strength," I tell him stiffly.

"I doubt it."

"You're also underestimating my weight."

"Come on, Eliza." He rolls his eyes. "You're, like, five foot one at the most."

"It's five foot *three*," I grumble.

He holds up his hands, using one of them to shield his head from the downpour. "Look, would you rather stand out here bickering in the rain over your height—which definitely isn't five foot three, by the way—or go somewhere warm and dry?"

Which is how I end up getting a piggyback ride home from Caz Song, the rain pelting our skin every step of the way, water sloshing at his feet, the clouded sky churning violently overhead. My arms wrapped around his neck. Everything looks darker, more saturated: the passing trees a rich brown, pink blossoms just starting to sprout. The compound is empty now save for us.

It feels like we're the last two people left in the world.

"I've been meaning to talk to you, you know," Caz says some minutes later as we round a bend in the lane. His grip on my legs remains firm, but I can hear the strain in his breathing, the slight falter in his footsteps. I do my best to stay very still.

"About what?" I ask.

"Last Friday . . ."

And suddenly my heart is pounding louder than the rain. "You're right, we should talk about the—the public response," I tell him, panicking. "Have you heard anything from your manager? Because I was looking at some of the comments, and there's still a significant segment online who need more convincing, and I feel like the upcoming interview would be a great opportunity—"

"You must know that's not what I care about."

Cold creeps into my veins. My teeth chatter. "What—what do you care about, then?"

"You," he says quietly. "I want you, Eliza."

The words hang in the misty gray air, and I'm glad he can't see my face. *You already have me*, I'm tempted to tell him. *More than I was ever planning to give.*

"I—"

"But not as part of a secret arrangement," he continues, talking faster, like he has to get this off his chest and he's not sure if he'll have the chance to do so again. "Not for show. Not for 'a strategic, mutually beneficial and romantically oriented alliance to help further our respective careers'—"

"You—you memorized that?"

"Of course I did. Even though I still feel like we could've used a better name." Without missing a beat, he goes on. "I don't want to act like we met while you were apartment hunting and hit it off, when the first time we *really* met, you were sitting two seats in front of me in English class and the teacher was reading out one of your essays and I just thought—I've never known anyone who can write like that before. I don't want to constantly keep my guard up around you when you're the only one who's ever made me feel like I can just be . . . honest. Myself. Like I matter even when all the cameras are off.

"I don't want to wait for an excuse to kiss you only when there's a literal crisis going on and when half our school is standing around to watch. I don't want our whole relationship to be built around a lie. And I know that's asking for a lot, because you have your readers and their expectations and there's already enough scrutiny but . . . I just want—" He sucks in a breath, and he might have once claimed to never beg anyone for anything, but his voice is painfully close to pleading when he says, "I want this to be real."

My heart seizes.

How many times have I dreamed of him saying something like this? A hundred. A thousand. But it was only that—a *dream.* I am totally, utterly unprepared for this speech in real life.

"What . . . about the essay?" I hear myself ask. There's water in my eyes, on my tongue. It tastes like salt. "People are already saying it's a publicity stunt—we've just spent all our energy trying to convince them it's not. If we— If I go out there and say the *whole story* is made up—"

"We can figure that out," he promises. God, he always makes these things sound so easy.

If only.

"I just—I don't understand why you're telling me this," I blurt out. "Why now? Since when did you even—"

And he actually laughs, though there's no humor in it. "Well, you haven't exactly made it easy for me."

"What's that supposed to mean?"

"Eliza," he says, shaking his head. "I'm usually pretty good with this stuff, but when it comes to you—one second you're saying things that sound so sincere, like you might really like me, and you're making me those paper cranes . . . And the next you're telling me that you're only doing this for your internship, that every sincere-sounding thing that comes out of your mouth is just flowery bullshit, and you're planning out our every single interaction three weeks in advance. If you hadn't kissed me back like that . . . I still wouldn't know."

I stare ahead, fully convinced now that I'm in some sort of alternate universe, where *Caz Song* is the one second-guessing *my* feelings toward him.

"Besides," he goes on, voice low, "a lot of people might like me for my—reputation. But that's the side I show to them on purpose to *make* them like me. Nobody's ever gotten to know me as well as you have. I wasn't sure . . . I didn't know if those other parts of me were worth wanting too."

And my heart shatters.

But my resolve doesn't.

"Of course they're worth wanting," I say, in disbelief that I'd even need to affirm this out loud. "Caz, you don't know how hard it's been to pretend like—like I *don't* want you. But this isn't going to work."

He stills; I feel the muscles in his shoulders bunch. "Why not?"

"Apart from the thousands of logistical reasons, you mean? It's— Okay. Okay, you know Zoe? Zoe Sato-Meyer?"

"I remember, yeah." His voice is carefully neutral. "The one who gave you the bracelet."

"Exactly. She is—she *was* my best friend." The correction makes my chest ache like a bruise, but I continue. "We didn't even have a fight or anything. It was just—we drifted apart. That's what always happens when I'm involved, Caz. Every single fucking time. And you might say or think you want me now, but . . . that's what will happen with us too. I'm certain of it."

This is the closest I have ever gotten to voicing the truth: that I'm afraid. That for a long time now, between maybe the third and fourth move, the fourth or fifth friend I lost along the way, I've suspected that there's something fundamentally unlovable about me. Something that makes it easy for people to forget me the second I leave, to drift out of touch no matter how hard I try to keep them in my life.

I've said before that my default setting is loneliness, but maybe I was wrong.

Maybe it's really fear.

"You can't keep doing this, Eliza," Caz says. We've reached my building now, and I slide off his back before he can carry me farther. Then I stand up unsteadily, soaked through and shivering, and bring myself to look at him. His jaw is set, tiny jewels of rainwater glistening on his skin, his eyes darker than the sky behind him. This feels, in every way, like a finale.

"Doing what?"

"You can't control everything. You can't decide how other people feel—how *I* feel—"

"But I already know how it's going to end," I choke out. "I *know.* And when it happens—*I'm* going to be the one heartbroken. Not you—"

"That's not true—"

"You think that now. But you don't know—you can't know—" My voice threatens to waver, to give me away, but I catch myself. Draw in a deep breath. Assume some semblance of professionalism, hide behind it like armor. "Look, this is my fault for not sticking strictly to our business arrangement. That's all it was supposed to be; that's all it really *can* be. And I'm close to finishing up with my internship. Once we do the interview together, and clean up this whole mess—we can stage a proper breakup. Part ways for good."

His eyes flash. "So that's it? You're just not going to give it a chance? You don't have the guts to even *try*?"

I want to answer him. I really do, but there's a fist-sized lump in my throat and I can barely swallow, let alone talk. So I just nod.

And Caz waits. He waits, and I disappoint him again and again with every new second that passes between us, until he understands. "Fine," he says at last, backing out into the rain. Already, his outline is blurring, like something from a dream. "If that's what you want."

"Whoa. What happened to you?"

Emily's eyes widen as she opens the front door to see me standing here, dripping wet and shivering, my hair in dirty tangles, my feet completely bare after abandoning my disgusting sneakers outside the entrance.

"It rained," I say, and I realize I sound like I've been crying.

"Yeah, *clearly*." She gapes at me a few moments longer,

opens and closes her mouth a few times, probably deliberating how appropriate it would be to make some joke about my sad, disheveled appearance, before sighing and hurrying off into the laundry.

She returns with two thick towels that smell faintly like pine.

"Thanks," I croak out, stepping through the doorway, leaving wet footprints everywhere behind me. But when I bend down to wipe them, I only end up spraying droplets of mud and water all over the marble surface and slipping on the mess I've just made, my left hip bone hitting the damp floor with a painful thud.

That's it, I decide as I pull myself slowly back up. I wince. *This is without a doubt the most miserable moment in my whole life. It is literally impossible for things to get any more depressing than this.* "I think I'm just going to take a shower first."

"Um," Emily says.

"Um, what?"

"The showers aren't really . . . working right now," she informs me. "I think something got stuck in the main pipes when it was raining. Ma and Ba went to find the wuye downstairs, but they said it's, like, a whole-building issue. Might take them a while to fix it."

And once again, the universe has managed to prove me wrong.

"Right," I say, wrapping both towels tight around my soaked clothes. "Cool. Very cool. Well, then I guess I'll just wait here."

"I can wait here with you," Emily offers.

I start to tell her *No, it's okay, just go play*, but my throat's closed up again, and maybe I don't want to be alone right now. Even if I already feel lonelier than I've ever felt.

We're both silent for a long time, listening to the light tap of rain against the windows, the distant rumble of thunder, the steady drip of water from my hair.

Then, as if she can't help herself, Emily blurts out, "Did you have a fight with Caz?"

The sound of his name sears like salt on an open wound. Swallowing hard, all I can think to say is "I'm sorry." Though I'm not sure what exactly I'm apologizing for. Lying about my relationship with him to everyone, even now? Making my personal essay up in the first place? Introducing him into her life, when she knows just as well as I do how horrible it is to be pulled away from the people you care about, how rare it is to move to a new place and find someone there who can make it feel like home? There's just *so much*. So many ways I've screwed up. So many things I've done wrong. "I know you really like him."

"I do like him," Emily says slowly. Then she looks up at me, and I'm struck by two things: First, how tall she's grown without my realizing, her head now almost level with my nose. And second, that fierce, protective look in her eyes, like our positions have been switched and *she's* the older sibling who'd tear down the world for me. "But if he was mean to you, I'll stop liking him immediately. I won't even invite him to my next birthday party."

I choke out a small laugh, but the sound's tinged by sadness.

"No, no. It's not that. If anything . . ." *If anything, I'm the one who wronged him.*

"Well, either way," Emily continues, leaning back against the wall, "the main reason I liked him was because of how you act when you're together."

This surprises me. "What . . . what am I like around him?"

"Happy," she says simply.

CHAPTER NINETEEN

Caz doesn't show up at school the next day.

Or the next day. Or the next. He doesn't read any of my texts asking if he's okay, or return my voicemails asking if we can make a plan for the interview, and I end up finding out through a dodgy media site that he's requested a two-week break from school to finish filming his drama.

And I—

Well, I survive. I brush my teeth and go to class and take my notes. I even write up that longer, official article I promised Sarah Diaz—a much more serious one this time about the slow collapse of the tutoring center industry in China, to be printed in the spring edition of Craneswift—and email it to her, shoving down a surge of anxiety when she confirms receipt alongside the question: *Are you all set for the interview?*

I don't know how to tell her that I'm not sure if Caz will even be coming. If we'll ever speak again. That every time I remember the knife-bright flash of hurt—then anger—in his eyes, the sound of his footsteps in the beating rain, it feels like someone's squeezing my heart inside their fist, like there's no chance we can ever find our way back from this. But there's too much riding on the interview: my career, Caz's reputation, the public's opinion of us, all our efforts so far. So instead I write, in the vaguest way possible, *It's all going just fine.*

And maybe when everything's over and done with and I'm lying alone in my bedroom, staring around at my four blank walls, I'll think of Caz and a terrible, burning pressure will build in the back of my throat. Maybe I'll imagine him shooting his dramas, laughing with Mingri, singing karaoke with his gorgeous costars, and dig my nails into my pillow. Maybe I'll miss him and hate him and curse his name.

But other than that, I'm doing fine. Great.

There's a new email in my inbox the next Saturday, barely two lines long:

I've just finished reading your piece. Please call me when you're free. —Sarah

At first all I can do is stare at the screen, not really registering any of it. Then I read the email again, my heart kicking faster and faster against my ribs, dread rising to my throat like bile.

Don't freak out, I scold myself. *You don't know that it's bad.*

But I don't know that it's good either.

I'm shaking as I retreat alone to the balcony and dial Sarah Diaz's number, gripping the phone tight in both hands.

She answers on the first ring. Like she's been waiting for me. "Eliza. How are you?"

I feel like I'm about to throw up or have a mini panic attack because of your email, thank you. And how are you? "I'm good," I manage.

"Well, that's good to hear. I'm sorry to reach out so suddenly, but I really wanted to talk to you about your article . . ."

"What did you think?" I sound so desperate. So *young.*

"It's . . ." And then she pauses. For at least twenty seconds. Nobody pauses like that when they're about to tell you your article was the best thing they've ever read. It's an I'm-sorry-to-inform-you-your-missing-relative-was-found-dead-in-a-ditch kind of pause. An I-might've-accidentally-run-over-your-dog-on-my-way-to-work kind of pause.

Sweat slicks my palms, my skin flashing hot and cold, then hot again. I start pacing around the balcony, as if moving might help redirect all my nervous energy.

"It's . . . different," Sarah finally says. Her voice is strained. "It's very different from your blog posts."

I don't know what to say to that, so I just stay silent, and all the while my stomach clenches tighter and tighter.

Then she releases an audible sigh. "I'm just going to be honest with you. You know how important authenticity and passion is to our brand, and I'm afraid I didn't really feel any of that come through as I was reading. I mean, it was clearly well researched, but the writing fell flat, and I couldn't really see a message to the piece, you know? As a whole, it felt very . . . hollow."

"Oh" is all I can manage at first. I swallow hard, fighting the sudden, overwhelming urge to cry. "Oh, that's—I mean, that's fair. That's fine."

"I hope I'm not coming across as too harsh, Eliza," Sarah continues, and the creep of sympathy in her voice—of pity, even—somehow makes me feel a thousand times worse. "Because I wanted to love this. I truly did. And you know how much I *adore* your work overall. I mean, that first essay was so joyous and authentic and sincere—which, I think, is the crux of the issue here."

A buzzing fills my ears, the irony of her words hitting me like a slap in the face. How could an essay I'd completely made up be *sincere*? An essay on a kind of feeling I'd never even experienced?

"What do you mean?" I ask.

"Well, it seems you write best when you truly believe in what you're writing about."

"Right. Okay. That's—okay."

"But don't despair," Sarah adds. "I've spoken with my team, and we're all happy to give you one more chance with this. To write on a topic of your choosing. Of course, if we run into similar issues again . . ."

The unspoken end of her sentence is clear. If I don't produce something she loves, there won't be a next chance. This will be the end. My recommendation letter gone and my potential writing career over before it even properly began.

I stop pacing and press my forehead to the cold glass of the balcony window, letting my breath cloud the surface. If I squint, I can make out the bare, crooked trees planted down below, the children racing through the playground, the couple walking in leisurely circles around the still lake, the dim afternoon sun painting their silhouettes a gentle blue gray.

All of them seem hundreds of miles away.

"Don't worry," I hear myself say. "I'll give you something else. Something better. I swear."

"Well, I'm glad to hear that, Eliza." She sounds relieved. "I sincerely hope you do. Oh, and just to double-check—is everything still good to go for the interview?"

Again, my thoughts drift to Caz, and my throat constricts. There might've been a time where I could give her a gentle disclaimer about him possibly-very-likely not showing up, but that's no longer a viable option. Right now, my role at Craneswift is hinging on my personal essay and my relationship with Caz; I can't screw *that* up too.

"Yes," I say with false cheer. "Yep. Of course."

As soon as I hang up, I grab my laptop from my bedroom and read through the article I sent her. I'm about four paragraphs in when I realize with a sharp pang that Sarah Diaz was right. It *does* feel hollow. Despite it being an opinion piece, the whole thing reads like one of those awful AI-generated news reports. There's no passion. No flow. No *spark*.

Because if I'm being totally honest with myself . . . I don't care about the topic. Never did. I just thought it was the kind of thing that would seem impressive.

Even the tightness in my chest now has nothing to do with the article itself but with the thought of having disappointed Sarah and the others at Craneswift, and the terrifying prospect of failing again.

Which is why I can't let that happen.

I turn away from the window. Take a deep, steadying breath to clear my head. I promised Sarah something better, and I'll deliver. I have to. All I need is to figure out what specific ingredient it was that made Sarah fall in love with my completely fictional personal essay and replicate it, and everything else will work out. Easy.

I can do this.

I can't do this.

It's midnight, according to the alarm clock beside my bed, and I've been staring at a blank Word document for the past six hours. I'm fairly sure my brain started disintegrating at the two-hour mark.

"God help me," I mutter, rubbing my temples to ward off a growing migraine.

You write best when you truly believe in what you're writing about, Sarah had insisted. But what do I truly believe in?

Nothing.

Everything.

I'm seriously debating whether or not banging my head against the wall might help force some words out when I hear the soft click and creak of the front door sliding open. The rattle of keys. Then the familiar *clack-clack-clack* of heels on hardwood.

Ma's home.

Grateful for an excuse to temporarily put aside the Blank Screen of Doom, I tiptoe toward the living room to greet her.

She's in her usual work attire: a fitted, perfectly ironed blazer; a plain silk blouse; and a few minimalist silver accessories. Between that and her knife-straight posture even as she's kicking away her red bottoms, she looks like she's ready to conquer the world.

As I step closer, however, the sour-sweet odor of alcohol and faint cigarette smoke wafts toward me. I grimace and change directions at the last second, heading into the kitchen instead.

The herbal medicine packets have all been labeled and divided into neat, colored containers: *For headaches. For period pains. For excessive internal heat.* Still, it's more due to muscle memory than Ma's exemplary categorization skills that I quickly locate the box I need: *For hangovers.*

I empty one of the packets into a glass of hot water and stir the brown powder until it dissolves, trying not to gag at the smell.

For reasons I'm yet to fully understand (though it has *something* to do with "renqing," or personal connections), the business culture here involves a lot of late-night dinners and alcohol, to the extent where it's almost impossible to get a big promotion if you don't drink at all. Case in point: Most of Ma's major contracts have been signed over glasses of baijiu or red wine.

The problem is that Ma actually hates alcohol, but I suspect she'd drink liquid fire if she thought it could help her close a deal.

"Ai-Ai? What are you doing up so late?"

I turn around at the soft shuffle of slippers and extend the cup of medicine to Ma. "Making sure you don't wake up hung over tomorrow, of course." I lean back against the counter. "You know, I'm pretty sure our roles are meant to be reversed right now."

She rolls her eyes, but the smile she gives me is warm. "Hao haizi. You're very thoughtful."

"Yeah, yeah," I say. Compliments always make me feel weird. "Just drink it while it's still warm."

She does in two great gulps, then makes such an exaggerated expression of disgust that I cackle despite myself.

"I guess what they say is true," she says, shaking her head, a contemplative look in her eyes. "Sometimes the things that are good for you . . . really taste bad."

"Wow, that's super deep, Ma." I snort. "Maybe you should tell that to Ba for his next poetry collection."

"Maybe I will," she says very seriously; then we both start laughing. But somewhere between one moment and the next, my laughter weakens at the edges, and I start thinking of all the things I shouldn't be thinking about, like Caz and my failed writing career and the lies I keep holding inside me like parasites, and my face crumples. Then I'm crying as if I've never cried before. As if I'll never stop.

"Ai-Ai?" Ma sounds bewildered, which is understandable, considering my emotions just did a complete one-eighty within the matter of seconds. "What's wrong?"

"N-n-nothing." It's the ugly kind of crying, all loud heaves and hiccups and hyperventilating, snot dribbling down my face. "I—I'm fine. I'm fine."

“Is it because of that Caz boy?” Ma asks, putting an arm around me, and I breathe in the sour scent of wine layered over her jasmine perfume.

I nod and shake my head at the same time, more harsh sobs jolting through my body. “It’s not . . . It’s . . .” I don’t know how to explain it.

Because *yes*, it’s Caz, of course it’s him, the boy who carried me through the rain and never showed his face again. But Caz isn’t the only one I’m heartbroken over.

There’s Zoe too.

And even though I miss them both intensely, with all my heart, in different ways, missing Zoe is almost worse. Because there aren’t thousands of books and poems and movies out there to describe exactly what I’m feeling, or lyrically beautiful songs for me to cry to and sing along with in the car. There’s no guidebook on how to survive this kind of fallout, no prescribed remedy to soothe this particular kind of pain. Romantic breakups are romanticized constantly, talked about everywhere by everyone, but platonic breakups are swept to the side, suffered in secret, as if they’re somehow less important.

“Are you trying to tell me that your relationship with Caz is fake?” Ma asks gently.

This stuns me into silence. Even my hiccups stop for a few seconds.

“How . . . how did you know?”

“You’re my daughter” is all she says, like that’s explanation enough. Maybe it is.

"I'm sorry." I rub my eyes, still sniffling. "Are you mad at me?"

"I suppose I should be," she says slowly, tucking my hair behind one ear. Then she grabs a tissue from the kitchen counter and wipes my face dry, and it's such a natural, motherly thing to do that I almost burst into tears again. "But no, I'm not."

We stay like that in silence for a while, her arm warm around my shoulders, bits of wet tissue stuck to my cheek. And it's nice. It's peaceful. I still feel like the apocalypse is happening, but I'm grateful that there's shelter here.

"I just—I don't know what to do," I croak out at last. "I don't know what I'm doing."

"That's okay," she says.

"No. No, it's not. No one likes me and I keep *ruining everything* and—" I stop short before my voice can crack.

Ma studies me for a moment, then she moves to the couch and sits me down beside her, her mannerisms suddenly businesslike, serious. "Do you know," she begins, folding one leg over the other, "the first time I announced that we were moving all the way across the world, to a country where you couldn't even speak the language, I expected you to throw a tantrum. Smash something, or at least slam a door. You were only a child, after all; it would've been understandable. But you know what you did?"

I sense that this is more of a rhetorical question, but I shake my head anyway.

"You simply nodded, with complete calm, and asked me if you could bring your favorite sweatshirt. At first I thought you were maybe too young to understand the—the *significance* of a move like that, but then I realized that you understood it very well, and that you cared deeply. More than any of us. You just didn't want to cause any trouble for me or your father.

"You hold everything in here, Ai-Ai," she says sternly, pointing to her own heart. "For better or worse. But not everyone is going to guess at what you're thinking like I do. No one is going to know how you feel if you don't tell them. And until you do—you can never really know what's going to happen."

I don't go to sleep after that. I *can't.* Ma's words keep clattering around my brain, until the noise gets so loud I find myself reaching for my phone. Opening it up to my last conversation with Zoe.

My fingers hover over the keys. My pulse speeds.

This whole reaching-out-to-the-people-you-care-about thing feels as counterintuitive and masochistic as sticking my hand into an open flame.

But this is *Zoe.* The girl who suffered through Ms. Betty's biology lectures and pop quizzes with me; who once lent me her jacket to cover up an embarrassing food stain even though the weather was freezing; who always cheered the loudest when I did the smallest things, like hit the volleyball over the net in PE class. The girl who threw me a surprise farewell party at the end of ninth grade before I left LA and listened patiently to my pointless rants and understood my dry humor and irrational fears when no one else did.

If I can tell anyone how I really feel, it should be her.

So I hug my knees close to my chest, draw in a shaky breath, and type out:

hello! i just wanted to say that i really miss you and

And what? Where do I go from there? Besides, who starts a spill-your-heart-out message with a *hello* and an exclamation point? She's going to think I'm someone from customer service. She's going to think my phone was hacked, or I've lost the ability to text like a normal teenager.

No.

I delete the entire message and start an email.

Hey, it's me.

I know we've both been kind of distant lately so I guess I just wanted to reach out. Give you an update on my life.

These days I've been listening to that playlist we made together in eighth grade, and it got me thinking about all those car rides back to your house when we played our music so loud your dad would pretend to get mad at us, even though he was always smiling. And also that day after Carrot dumped you (and since we're being totally honest here, I never liked him anyway—he always wore his muddy shoes inside your house, and he absolutely does NOT look like a young Keanu Reeves), when we had our school trip to the beach and you were chucking rocks into the waves as if the sea had personally offended you while I went through every post-breakup cliché I knew, and the water was the same flat gray shade as the sky, and everything was both horrible and wonderful because afterward we shared a packet of salt-and-vinegar chips and added like twenty depressing songs to our playlist. Then I said something that made you laugh for the first time that day and soon we were both laughing at nothing until our stomachs hurt. We did that a lot, actually. Sometimes I felt like we could turn anything into an inside joke.

And so I guess the point of my nostalgic rambling is that I miss you. Obviously. And I realize that it's hard for us to make new memories like the old ones when we're not even in the same country, and so many friendships drift apart after one of them moves schools/cities/gets a job etc. But . . .

I figured it'd be better to just tell you all this, instead of writing more sad, dramatic monologues in my head. And I figured there might also be a (small) chance that you've been listening to the songs on our old playlist too. Or at least thinking about it.

Besides, even if this does happen to be the last message I ever send you, I'd much rather we leave it on a good note. Though of course, I'm hoping we don't have to leave things on any note at all.

Just shoot me a message if you want to talk. Or give me a call. Anything. You know how to find me.

Hope is such a terrible thing.

It's like a bad habit you can't shake off, a stray dog that keeps showing up outside your door for scraps, even when you have nothing left to give. Every time you think you're rid of it at last, it manages to sneak its way back in. Take over. Cling on.

And though I *know* this all too well, I still can't help feeling a sharp, bright spark of hope when my phone rings the next morning.

A video-call invite from Zoe.

I pick up so fast I nearly drop the phone, but I manage to set it up on my bedside table, position myself in front of the camera just as Zoe's face fills my screen. And it's just—

Hope.

There's so much hope in me.

"Hi," I say.

She smiles. It's an awkward smile, but earnest. "Hi."

I'm suddenly reminded of that day in eighth grade, the first time we really spoke. I was new but already loved by the English teachers, and Zoe was the long-reigning star student in every subject, so most people thought we'd hate each other. But then, after I'd read one of my creative writing pieces out loud for a presentation, she'd approached me. She'd been smiling like this as well, while I was wary and hopeful and nervous—until she opened her mouth and said, "God, your writing is so beautiful."

That's how we became best friends.

It's actually funny, looking back at it. How writing has always been the string tying me to people.

"I read your message," Zoe says now. "Thank you. Really. And—sorry. I know things have been kind of weird . . ."

"You don't have to apologize—"

"No, no, but I do." She sighs, long and loud. "It's just been so hectic over here with college applications and it's—well, *you* remember how competitive it was. People ready to kill each other over a good grade. Now imagine that, but like on freaking steroids. And then this new girl, Divya—I'm not sure if you know—"

"I remember," I tell her.

"Yeah, so it turns out she's applying for the same college *and* major as me, and—I mean, it's still competitive as hell, but it's also nice having someone who understands, you know?"

I nod, letting her talk.

"And meanwhile, you're going out with a *celebrity* and doing all this cool shit and I didn't want to pile my stress on top of yours so . . . So, yeah," she finishes, giving me that stiff, awkward smile again.

"Wow."

"I know it's—"

"*Wow*, Zoe." I shake my head and laugh. "Are you kidding me? You once let me rant to you for an hour about those mini shampoos they give out in hotels, but you didn't want to bother me with your very valid stress about your literal future?"

Finally, her smile widens. Turns into the grin I know so well and missed so much. "Well, when you put it like that . . ."

"I'm right. You know I'm right."

"I *suppose* so . . ."

And maybe hope isn't so terrible after all. Because we spend the next hour chatting and catching up, and even though it's not *exactly* the same as it used to be—there are more pauses, and those small hints of awkwardness—I don't think I've lost her.

If only it could be like this with Caz too, a small voice whispers in the back of my head. *If only I could just fix everything.* But I quickly drown it out. Zoe's been my best friend for years. Caz Song, on the other hand, is ranked in the top three of China's biggest heartthrobs; the distance between us is irreconcilable.

Before I can dwell on it longer, the conversation turns to Craneswift, and my writing.

"It's going horribly," I tell her up front. "I sent Sarah my final article, and she thought it was the worst thing in the world."

"I *doubt* she said that."

"She strongly implied it."

"Come on," she says once she stops laughing. "You're talented, I know you are. Did she tell you what was wrong or—"

"It was too . . . stiff, apparently. It didn't feel as genuine as my blog posts."

"Then change it," she says, like the answer is obvious.

"But I can't be the person who exclusively writes these personal, sentimental, wholly sincere essays about love and joy," I protest. "I can't. That's not me. I wanted to write something serious."

"Well, why not?"

"It's just. Because it feels . . ." I scramble for the right word. "It feels embarrassing."

Zoe just shrugs. "Most sincere things feel at least a little embarrassing. It's part of our defense mechanisms. Our heart's way of protecting us from potential hurt."

Before I can argue with that, I hear her mom shouting for her from the other room.

"Shit. Forgot to take out the laundry," she mutters, getting up to leave. Then she pauses. "I'll call you later, okay? Promise."

"Okay. Bye. Miss you," I say in a rush, and I realize she might have a point about the kind of things that are embarrassing.

She laughs, lifts her hand to wave at me, and it's only then that I catch sight of the frayed blue string around her wrist. A bracelet identical to my own. She's kept it all along. "Miss you too."

CHAPTER TWENTY

The interview is scheduled for 4:00 p.m. the following Monday.

At 2:00 p.m., I swallow my pride and write, then rewrite, a text to Caz, my fingers shaking as I type out the time and location, alongside the question: *Will you be there?* At 2:30 p.m., the little read icon pops up below the message, but there's no reply.

At 3:30 p.m., I show up alone to the senior library, my gut roiling.

The interviewer, Rachel Kim, wanted us to meet here. Something about it offering "insight" into my daily life as a student, which is pretty funny since I haven't set foot into the library once in all my time here. I obviously didn't tell her that, though. I mean, it's not as if this interview is going to be grounded in truth anyway.

When I walk through the library's sliding glass doors, the camera crew is already setting up inside. There's equipment everywhere, professional cameras and microphones and screens resting on top of children's bookshelves, long metal rods leaning against the pastel walls. A chair and two vintage sofas placed at the center of the room. Someone has even left out a tray of cupcakes and water, all still untouched.

I'm actually trembling as I make my way over to the sofas. I sit down and cross my legs. Uncross them. Fidget with a stray thread in the cushions.

I resist the sudden urge to throw up.

It's just nerves, I tell myself. Nerves, and the fact that Caz isn't here with me.

The next half hour crawls by at an excruciatingly slow pace. My mouth always gets dry when I'm stressed, so I keep getting up and chugging water and running to the bathroom and back again, all the while trying to look cool about the whole thing. The camera crew must think I have food poisoning.

I'm onto my eighth cup of water when the front doors slide open.

A pretty young woman with a pixie cut and the longest false lashes I've ever seen glides into the room, her eyes instantly landing on me.

"You must be Eliza!" she gushes, extending a manicured hand. Her nails are painted the same glossy peach pink shade as her dress. "I'm Rachel."

"Yes. Hi." I stand up quickly, praying she doesn't notice the sweat stains on the sofa, and give her hand a firm shake.

"It is *so* lovely to meet you in person," she says, all Colgate-ad smiles. Her breath smells like spearmint. "God, I've been looking forward to this interview for ages."

"Yeah." I try to match her level of enthusiasm and fail miserably. "I mean, same here."

We both sit down. Or, at least, *I* do—she kind of pauses

halfway and cranes her neck left and right, like I might be hiding something behind me.

"Sorry," she says after a beat. "It's just that . . . Is Caz not going to be here?"

My heart twists at the name. My throat burns.

But just as I'm about to feed her some excuse about Caz being called away last minute to reshoot a scene, the library doors slide open again, and Caz strides in like he had planned to come here all along.

A giddy, overwhelming surge of relief—mingled with disbelief—shoots through me.

"Sorry I'm late," he says to Rachel, shaking her hand. "You know how Beijing traffic can be." Then he turns to me for the first time since that day in the rain and smiles.

And my heart falls. Breaks upon impact.

Because it's his formal smile, the same smile he gives strangers and fans and interviewers like Rachel, the corners of his mouth curving up just slightly, neither of his dimples showing.

It shouldn't hurt this much. I should just be glad he's still honoring our agreement after everything that happened between us. Yet as I force myself to smile back at him and watch him take the seat beside me, so close his shoulders almost brush my own, I can't help feeling like there's an axe lodged in my chest, twisting deeper with every passing second.

"It is *so good* to see you two together," Rachel gushes as she sits down opposite us, hands folded neatly over her skirt. "I'm sure you've heard this, like, a million times already, but you really do make the *cutest* couple."

Just smile and play along, I command myself, squashing the urge to glance over at Caz, to assess his reaction at her words. *It'll all be over soon.*

But the interview drags on forever. After launching into a long, complimentary introduction, covering everything from my cultural background to the schools I've attended to how my essay went viral in the first place, Rachel pivots to Caz's acting career, her Colgate beam widening.

"You've starred in quite a few popular works, haven't you?" she says once she's listed them all. "From campus dramas to costume and xianxia dramas."

"Yeah, guess I have." Unlike me, Caz obviously has no problem doing interviews; his answers come out smooth and easy, the result of years of practice and experience under the spotlight. But there's an uncharacteristic tension to his body that, while I doubt is noticeable to onlookers, pulls at the narrow space between us like a taut cord.

Maybe, I dare think, *it's killing him the way it's killing me, sitting this close together, acting like everything's fine, like we're dating and* in love, *when we haven't even spoken in more than a week—*

"And what do you think of his work, Eliza?" Rachel asks. "Do you watch his dramas often?"

I blink, not expecting to be cued. "Um." I clear my throat. "I do, of course I do. Often. He's great in them." This part requires no bullshitting—he *is* great in his dramas, and by now, I've watched everything he's ever acted in, including his first minor role as the prince's guard in an early palace drama.

Even then, he was beautiful.

"What about you?" Rachel turns back to Caz, pausing to take an *incredibly* small, elegant sip of water, then another, as if determined to stretch this interview out for as long as possible. "Would you call yourself a fan of Eliza's writing?"

"Yes," Caz says quietly, and this time, I can't stop myself from sneaking a glance at his face. Though his eyes are dark and steady, staring straight ahead, there's some subtle, complex interplay of emotions just beneath that mask of nonchalance, something that makes his next words sound like a confession. "I've always been her fan."

"Oh, how sweet," Rachel coos, then adds something else about my blog posts for Craneswift, but I barely hear her.

I'm remembering what Caz said the other day:

The first time we really *met, you were sitting two seats in front of me in English class and the teacher was reading out one of your essays . . .*

And then, as if I've accidentally unlocked some mental vault of all my forbidden, repressed memories, everything he said after that comes rushing back to me too.

I want this to be real.

The library seems to spin, the artificial heat swelling around me, the camera lights blinding, recording every little shift and flicker of emotion on my face. The space between Caz and me somehow feels both smaller and wider than ever.

". . . okay, Eliza? Do you want a drink of water?"

When I glance up, Rachel and Caz and the crew are all staring at me, variations of confusion and concern playing out in their expressions. Well, mostly confusion. It's Caz who looks most concerned—though only for a fleeting second, before his jaw tightens and his features smooth over again. I can't bear it. I can't bear it, yet I have to. I need to see this performance through to the end.

"Sorry," I say, wrenching my attention away from him. "Just, um, spaced out there for a second. I'm good."

"Oh, well, we *have* been talking for a while, haven't we?" Rachel says as she checks her watch in mild surprise. "Don't worry, we'll be wrapping up soon."

I haven't even had the chance to release a silent breath of relief before she reaches into her bag and retrieves a thin, laminated script.

"What . . . ?" I begin.

"Just a fun thing we thought we'd try," Rachel explains cheerily, tossing the script over to me.

I study the script, and my heart stumbles over its next beats. The translated lines are from a famous scene Caz shot for his last costume drama, where he played a ghost king desperately in love with a banished princess over the course of ten lifetimes. And it's not just any famous scene—it's *the* famous confession scene, set right after the ghost king transfers his own powers to the princess to save her. I've seen screenshots and quotes of it floating around all over social media.

"Basically, we'd love for Caz to reenact this iconic scene with you," Rachel says with a wink. Or maybe something's just gotten stuck in her false lashes. "And I know you're not an actor, Eliza, but your lines are super short. Plus," she adds, grinning, "since this is your boyfriend, it's not like there's much actual acting needed."

I'm probably more of an actor than you realize, I think, mouth dry.

A half-formed protest rises to my lips, but I swallow it back down again, unsure how to phrase it without inviting suspicion. Besides, Caz doesn't seem to have any major issues acting out one of his most dramatic, romantic scenes right here with me. He just glances over my shoulder at the script, repeats the lines to himself a few times, nods, and says, "Okay. Sure thing."

And if I notice him swallow right after, his fingers flexing over the sofa cushions, it's still nothing compared with the panic worming in my gut. I'm honestly not sure how much longer I can maintain my composure, hide my hurt, before I fall apart.

"Whenever you're ready," Rachel calls, waving for the cameras to move closer to us.

Caz leaves his seat and promptly kneels down before me, right on the library floor, already slipping into character like a second skin: There's a new hardness to the planes of his face, a brilliant intensity to his pitch-black gaze. Taking my hand in his, he asks, voice low and much deeper than it usually is, "How do you feel?"

My mind blanks for a moment, registering nothing but the cool, firm press of his fingers, before I realize that it's my turn to say my lines. "Better. I . . . um . . . No—wait—" Flushing, I scan through the script again. "I should be asking you that, you fool. How could you—"

"It's nothing," he says, fully immersed in the scene. He lifts his hand up to my cheek, tucks a loose strand of hair behind my ear, and I try to keep my breathing even, to conceal how much his proximity hurts. *Only stage directions*, I remind myself, again and again. *Only that.*

"It's not nothing," I continue from memory. "Your powers . . ."

"I can survive this world without my powers, but I can't survive it without you." Slowly, he says, "I've waited ten lifetimes for you, lost you ten times, fought my way through the underworld to retrieve your soul. You are my light, Your Highness; the only home I've ever known. I'd gladly die before I let you slip through my fingers again."

Upon his last words, the library falls into complete silence; even the crew seems entranced by his performance.

And though I know—I *know*—it's all fake, the hot tangle of emotions in my throat isn't. Our gazes lock, me sitting down, him still on his knees, that invisible string between us tightening, and something seems to ripple over his face too.

Then Rachel's loud, abrupt applause shatters the stillness.

"Oh, that was *wonderful*," she enthuses, long nails fluttering at her chest. "Even better than I could've hoped. I'll be sure to add this into the promo video." She then goes on for a while about how great the interview went, how much she loves my blog posts, how excited she is to see my career with Craneswift take off further, and I think:

This is it. This is exactly what I wanted—or what I thought I wanted. The promise of a good career. The opportunity to impress the interviewer, and whoever ends up watching this at home. The safety of keeping Caz Song at a distance, of keeping everything between us purely professional.

So why do I feel so miserable?

When Rachel finally releases me from the conversation and busies herself packing up the interview equipment, I hurry after Caz out the library without hesitating. Without any instinct for self-preservation. Instead, there's just the horrible hope blooming inside me like a severe bruise, the old, foolish thought resurfacing: *Maybe there's a way to fix this.* To tell him how I feel, the way I did with Zoe. Some way to keep him in my life, even if it's only as friends. Now that I've experienced the alternative firsthand—no calls from him, no real smiles, nothing, as if I don't even *exist* in his life—I realize that pain might be inevitable. But some kinds of pain are worse than others.

Caz stops halfway down the empty corridor, and I almost crash into him.

For a moment, he just stares down at me, an unfathomable look in his eyes.

"What are you doing?" he asks, his voice quieter now that we're alone, distant. It kills me, but I know I also can't blame him. *I* was the one who put that distance between us.

"I—I'm—" I chew my tongue, the irony of it hitting me. How supposedly good I am with words, except when it comes to this. To *him*. "I just wanted to say—to tell you . . ."

He tilts his head slightly, something behind his gaze shifting. Like he cares what I have to say next, despite himself. "Yeah?"

"I'm sorry," I blurt out. "I didn't mean—the other day, when you said—I was lying—"

"You were lying," he repeats. "About which part?"

"I—"

He shifts position, so that my back's facing the closest wall, and moves forward. His voice remains soft, gentle even, yet each word cuts through the air like knives. "About how I should trust you? How I could be myself around you? How about that apparently you know better than I do how I really feel, even when I've just laid my heart out to you? Which one is it, Eliza?"

A flush rises through me. This is going so terribly wrong.

But he isn't finished yet. He steps forward again, just like that day on the roof, and the back of my head touches the hard wall. "Those are all your words, not mine," he says. "You ask me to feel comfortable around you, but the second I do, you just—you retreat. You run away. Do you know what it's like for me? I trusted you with my hurt, my fears, my doubts, my heart—things I've never told anyone else, and you *left*."

"I know that now," I babble, my eyes stinging. "I know it wasn't fair but . . . you came today." There's so much hope in my voice it's embarrassing. *You came for me, right?*

Yet the hope inside me wilts when I see his expression.

"I came because we made a deal, and because I understand how much it means to you and your career. But, Eliza . . ." He shakes his head with a laugh that sounds more like a sigh. He moves away from me, and the space between us—the space I'd once tried so hard to manufacture—feels cold, cursed. "Whether they're real or not—all your words have consequences. You can't just take them back."

It takes me too long to recover, to pick my heart up from where it's fallen like shattered glass. By the time I do, Caz is already gone.

CHAPTER TWENTY-ONE

The next week, I'm in math class when the interview goes up.

Ms. Sui is out today. We've been left without a sub and instructed to use the hour as a study hall, so everyone around me is already scrolling through their socials, a tab of our algebra questions left open in the corner just for show. Then there's a small flurry of activity: quiet, half-muffled giggles, chairs squeaking as friends turn from their desks to watch, curious eyes swiveling from their screens to me.

And the empty seat beside me.

A now-familiar pang fills my gut. Caz has been absent from school all week. Busy shooting again.

Although, as Savannah sets her laptop on the teacher's desk, in clear view of the whole classroom, and starts playing that dramatic reenactment Caz and I did, I'm not so sure this isn't a good thing.

"Oh my god. *Look* at you two," Nadia says, grinning over at me while the others giggle.

I don't really want to, the same way you wouldn't want to scratch at an open wound, but the video volume's now playing too loud for me to ignore, my own stilted voice drifting toward me:

"I should be asking you that, you fool . . ."

Resisting every impulse to cringe, I look up.

Whoever edited our interview has gone through the trouble of placing my clip with Caz beside a reference clip from the original drama he starred in. And as the video plays on, the camera zooming in on Caz's face while he makes his famous confession, I can't help noticing a difference between the two versions. I mean, there's *obviously* a difference; the original actress is far more beautiful and natural on-screen than I'll ever be, and with the peach blossoms unfurling around them in the background and their long, blood-splattered, traditional-styled robes, their scene together looks like something from an epic tragedy.

But the look in Caz's eyes is somehow different too.

Because when Caz tells the actress how he waited for her, how he missed her, how he refuses to lose her again, his acting is impeccable, wholly convincing. Yet it's only that—*acting.* When he murmurs those same lines to me, however, the raw, piercing intensity of his gaze is undeniably real.

What was it that Daiki had teased us for on Caz's birthday?

We can see it in your eyes . . .

I grip the edge of my desk, a startled breath rattling in my throat. Caz had told me, of course. Both the day we kissed, and the day in the rain, and again after the interview. But maybe, up until this very instant—with the evidence playing right before my eyes, the camera forcing me to see myself and him through its objective lens—I'd never *truly* trusted that he could mean it. That Caz Song could feel something real for me. That there isn't something fundamentally broken about me, something that will inevitably drive him away.

And now the only identifiable thought in my head is:

Shit.

Shit. I've messed up. Miscalculated. The whole time I've been trying to protect myself from getting hurt . . . I've hurt him too. More than I could've possibly imagined. I have to talk to him, set things right. Ask for one more chance.

I start to rise to my feet, but at the front of the classroom, Savannah lurches back first. "Oh my god," she whispers, staring at something on her laptop. Her widened eyes cut to me, and confusion rolls through my gut, merging with something sour like dread. "Um, Eliza—I think you should . . . I don't . . ."

The interview clip has ended now, but a notification has popped up. There's a new article about Caz waiting, posted only a few minutes ago. I peer closer, heart speeding, and the words leap out at me in fragments, sinking in like shards of glass:

Young actor Caz Song . . . while filming highly anticipated xianxia drama . . . accident on set . . . injuries unknown . . . Lijia Hospital . . . waiting for comment—

I go completely still.

Still as death.

What? I want to say, but the word never leaves my mouth. *You're joking*, but that doesn't make it out either. I want to throw up. My heart is self-cannibalizing, I swear, shrinking smaller, shrinking into nothing, and I can't do anything except stand there. Suck in breath after breath after breath until I manage to unhook my voice from my throat.

Even then, it comes out as a weak rasp. "I don't . . . I don't understand."

"It says something about a broken wire," Savannah says, reading fast, and the temperature in the classroom seems to plummet a hundred degrees. Everyone is frozen beside me. "Or the equipment when they were shooting. Some kind of malfunction—"

And I'm officially panicking. Hyperventilating. My mind fogged with white.

I think of Caz and the pale scar running down his forearm and those cursed, worn-down wires that should've been replaced months ago. It already happened to him once. It could always happen again.

"I'll call him," I croak, because that small, hopeful, foolish part of me is still praying this is all a misunderstanding. Maybe he wasn't even shooting today. Maybe he wrapped up his scene early and left before the accident.

Maybe.

Please.

The entire class stays silent as I scroll through my contacts, find Caz's number on my first try. It's so familiar I almost have it memorized by now. Then I click the call button and put it on loudspeaker and it rings—

And rings.

My heart lurches to my throat in beat with every new, unanswered sound of the dial. I feel nauseated. Faint. If I close my eyes I can imagine Caz's voice on the phone now, smooth and low and slightly confused as to why I'm calling him in the first place, and for a brief moment when the ringing stops, I swear it's him.

But all that comes through is his voicemail.

I stuff my phone away and look up, will myself not to see the pity swimming in Savannah's eyes, the open concern laid out on Nadia's face. "If a teacher asks, just tell them I had to leave."

"Wait. Where are you going?"

It's such an absurd question that I almost burst into hysterical laughter. Where else could I go? Where else, but to him? It doesn't matter that he's more or less rejected me already, that this could very well end badly. I just need to *see* him, to be there for him, confirm for myself that he's okay. No matter how much it hurts.

"The hospital," I call over my shoulder, already twisting away, punching Li Shushu's number into my phone with trembling fingers.

Then I run—

But this time, I'm not running away.

The drive to Lijia Hospital takes an eternity, every passing minute dragging like a knife across my skin.

But somehow, before I can lose my mind or my heart can explode, the sign for Lijia Hospital comes into view. It looks brand-new, the blue paint gleaming.

I don't wait for Li Shushu to park the car properly before I run out, yelling back over my shoulder for him to drive home without me, because if Caz is safe, then we can talk and figure out a way back to the compound ourselves, and if he's not, well—

I smother the thought to death and run faster.

The air smells different the second I burst into the hospital. Like antiseptics and lemon pine to cover up something nasty and the sharp, metallic tang of stainless steel or maybe just old blood. Like desperation and sickness.

And now comes the tricky part—

I have no idea where Caz's room is.

If I simply walk up to a receptionist and ask for Caz Song's room number, they'll most likely dismiss me as a fan, or maybe a stalker. They might even kick me out.

Which means I have to figure out where he is myself. It's manageable—there are only four levels in the hospital. That's what the signs beside the main staircase say. And since the first floor is mainly for administrative purposes and the second floor is the labor ward, I can start on the third floor, search around from there . . .

No sooner than the vague plan forms in my head, I'm already moving, taking the stairs two at a time.

The third floor opens up into a vast, white-walled room lined with uncomfortable-looking plastic seats. Colorless afternoon light drifts in through the windows. There are more doctors up here, and patients too: a sniffling child hooked to an IV, a too-big military coat resting around his skinny shoulders; a weary mother fumbling through her purse for receipts, medical details.

I check every face I pass, every curtained room on both ends of the hall. I don't know what exactly I'm looking for. Maybe Caz himself, alive and well, or a cast member, or—

Someone.

Anyone.

Even just one tiny sign that he's all right.

My heart hammers against my ribs as I move deeper in, searching and finding nothing. My skin buzzes, a new tide of panic rushing to shore.

Then I spot a familiar figure waiting outside one of the closed rooms—broad jaw and cropped hair and even broader shoulders, half his body still covered in plates of fake armor.

Mingri.

Relief crashes through my chest, but it's cut short by the look on his face.

His lips are set in a hard, tired line, his eyes vacant and rimmed with red. As I stare, he wipes his face roughly with one hand. Is he . . . crying?

No.

My footsteps falter, and suddenly I want to turn right back around. Get out of here. Go back to not knowing. But he's already seen me.

"Eliza?" Mingri rubs his eyes one last time and straightens, walks over slowly, exhaustion written all over his body. Exhaustion, or . . . grief. His voice is hushed. "What are you doing here?"

"I . . ." There's something stuck in my throat, something painful. I try to clear it. "Where's Caz?"

His features pinch, and I know—even before he says the words—I know. I steel myself with every cell in my body, but it's still not enough to stomach what he says next, in Mandarin:

"Ta bu zai."

I do a quick translation in my head—*he isn't here*—and everything stops. My ears ring. Ring on and on and on like an unanswered call before the static turns to silence. I think I collapse to the ground, because next thing I know my knees are bruising against the gray tiles, the cold of the floor creeping into my skin, into my bones, sinking its sharp teeth into everything. Mingri moves forward with hands outstretched, starts to say something else, but I can't hear him. Can't even think.

Not here. Not anymore.

Dead.

A nail deep in my chest, twisting. That's what it feels like, and I don't want to feel this, but when did that ever stop anything? It's over. All of it. And I never even got the chance to tell him how I really felt, never even got to give him a real apology. I breathe in and out and the world is still moving, it must be, but everything is frozen inside me. I had always feared Caz Song would break my heart, but this—

This is the kind of heartbreak you never recover from.

CHAPTER TWENTY-TWO

Two hands touch my shoulders. Gentle.

I don't know who they belong to. I don't care. My eyes blur, the hospital lights bleeding into the corners of my vision like a white haze of stars, and it's not until I hear his voice, feel his shadow reaching over me, that I freeze.

"What happened? What did you say to her?"

His voice. Not Mingri's, but—

My breathing stutters. My heart crashes and picks up again at a thousand miles a minute, and I twist around so fast my spine cracks, because it's not real *it's not real it can't be real it can't be except it is.*

It is.

Caz Song is standing in the center of the hospital corridor, gazing down at me, long lashes shadowing his cheeks, eyes liquid-black with concern. He's alive. He's alive and right there and he's never looked so beautiful and even though I can't bear to look away from him, I turn to Mingri for confirmation that I'm not hallucinating.

And Mingri is turned toward Caz, which means I must not be.

He's really here.

"Eliza?" Caz says, and his voice is so exquisitely tender that I forget myself, forget everything, just spring up from the ground with more strength than I knew I possessed and throw my arms around his body, crash headfirst into his chest. He wobbles slightly upon impact, caught off guard, but he manages to regain his balance.

And I hold him. Hold on to him.

I breathe in the summer scent of his shampoo and feel the firmness of his shoulders, the hard places where his muscles connect, the slope of his neck, and it all feels so nice I could cry.

Then Mingri clears his throat.

We pull apart, but the moment lingers somewhere in the space between my fingertips, the leftover heat from his body warming my skin.

"Sorry. I had no idea—" Mingri says, hands half thrown up in bewildered defense. "I didn't think—"

"What did you tell her?" Caz repeats, his eyes still on me. All the tenderness is gone. In fact, he sounds more pissed off than I've ever heard him. Pissed off at *Mingri*.

"I . . ." Mingri brings one hand to the back of his neck, rubs it over flushed skin. "I just told her you weren't here anymore. That you'd left. *To get water* is what I meant, but I can see how she *may have* mistaken *here* for, ah, the general physical realm of the living, instead of this specific space—and maybe I shouldn't have used Mandarin . . ."

Caz stares at him for a long, disbelieving beat. Then he punches Mingri's shoulder. It's not a particularly aggressive punch—not the kind intended to beat the crap out of someone or start a fight—but judging from the thud it makes and Mingri's immediate wince, it's not particularly gentle either.

"How could you say that?" Caz demands.

"I thought she already knew you were okay! And besides, I mean, I didn't exactly get a chance to clarify before she—"

"You might have considered your word choice better," Caz cuts him off.

"Well, it's not like I was lying," Mingri mumbles.

By now my despair has receded into only confused embarrassment. I brush my cheeks as casually as I can, as if I haven't just been caught breaking down. Then I look back and forth between the two of them before settling on Mingri.

"But you . . ." I say, remembering. "You looked so out of it, and you were rubbing your eyes . . ."

"Yeah, because I was *yawning*. And that look on my face is what happens when you shoot the same scene forty times in a boiling tent without any breaks." He tosses Caz a not-so-subtle look of irritation. Jerks an accusing thumb toward him. "Thanks to this guy, we've been working hard-core for weeks. I mean, he used to be all dedicated and shit, but recently—"

"Mingri." Caz clears his throat.

Mingri ignores him. "Recently he's been extra intense. Won't even stop for lunch. Even the *director* was asking him to take it easy. Anyway, we figured it had something to do with you—"

"Mingri."

"But he was scaring the shit out of us, so we didn't—"

"I think that's enough," Caz says loudly, and Mingri throws a hand up in surrender.

"Okay, okay, I'll give you two some space." Then a small, wistful grin flits over his face. "I'm meant to be meeting Kaige outside anyway, so . . ."

"Yes, go, have fun," Caz tells him with some force.

But Mingri lingers for a beat and winks. "Good to see you again, Eliza. Really. For the sake of the entire cast and crew, please take care of him"—he dodges another punch from Caz—"and, um, sorry again about the death thing."

"It's fine," I say in a rush, because I kind of really want to speak to Caz alone. Mingri seems to get the message; he waves at both of us and then he's off.

As his footsteps retreat down the corridor, I turn back to Caz.

"Are you injured or—"

"Just a shallow cut on my arm," he says, rolling up his sleeve to show me. There's a bandage stretching from his elbow to his wrist, running almost parallel to his old scar. "We didn't even need to come to the hospital for this, but they were scared it'd be infected or something." He shrugs and pushes his sleeve back down before I can look closer. "It's really fine."

"And are we—" I swallow. Make myself finish the sentence. He's already rejected me once. The worst that could happen is he rejects me again, and I lose him, and I spend the rest of my life nursing a broken heart. But if I don't tell him how I feel, when I feel it? That's another kind of heartbreak: more fatal, more terrible. "Are *we* fine? Are you—are you still mad?"

Surprise dances over his features. Then he stuffs his hands in his pockets, leans back, and looks at me with such intensity that for a moment I forget how to breathe. "What do you think?"

"I . . ." I'm forced to trail off when two nurses appear down the corridor carrying dark vials of blood. They smile and nod at us as they pass. We smile back. Everyone's very polite, and I want to tear my hair out. My heart feels like it's trying to fight its way free from my ribs.

As soon as they're out of earshot, I try again. "I was thinking—"

Another group of nurses walk past us, chatting, seemingly in a competition to see who can walk the slowest. We repeat the whole excruciating process again. I smile until my teeth grind into dust, until my jaw physically hurts from my effort to keep from screaming.

"You know what?" I decide, unable to stand it anymore. "Follow me."

All the hospital rooms are completely occupied, as are the waiting areas and the downstairs lobby, so we end up sneaking into a cleaning closet on the far corner of the second floor.

"Feels like home," Caz remarks as I push him gently against a cabinet of disinfectants and shut the door behind us. The space is even smaller than the janitor's closet at our school; a few more inches, and we'd be touching. We're standing so close, in fact, that I can feel the subtle change in his breathing when he looks at me. "So. What were you saying before?"

All this time, I've prided myself on my ability to lie, to spin a story out of nothing, to act like I don't care about anything. But insincerity is easy. Bullshitting your way through things is easy. It doesn't require any emotional attachment; there aren't any stakes involved. It can't hurt you, because you never believed in any of it anyway.

But telling the truth—saying *exactly* what you mean, how you feel, to the people you care about most . . . That's one of the hardest things in the world. Because you have to trust them. Trust that they won't hurt you, even when they have the power to.

I take a deep breath. Open my mouth.

My only source of comfort is that I've already done this with Zoe, and it didn't kill me. Maybe, just maybe, I can do it again.

"Before I came here," I begin, reaching for the right words, "I was actually watching that interview we did. With the confession scene. I mean, okay—that was, like, the catalyst, but I guess I've been thinking about this long before . . . But I just didn't *know it*, you know?"

Caz's brows crinkle faintly, and I realize I'm making no sense. God, I'm terrible at this.

I flush, try again. "What I mean is—well, first, if I'm going to be serious about my writing, I don't want my whole career to be built around a lie. More than likely the truth is going to come out one day, and I think . . . I was just trying to delay it, because I'm a total coward, and there are too many people out there I didn't want to let down. Except by continuing the lie, I was letting them down anyway.

"Second, I realized that—and trust me, believing you were dead for a few moments back there has really reaffirmed this—I don't want our relationship to be built around a lie either. I want to be with you," I say, and my voice softens on its own, like the words are too sacred to be spoken aloud in this dim, cramped room of bleach and feather dusters and tangible longing. I move forward, tilt my head up. The excruciating distance between us narrows down from three inches to two to one. "For real, this time."

The seconds that follow are some of the most terrifying ones in my life. Maybe I'll always be scared. Maybe the fear of getting hurt, of being left alone, will never truly go away. But even if it's my default setting, I can fight it. So many beautiful things lie on the other side of fear.

Like love.

Like this.

Caz stares down at me for forever, the look in his eyes asking and answering everything. Then he brings his fingertips slowly to my jaw, as if he's not entirely convinced I exist. "Really?"

"Really." I inhale. It seems impossible that half an hour ago I felt like I would die, and now here I am, more alive than I ever thought I could be. "Hey, your face isn't injured or anything, right?"

He stills, confused. "No, why—"

"Good," I tell him, smiling, and I press my lips to his.

CHAPTER TWENTY-THREE

And now comes the real damage control.

After I get home, I write out a quick email to Sarah telling her that I have a plan for my second piece. It'll be different from my personal essay, I explain, and much longer in length, but I'm ready to pour my whole heart into it.

All of this is true.

There's an idea that's been brewing in the back of my mind ever since I entered the cleaning closet with Caz, and it's risky and absolutely terrifying, but I'm learning that most valuable things are.

Around midnight, Sarah sends me a reply.

I look forward to reading it.

Once I have the green light, I get to work right away. I open up a blank Word document and title it "THIS_TIME_IT'S_REAL.docx." Then I start from the very beginning. The *actual* beginning, including—

The English assignment I didn't want to do. The parent-teacher interviews. Stumbling across Caz out in the corridor. Every awkward, heart-pounding, embarrassing detail.

It's a confession and an apology and a love story all wrapped in one, and the more I write the more I realize that I was wrong before. Writing isn't a form of lying—not the good kind anyway, the kind that makes you feel something.

Writing is a means of telling the truth. Both the beautiful and the ugly.

It also occurs to me that maybe, *just maybe*, I meant half the things I wrote in my original essay. Maybe there is some small, weak part of me that wants to be wanted, to hold hands with someone beautiful in the blue-dark, to breathe and hear its echo, to walk through the alleys of Beijing with another shadow falling naturally beside mine.

No, not weak. This is what I need to get into my head. Hope is not weakness. It's oxygen, a crack in the window, the pale slash of moonlight across a dusty room.

Maybe I should start learning to invite it in.

Between my writing sessions, I paint my bedroom walls blue.

Emily and Ba come in to help. We blast music from my laptop and wear old raincoats fished from boxes and cover the floor with last month's newspapers and we paint and paint and paint. Emily loves this task more than anyone. Her brush flies everywhere over the white canvas, splattering droplets of color onto her rosy cheeks and bare feet, so her toes look like they might be an alien's. We know Ma is going to scold her for making a mess when she sees, but Ba just laughs. There are specks of paint in his hair too. In the creases of his skin when he smiles.

I smile back at him, grateful for everything.

We finish painting less than an hour before lunch, and we all stop to admire our work. I've chosen a bright, cheerful shade of blue, as blue as the spring sky outside my window. As blue as fresh cornflowers. And when the sun hits the room at the right angle, lighting up everything from within, the walls look almost turquoise, the same shade as the shallowest ends of the ocean, or a cliffside pool.

I want to wake up every day and look around my bedroom and feel what I feel now: Happy. Hopeful.

After the paint has dried, I hang up the string of fairy lights I bought on Taobao and carefully arrange a series of photos onto the wall beside my bed.

In the first few photos, I'm with Zoe. Both of us are laughing so hard our faces look close to distorted, hands clutching our sides.

There are more photos: of the frozen-over compound lake in winter; my family crowded together at the seafood restaurant, chopsticks in hands; the Westbridge school buildings at sunset, the sky blushing pink over the courtyard. Of me and Caz that day in Chaoyang Park, my lips touching his cheek, his eyes wide with faint surprise.

I stare at the photos on the wall and lie back down on my soft covers, and this strange, tender feeling in my chest—it feels a lot like home.

I'm sitting on the rooftop again, but this time, I'm not alone.

"Hey," Caz says, hopping onto the swings beside me, a folder in his hand. He's grinning, and I can't tell if something incredible has happened or if he's just glad to be here. I mean, that's definitely why *I'm* grinning like an idiot. It's weird how everything feels new and familiar at once, the future stretching ahead of us both like a gleaming, open road. New, because I'm not afraid to open up to him anymore, and maybe, eventually, other people too; I've already made plans to go shopping at Indigo with Savannah and have lunch the next day with all of Caz's friends.

And familiar, because it's him.

"What's that?" I ask, nodding at what he's holding.

"A college application."

"I thought I already helped you write all of them," I say, confused.

"This is different." He drums two fingers over the folder, a small, nervous habit of his that few others seem to know, then holds it out for me to read. "This one—this is for the Beijing Film Academy."

It takes a moment for the name to register. Then my eyes widen. "Caz. Wait, you mean—"

"I've been thinking a lot about what you said," he explains as I open the folder, flipping carefully through the pages inside. They've already been filled out in his messy handwriting. Warmth rushes through my chest. I know better than anyone how hard it is to share your writing with others, how vulnerable it leaves you.

"And I still want a college education," he continues. "I'm sure of that, but I guess . . . it can't hurt to study something I'm actually interested in, can it? A bunch of famous actors have graduated from here too."

"Oh my god. *Caz*. That's amazing."

He shrugs and rubs a hand over the back of his neck like it's no big deal, but he's so clearly trying not to smile. "I might need your help with it, though. You don't have to write anything—just read over it, tell me what you think, if it's not too inconvenient—"

"Of course I'll help," I say. I almost start to justify this with a clause from our arrangement, or a complete lie about how I enjoy editing people's college applications anyway. Then I remember that we don't have to pretend anymore, we can both just be ourselves, and it's relief and sharp delight all at once, the very best feeling in the world. "Caz, I'd love to be inconvenienced by you. I wouldn't mind being inconvenienced by you for the rest of my life."

"Thank you." He sounds almost shy. "I seriously owe you—"

I hold up a hand before he can say any more. "Okay, stop being so polite. It's scaring me."

He scoffs. "What, you'd prefer if I never thanked you for anything?"

"See?" I point a finger at him; he makes a half-hearted attempt to bat it aside. "That attitude right there? That's much better."

"You're so weird sometimes," he says, and it somehow sounds more affectionate than *I love you*. He kicks the swing back, and my stomach dips pleasantly with the motion. "Anyway, what about you? How's the writing?"

"I'm about two-thirds done. But, like, I have no idea how people will respond to it."

And that's the thing. That's always the thing: It might not go well. It might go *terribly*. I might wake up one day having given my heart to the world, revealed all those vulnerable and embarrassing parts of me, spelled out my innermost thoughts, and discover that no one likes them. Or worse, that no one cares in the first place.

It's the same with Caz. There's still every chance that what we have won't last the year, or even the season. Maybe we'll graduate and end up on opposite ends of the world and slowly drift apart. Maybe he'll change irrevocably, shedding the self that once wanted me and discarding it like an old winter coat. Maybe I will.

But certain joys, I'm discovering, are worth the potential pain.

"Are you happy?" I ask Caz, tilting my head to properly look at him, to study the familiar curve of his jaw, the deep dimples in his cheeks when he smiles and pulls me closer. The city rises up behind him, and if someone were to assign me an essay about *home* again, I know exactly what I'd write.

"I am," he says softly. "Are you?"

I breathe in the sweet scent of magnolias from the gardens, feel the spring air on my skin, the scratch of his jacket against my neck. His presence beside me, warm. Whole. My heart threatens to overflow.

"I'm so unbelievably happy right now," I tell him.

And I mean every word.

ACKNOWLEDGMENTS

Despite the title of this book, the journey to getting it published has been absolutely surreal in the very best way, and would not be possible without any of the following people:

Thank you to Kathleen Rushall, my brilliant agent. It's impossible to talk about you without gushing about you. I can't express how grateful I am for your support, your patience, your faith, and your advice. You've truly changed my life, and every day I marvel at how lucky I am for it. Thank you also to the wonderful team at Andrea Brown Literary Agency.

Thank you to Maya Marlette, for your endless enthusiasm and hard work and delightful emails, and for believing in this book from the very beginning. A huge thank-you to everyone in the Scholastic family, including the incredible Mallory Kass and Jalen Garcia-Hall. Thank you to the immensely talented Caroline Noll, Elizabeth Whiting, Alan Smagler, Dan Moser, Jarad Waxman, and Jody Stigliano, as well as Rachel Feld, Erin Berger, Brooke Shearouse, Shannon Pender, and Jordana Kulak for championing my work. More thanks to my audio team, led by Lori Benton and John Pels, for helping bring my book to life. Thank you to my all-star production editor Janell Harris, my amazing copyeditor, Priscilla Eakeley, my proofreaders, Jody Corbett, Jackie Hornberger, and Jessica White, and the most lovely library/

conventions team, Emily Heddleson, Lizette Serrano, and Sabrina Montenigro. Many thanks to David Levithan, Ellie Berger, and Leslie Garych. And the biggest thank-you to Maeve Norton, Elizabeth Parisi, and Kanith Thailamthong, for your passion and expertise in putting together my final cover.

Thank you so, so much to the fantastic Taryn Fagerness at Taryn Fagerness Agency. Your support really means the world.

All my thanks to everyone who's worked on shaping and selling this book, both in the US and abroad.

Thank you to Fi and Phoebe, for reassuring me when I'm stressed, which is most of the time, and for constantly inspiring me to be better.

Thank you to my little sister, Alyssa, for reading every version of this book and cheering me on. I don't like to admit it often, but you're the best reader and sibling I could ever ask for, and the house is always warmer when you're around.

Thank you, again and forever, to my parents, who have given me all I've ever needed and more. I hope to make you proud.

ABOUT THE AUTHOR

Photo by Alyssa Liang

Ann Liang is a graduate of the University of Melbourne. Born in Beijing, she grew up traveling back and forth between China and Australia, but somehow ended up with an American accent. When she isn't writing, she can be found making overambitious to-do lists, binge-watching dramas, and having profound conversations with her pet labradoodle about who's a good dog. You can find her online at annliang.com.